FAIRY GOLD
A BOOK OF OLD ENGLISH FAIRY
TALES CHOSEN BY ERNEST RHYS

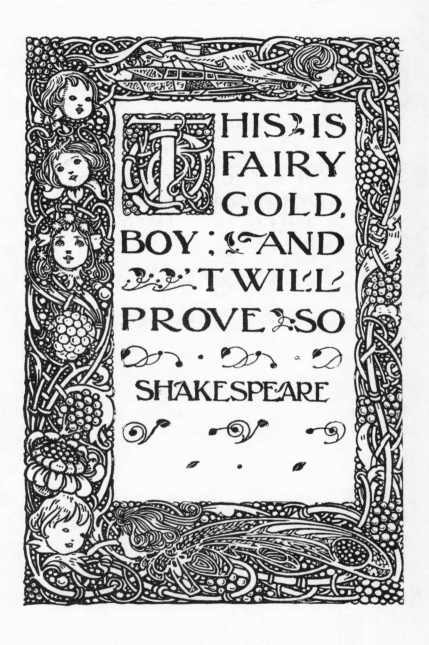

THIS IS
FAIRY
GOLD,
BOY ; AND
'T WILL
PROVE SO

SHAKESPEARE

FAIRY GOLD
A BOOK OF
OLD ENGLISH
FAIRY TALES
CHOSEN BY
ERNEST RHYS

BOOKS FOR LIBRARIES PRESS
FREEPORT. NEW YORK

First Published 1907
Reprinted 1970

STANDARD BOOK NUMBER:

8369-5317-7

LIBRARY OF CONGRESS CATALOG CARD NUMBER:

77-114912

PRINTED IN THE UNITED STATES OF AMERICA

THE PREAMBLE

" When we came to the door of gold,
The pipes within did whistle and play."

THE Fairyland that is entered through the golden door of this book is pictured in tales and rhymes that have all been told at one time or another to English children. Some of these tales have been forgotten and some have been lost or long-buried, and so there are several that will seem new to you who read them here to-day. Such a story is that of the elfin Green-Knight, which is a case of a delightful old fairy-tale that grew into as delightful a romance. A romance indeed is little else than a fairy-tale for older folk; and with an eye to the close kinship between the two the first part of this book of "Fairy-Gold" tries to show in a new way how the fairy-tale-tellers and the romancers "swapped" (as school-boys say) their good things. There you have a story like that of King Arthur and the Giant of St. Michael's Mount, which comes from that noble old romancer, Sir Thomas Malory. For a fairy-tale, like a cat, has nine lives; it can pass into many queer shapes, and yet not die. You may cut off its head, or drown it in sentiment or sea-water, or tie a moral to its tail; but it will still survive, and be found sitting safe by the fire some winter night.

In some cases, north-country and other friends have

vii

helped me to find new versions of old favourites like "The Lambton Worm." And using a ballad-monger's right, I have put into its natural shape that other "Laidley" or "loathly" worm of Spindleston. Every change in these tales has been made with a real regard for the jealous love that children feel for their favourites; and so the literary touches added by some earlier collectors have been got rid of here, and the simpler colours of folk-lore and nursery-lore restored.

The genuine teller of fairy-tales long ago was an old woman or gossip of the Mother Goose kind. I am sure that "Mother Jak," who was nurse to the small prince who became Edward VI., was one of these. Another "Mother Jack," formerly cook and housewife at Castle Fortune, who nursed several of the children, has been made godmother to the second part of this book. It is sure and certain that she must have told every tale and sung every song there put down to her.

This too may be said of her,—she could have told us many things which, now that she has long been dead, must remain unexplained for ever. She could have told you what to do if you were "pixy-led,"—like that west-countryman "who declared and offered to take his Bible-oath upon it, that, as sure as ever he was alive to tell it, whilst his head was running round like a mill-wheel, he heard with his own ears they bits of Pisgies a-laughing and a-*tacking* their hands, all to see he led-astray, and never able to find the right road, though he had travelled it scores of times long agone, by night or by day, as a body might tell," or she could have told you of that girl, who once knew a man who, "one night, could not find his way out of his own fields, all he could do, until he recollected to *turn his coat*." The moment he did so, he heard the Pixies all fly away, up into the trees, and there they sat and laughed. "Oh! how they did laugh!"

In "Mother Jack's Fairy Book," will be found many of those shorter fairy-fables and stories, which, just because they are brief, are in danger of being lost sight of altogether. In Part III., which follows, are fairy tales and poems from some later writers and poets. Among them will be found Browning's "Pied Piper of Hamelin," because there is every reason to believe that Hamelin was as near home as Newtown (Isle of Wight), and that "the river Weser deep and wide" was the Solent. Of the stories in the third part, one, "the Defeat of Time," is by Elia ; "Melilot," "Bacon Pie," and four others are from the "Oberon's Horn" of Henry Morley. And of the songs and poems, Wordsworth, Keats, Tom Hood, each, have given you one. It was "Robin" Herrick who wrote the "Queen Mab" poems and the "Fairy Beggar," that appear in the first part; and John Lyly who wrote the "Fairies' Frolic." "Catskin," in the same part, has simply made another change of dress, very much as she does in the story itself.   E. R.

CONTENTS

PART I

FAIRY TALES AND ROMANCES

Contents

PART II

MOTHER JACK'S FAIRY-BOOK

Contents xiii

PART III

LATER FAIRY TALES AND RHYMES

LIST OF ILLUSTRATIONS

PART I

FAIRY TALES AND ROMANCES

⚘ THE IMP TREE ⚘

NCE there was a King of Winchester called Orfeo, and dearly he loved his queen, Heurodis. She happened one hot afternoon in summer-time to be walking in the orchard, when she became very drowsy; and she lay down under an imp tree,[1] and there she fell fast asleep. While she slept, she had a strange dream. She dreamt that two fair knights came to her side, and bade her come quickly with them to speak to their lord and king. But she answered them right boldly, that she neither dared nor cared to go with them. So the two knights went away; but very quickly they returned, bringing their king with them, and a thousand knights in his train, and many beauteous ladies drest in pure white, riding on snow-white steeds. The king had a crown on his head, not of silver or red-gold, but all of precious

[1] The "Imp Tree" is not as you might suppose, a tree of the imps, but a tree on which a branch of another tree has been "imped" or grafted.

stones that shone like the sun. By his side was led a lady's white palfrey that seemed to be prepared for some rider, for its saddle was empty. He commanded that Heurodis should be placed upon this white steed, and thereupon the King of Faërie and his train of knights and white dames, and Heurodis beside him, rode off through a fair country with many flowery meads, fields, forests and pleasant waters, where stood castles and towers amid the green trees. Fairest of all, on a green terrace overlooking many orchards and rose-gardens, stood the Faërie King's palace. When he had shown these things to Heurodis, he brought her back safe to the Imp Tree; but he bade her, on pain of death, meet him under the same tree on the morrow.

When Heurodis awoke from this dream, it was to find Orfeo standing at her side. She told him of all that had happened; of the Faërie King and of the green faërie country she had visited. He resolved that on the morrow he and a thousand knights should stand armed round the Imp Tree to protect her from the Faërie King. And when the time came, there they stood like a ring of living steel or a hedge of spears, to guard Heurodis. But in spite of all, she was snatched away under their very eyes; and in vain were all their efforts to see which way she and her faërie captors were gone.

Orfeo made search for his lost queen everywhere during many days, but no footstep of her was to be found in upper earth. And then in sorrow for her, and in utter despair, he left his palace at Winchester, gave up his throne and went into the wilderness, carrying only a harp for companion. With its tunes, as he sang to it, sorrowing for Heurodis, the wild beasts were enchanted and often came round about him—yea, wolf and fox, bear and little squirrel—to hear him play. And there in the forest, Orfeo (as the old story-book says):

> " Often in hot undertides [1]
> Would see the Faërie King besides,
> The King of Faërie with his rout
> Hunt and ride all roundabout,
> With calls and elfin-horns that blew,
> And hounds that did reply thereto,
> But never pulled down hart or doe,
> And never arrow left the bow."

[1] Afternoons.

And sometimes he saw the Faërie Host pass, as if to war, the knights with their swords drawn, stout and fierce of face, and their banners flying. Other times he saw these faërie knights and ladies dance, dressed like guisers, with tabors beating and joyous trumpets blowing. And one day Orfeo saw sixty lovely ladies ride out to the riverside for falconry, each with her falcon on her bare hand, and in the very midst of them (oh wonder !) rode his lost queen, Heurodis. He determined at once to follow them ; and after flying their falcons they return through the forest at evening to a wild rocky place, where they ride into the rock through a rude cleft, overhung with brambles. They ride in, a league and more, till they come to the fairest country ever seen, where it is high midsummer and broad sunlight. In its midst stands a palace of an hundred towers, with walls of crystal, and windows coped and arched with gold. All that land was light, because when the night should come, the precious stones in the palace walls gave out a light as bright as noonday. Into this palace hall Orfeo entered, in the train of the ladies, and saw there the King of Faërie on his throne. The king was enraged at first when he saw the strange man enter with his harp. But Orfeo offers to play upon it, and Heurodis, when she hears, is filled with longing, while the Faërie King is so enchanted that he promises to Orfeo any gift he likes to ask out of all the riches of the faërie regions. But Orfeo, to this, has only one word to reply :—

"HEURODIS !"

And the King of Faërie thereupon gives her back to Orfeo, and they return in great joy, hand in hand together, through the wilderness to Winchester, where they live and reign together for ever afterwards in peace and happiness. But let none who would not be carried away like Heurodis to the Faërie King's country dare to sleep in the undertide beneath the Imp Tree.

THE BLACK BULL OF NORROWAY

To wilder measures next they turn :
  The black, black bull of Norroway !
Sudden the tapers cease to burn,
  The minstrels cease to play !

ONCE upon a time there lived a king who had three daughters; the two eldest were proud and ugly, but the youngest was the gentlest and most beautiful creature ever seen, and the pride not only of her father and mother, but of all in the land. As it fell out, the three princesses were talking one night of whom they would marry. "I will have no one lower than a king," said the eldest princess. The second would take a prince or a great duke even. "Pho, pho," said the youngest, laughing, "you are both so proud; now, I would be content with the Black Bull o' Norroway." Well, they thought no more of the matter till the next morning, when, as they sat at breakfast, they heard the most dreadful bellowing at the door, and what should it be but the Black Bull come for his bride. You may be sure they were all terribly frightened at this, for the Black Bull was one of the most horrible creatures ever seen in the world. And the king and queen did not know how to save their daughter. At last they determined to send him off with the old henwife. So they put her on his back, and away he went with her till he came to a great black forest, when, throwing her down, he returned, roaring louder and more frightfully than ever. They then sent, one by one, all the servants, then the two eldest princesses; but not one of them met with any better treatment than the old henwife, and at last they were forced to send their youngest and favourite child.

Far she travelled upon the Black Bull, through many

4

dreadful forests and lonely wastes, till they came at last to
a noble castle, where a large company was assembled.
The lord of the castle pressed them to stay, though much
he wondered at the lovely princess and her strange companion. But as they went in among the guests, the
princess espied a pin sticking in the Black Bull's hide,
which she pulled out, and, to the surprise of all, there
appeared not a frightful wild beast, but one of the most
beautiful princes ever beheld.

You may believe how delighted the princess was to see
him fall at her feet, and thank her for breaking his cruel
enchantment. There were great rejoicings in the castle
at this, but alas! in the midst of them he suddenly disappeared, and though every place was sought, he was no-
where to be found.

The princess, from being filled with happiness, was all
but broken-hearted. She determined, however, to seek
through all the world for him, and many weary ways she
went, but for a long, long while nothing could she hear of
her lover. Travelling once through a dark wood, she lost
her way, and as night was coming on, she thought she
must now certainly die of cold and hunger; but seeing a
light through the trees, she went on till she came to a
little hut, where an old woman lived, who took her in,
and gave her both food and shelter. In the morning the
old wifie gave her three nuts, that she was not to break
till her heart was "like to break and owre again like to
break"; so, showing her the way, she bade God speed
her, and the princess once more set out on her wearisome
journey.

She had not gone far till a company of lords and ladies
rode past her, all talking merrily of the fine doings they
expected at the Duke o' Norroway's wedding. Then she
came up to a number of people carrying all sorts of fine
things, and they, too, were going to the duke's wedding.
At last she came to a castle, where nothing was to be
seen but cooks and bakers, some running one way, and
some another, and all so busy that they did not know
what to do first. Whilst she was looking at all this, she
heard a noise of hunters behind her, and some one cried
out,—

"Make way for the Duke o' Norroway!"

And who should ride past but the prince and a beautiful
lady.

You may be sure her heart was now "like to break and
owre again like to break" at this sad sight, so she broke
one of the nuts, and out came a wee wifie carding wool.
The princess then went into the castle, and asked to see
the lady, who no sooner saw the wee wifie so hard at
work, than she offered the princess anything in her castle
for it.

"I will give it to you," said she, "only on condition
that you put off for one day your marriage with the Duke
o' Norroway, and that I may go into his room alone
to-night."

So anxious was the lady for the nut, that she consented.
And when dark night was come, and the duke fast asleep,
the princess was put alone into his chamber.   Sitting
down by his bedside, she began singing :—

   " Far hae I sought ye, near am I brought to ye,
     Dear Duke o' Norroway, will ye no turn and speak to me?"

Though she sang this over and over again, the duke never
wakened, and in the morning the princess had to leave
him, without his knowing she had ever been there. She
then broke the second nut, and out came a wee wifie
spinning, which so delighted the lady, that she readily
agreed to put off her marriage another day for it ; but the
princess came no better speed the second night than the
first, and, almost in despair, she broke the last nut, which
contained a wee wifie reeling, and on the same condition
as before, the lady got possession of it.

When the duke was dressing in the morning, his man
asked him what the strange singing and moaning that had
been heard in his room for two nights meant.

"I heard nothing," said the duke ; "it could only have
been your fancy."

" Take no sleeping-draught to-night, and be sure to lay
aside your pillow of heaviness," said the man, "and
you also will hear what for two nights has kept me
awake."

The duke did so, and the princess coming in, sat down
sighing at his bedside, thinking this the last time she might
ever see him. The duke started up when he heard the

voice of his dearly-loved princess ; and with many endear-
ing expressions of surprise and joy, explained to her that
he had long been in the power of a witch-wife, whose spells
over him were now happily ended by their once again
meeting.

The princess, happy to be the means of breaking his
second evil spell, consented to marry him, and the wicked
witch-wife, who fled that country, afraid of the duke's
anger, has never since been heard of.   All was hurry and
preparation in the castle, and the marriage which took
place happily ended the adventures of the Black Bull o'
Norroway, and the wanderings of the king's daughter.

THE LAMBTON WORM

LONG, long ago,—I cannot say how long, —the young heir of Lambton Castle led a careless, profane life, regardless of God and man. All his Saturday nights he spent in drinking, and all his Sunday mornings in fishing. One Sunday, he had cast his line into the Water of Wear many times without a bite; and at last in a rage he let loose his tongue in curses loud and deep, to the great scandal of the servants and country folk as they passed by to the old chapel at Brugeford, which was not in ruins then.

Soon afterwards he felt something tugging at his line, and trusting he had at last hooked a fine fish, he used all his skill to play it and bring it safe to land. But what were his horror and dismay on finding that, instead of a fish he had only caught a loathly worm of most evil appearance! He hastily tore the foul thing from his hook, and flung it into a well close by, which is still known by the name of the Worm Well.

The young heir had scarcely thrown his line again into the stream when a stranger of venerable appearance, passing by, asked him what sport he had met with?

He replied: "Why, truly, I think I have caught the evil one himself. Look in and judge."

The stranger looked, and remarked that he had never seen the like of it before; that it resembled an eft, only it had nine holes on each side of its mouth; and, finally, that he thought it boded no good.

The worm remained there unheeded in the well till it outgrew so confined a dwelling-place. It then emerged, and betook itself by day to the river, where it lay coiled round a rock in the middle of the stream, and by night to a neighbouring hill, round whose base it would twine itself, while it continued to grow so fast that it soon could

encircle the hill three times. This eminence is still called
the Worm Hill. It is oval in shape, on the north side of
the Wear, and about a mile and a half from old Lambton
Hall.

The Lambton Worm now became the terror of the
whole country side. It sucked the cows' milk, worried
the cattle, devoured the lambs, and committed every sort

of depredation on the helpless peasantry. Having laid
waste the district on the north side of the river, it crossed
the stream and approached Lambton Hall, where the old
lord was living alone and desolate. His son had repented
of his evil life, and had gone to the wars in a distant
country. Some people say he had gone as a crusader to
the Holy Land.

On hearing of the dreaded Worm's approach, the
terrified household assembled in council. Much was said,
but to little purpose, till the steward, a man of age and

experience, advised that the large trough which stood in the courtyard should immediately be filled with milk. This was done without delay; the monster approached, drank the milk, and, without doing further harm, returned across the Wear to wrap his giant form around his favourite hill. The next day he was seen recrossing the river; the trough was hastily filled again, and with the same results. It was found that the milk of "nine kye" was needed to fill the trough; and if this quantity was not placed there every day, regularly and in full measure, the Worm would break out into a violent rage, lashing its tail round the trees in the park, and tearing them up by the roots.

The Lambton Worm was now, in fact, the terror of the whole country. Many a knight had come out to fight with it, but all to no purpose; for it possessed the marvellous power of reuniting itself after being cut asunder, and thus was more than a match for all the knighthood of the North. So, after many a vain conflict, and the loss of many a brave man, the creature was left in possession of its favourite hill.

After seven long years, however, the heir of Lambton returned home, to find the broad lands of his ancestors waste and desolate, his people terror-stricken or in hiding, his father sinking into the grave overwhelmed with care and anxiety. He took no rest, we are told, till he had crossed the river and surveyed the Worm as it lay coiled round the foot of the Worm Hill; then, hearing how every other knight and man-at-arms had failed, he took counsel in the matter from the Wise-woman of Chester-le-Street.

At first the Wise-woman of Chester-le-Street did nothing but upbraid him for having brought this scourge upon his house and neighbourhood; but when she saw that he was indeed penitent, and eager at any cost to remove the evil he had caused, she bade him get his best suit of mail studded thickly with spear-heads, to put it on, and thus armed to take his stand on the rock in the middle of the river Wear. There he must meet the Worm face to face, trusting the issue to Providence and his good sword. But she charged him before going to the encounter to take a vow, that, if successful, he would slay the first living thing that met him on his way homewards. Should he fail to fulfil this vow, she warned him that for nine generations no lord of Lambton would die in his bed.

The heir, now a belted knight, made the vow in Bruge-ford Chapel. He studded his armour back and breast-plate, greaves and armlets, with the sharpest spear heads, and unsheathing his trusty sword took his stand on the rock in the middle of the Wear. At the accustomed hour the Worm uncoiled its "snaky twine," and wound its way towards the hall, crossing the river close by the rock on which the knight was standing eager for the combat. He struck a violent blow upon the monster's head as it passed, on which the creature turned on him, and writhing and lashing the water in its rage, flung its tail round him, as if to strangle him in its coils.[1]

But the closer the Worm wrapped him in its folds the more deadly were its self-inflicted wounds, till at last the river ran crimson with its blood. As its strength diminished, the knight redoubled his strokes, and he was able at last with his good sword to cut the serpent fold by fold, and piece by piece asunder; each severed part was immediately borne away by the swiftness of the current, and the Worm, unable to reunite itself, was utterly destroyed.

[1]There is a modern ballad, which describes the death-grapple of the Worm :—

"The Worm shot down the middle stream
Like a flash of living light,
And the waters kindled round his path
In rainbow colours bright.

But when he saw the armed knight
He gathered all his pride,
And, coiled in many a radiant spire,
Rode buoyant o'er the tide.

When he darted at length his dragon strength
An earthquake shook the rock ;
The fireflakes bright fell round the knight
But unmoved he met the shock.

Though his heart was stout it quailed no doubt,
His very life-blood ran cold,
As round and round the wild Worm wound
In many a grappling fold."

During this long and terrible combat in the river, the household of Lambton had shut themselves within-doors to pray for their young lord, he having promised that when it was over he would, if conqueror, blow a blast on his bugle.   This would assure his father of his safety, and warn them to let loose a favourite hound, which they had destined as the victim, according to the Wise-woman's word and the young lord's vow.   When, however, the bugle-notes were heard within the hall, the old lord of Lambton forgot everything but his son's safety, and rushing out of doors, ran to meet and embrace him.

The heir of Lambton felt his heart turn sick as he saw his old father come.   What could he do?   He could not lift his hand against his beloved father; yet how else could he fulfil his vow?   In his perplexity he blew another blast; the hound was let loose, it bounded to its master; the sword, yet reeking with the Lambton Worm's blood, was plunged into its heart.   But it was all in vain.   The vow was broken.   What the Wise-woman of Chester-le-Street had foretold came true.   The curse lay upon the house of Lambton for nine generations.

THE LAIDLEY WORM OF
SPINDLESTON[1]

I

THE king has sailed from Bambrough sands,
    Long may May Margaret mourn!
Long may she stand on the castle wall,
    Looking for his return.

She has counted the keys of each chamber;
    And knotted them on a string.
She has cast them o'er her left shoulder,
    To bring good-luck to the king.

She trippéd out, she trippéd in,
    She tript into the yard;
But it was more for the old king's sake,
    Than for the new queen's regard.

II

IN two months but a day, the king
    Has brought his new queen home;
And all the lords in the north country,
    To welcome them are come.

"And welcome, father!" says May Margaret:
    "Unto your halls and bowers!
And welcome too, my step-mother,
    For all that's here is yours!"

A Scots lord said, that heard her speak:
    "This Lady Margaret's grace
Surpasseth all of womankind,
    She has so fair a face!"

[1] Worm was an old word for a serpent, and "laidley" means loathly, or horrible.

With that the new queen turned about :—
  "You might have excepted me ;
But I will bring May Margaret down
  To a Laidley Worm's degree.

I will bring her low as a Laidley Worm,
  That warps [1] about the stone ;
And not, till the Childe of Wynde comes back,
  Shall her witching be undone ! "

The princess stood at the bower door
  Laughing,—and who could blame ?
But e'er the next day's sun went down,
  A long worm she became.

For seven miles east, and seven miles west,
  And seven miles north and south,
No blade of grass or corn could grow,
  So fiery was her mouth.

The milk of seven white milch-kine,
  Was brought her at morning light ;
The milk of seven white milch-kine,
  She drank at fall of night.

Word went east, and word went west,
  And word went over the sea,
That a Laidley Worm in Spindleston Heughs,
  Would ruin the North Country.

Word went east, and word went west,
  Word went across the sea ;
The Childe of Wynde got wit of it,
  And it fretted him wondrously.

He called about him his men-at-arms,
  "To Bambrough we must sail :—
And we must land by Spindleston,
  This Laidley Worm to quell."

They built a ship without delay,
  With masts of the rowan tree,
With fluttering sails of silk and hemp,
  And set her on the sea.

[1] Wraps itself.

III

NEXT morn the wicked queen looked out,
   To see what could be seen :
There she espied a gallant ship,
   Before the castle green.

When she beheld the silken sails,
   Full glancing in the sun,
To sink the ship she sent away
   Her witch-wives, every one.

In vain, in vain! The witch-wives came
   Back where the witch-queen stood—
For know that witches have no power,
   Where there is rowan-tree wood.

O, then the queen sent the Laidley Worm,
   To make the top-masts heel,—
And the Laidley Worm has wormed the sand,
   And crept beneath the keel.

The worm leapt up, the worm leapt down,
   And plaited around each plank;
And aye as the ship came near the quay,
   She heeled till she nearly sank.

But the Childe of Wynde he put about,
   And he steered for Budley-sand;
And jumping into the shallow sea,
   He is safely got to land.

And there he drew his sword of proof,
   For the worm was close behind;
But ere he struck he heard a voice,
   So soft as summer-wind :

"Oh! quit thy sword, unbend thy bow,
   And give me kisses three;
For though I seem a Laidley Worm
   No hurt I'll do to thee!

Oh! quit thy sword, unbend thy bow,
   And give me kisses three!
If I'm not won ere set of sun,
   Won I shall never be."

He quitted his sword, and kissed her thrice,
   The wet sand at his feet;
She sank in the sand a Laidley Worm,—
   She rose up May Margaret.

She trembled in the cold sea-air,
   But his mantle has wrapt her round,
And they are up to Bambrough Castle,
   As fast as horn can sound.

The witch-queen stood upon the stair,
   Twisting her wicked hands:
"Oh! who is this?" said the Childe of Wynde,
   "That on the stairway stands?

Woe, woe to thee, thou wicked witch,
   An ill death mayest thou die;
The doom thou dreed on May Margaret
   The same doom shalt thou dree.

I will turn you into a Laidley Toad,
   That still in the clay doth wend;
And won, won, shalt thou never be!
   Till this world hath an end!"

SHE TREMBLED IN THE COLD SEA-AIR,
BUT HIS MANTLE HAS WRAPT HER ROUND.

B

THE GREEN KNIGHT

I

WHEN Arthur was King of Britain, and so reigned, it befell one winter-tide he held at Camelot his Christmas feast, with all the knights of the Round Table, full fifteen days. All was joy then in hall and chamber; and when the New Year came, it was kept with great joy. Rich gifts were given and many lords and ladies took their seats at the table, where Queen Guenever sat at the king's side, and a lady fairer of form might no one say he had ever before seen. But King Arthur would not eat nor would he long sit, until he should have witnessed some wondrous adventure. The first course was served with a blowing of trumpets, and before each two guests were set twelve dishes, and bright wine, for there was no want of anything.

Scarcely had the first course commenced, when there rushed in at the hall-door a knight,—the tallest on earth he must have been. His back and breast were broad, but his waist was small. He was clothed entirely in green, and his spurs were of bright gold; his saddle was em· broidered with birds and flies, and the steed that he rode upon was green. Gaily was the knight attired; his great beard, like a green bush, hung on his breast. His horse's mane was decked with golden threads, and its tail bound with a green band; such a horse and such a knight were never before seen. It seemed that no man might endure the Green Knight's blows, but he carried neither spear nor shield. In one hand he held a holly bough, and in the other an axe the edge of which was as keen as a sharp razor, and the handle was encased in iron, curiously graven with green.

Thus arrayed, the Green Knight entered the hall, with-out saluting anyone; and asked for the governor of the company, and looked about him for the most renowned of them. Much they marvelled to see a man and a horse as green as grass; never before had they seen such a sight as this; they were afraid to answer, and were as silent as if sleep had taken hold of them, some from fear, others from courtesy. King Arthur, who was never afraid, saluted the Green Knight, and bade him welcome. The Green Knight said that he would not tarry; he was seeking the most valiant, that he might prove him. He came in peace; but he had a halberd at home and a helmet too. King Arthur assured him that he should not fail to find an opponent worthy of him.

"I seek no fight," said the knight; "here are only beardless children; here is no man to match me; still, if any be bold enough to strike a stroke for another, this axe shall be his, but I shall give him a stroke in return within a twelvemonth and a day!"

Fear kept all silent; while the knight rolled his red eyes about and bent his gristly green brows. Waving his beard awhile, he exclaimed,—

"What, then—is this Arthur's Court? Forsooth, the renown of the Round Table is overturned with a word of one man's speech!"

Arthur grew red for shame, and waxed as wroth as the wind. He assured the knight that no one was afraid of his great words, and seized the axe. The Green Knight, stroking his beard, awaited the blow, and with a dry countenance drew down his green coat.

But thereupon Sir Gawayne begged the king to let him undertake the blow; he asked permission to leave the table, saying it was not meet that Arthur should take the game, while so many bold knights sat upon bench. Al-though the weakest, he was quite ready to meet the Green Knight. The other knights too begged Arthur to "give Gawayne the game." Then the king gave Gawayne, who was his nephew, his weapon and told him to keep heart and hand steady. The Green Knight inquired the name of his opponent, and Sir Gawayne told him his name, declar-ing that he was willing to give and receive a blow.

"It pleases me well, Sir Gawayne," says the Green

Knight, "that I shall receive a blow from thy fist; but thou must swear that thou wilt seek me to receive the blow in return."

"Where shall I seek thee?" says Sir Gawayne; "tell me thy name and thy abode and I will find thee."

"When thou hast smitten me," says the Green Knight, "then tell I thee of my home and name; if I speak not at all, so much the better for thee. Take now thy grim weapon and let us see how thou strikest?"

"Gladly, sir, forsooth," quoth Sir Gawayne.

And now the Green Knight puts his long, green locks aside, and lays bare his neck, and Sir Gawayne strikes hard with the axe, and at one blow severs the head from the body. The head falls to the earth, and many treat it roughly, but the Green Knight never falters; he starts up, seizes his head, steps into the saddle, holding the while the head in his hand by the hair, and turns his horse about. Then lo! the head lifts up its eyelids, and addresses Sir Gawayne :—

"Look thou, be ready to go as thou hast promised, and seek till thou findest me. Get thee to the Green Chapel, there to receive a blow on New Year's morn; fail thou never; come, or recreant be called." So saying, the Green Knight rides out of the hall, his head in his hand.

And now Arthur addresses the queen: "Dear dame, be not dismayed; such marvels well become the Christmas festival; I may now go to meat. Sir Gawayne, hang up thine axe." The king and his knights sit feasting at the board, with all manner of meat and minstrelsy, till day is ended.

"But beware, Sir Gawayne!" said the king at its end, "lest thou fail to seek the adventure which thou hast taken in hand!"

II

LIKE other years, the months and seasons of this year pass away full quickly and never return. After Christmas comes Lent, and spring sets in, and warm showers descend. Then the groves become green; and birds build and sing for joy of the summer that follows; blossoms begin to bloom, and noble notes are heard in the woods.   With the soft winds of summer, more beautiful grow the flowers, wet with dew-drops.   But then harvest approaches, and drives the dust about, and the leaves drop off the trees, the grass becomes grey, and all ripens and rots.   At last, when the winter winds come round again, Sir Gawayne thinks of his dread journey, and his vow to the Green Knight.

On All-Hallow's Day, Arthur makes a feast for his nephew's sake.   After meat, Sir Gawayne thus speaks to his uncle: "Now, liege lord, I ask leave of you, for I am bound on the morrow to seek the Green Knight."

Many noble knights, the best of the Court, counsel and comfort him, and much sorrow prevails in the hall, but Gawayne declares that he has nothing to fear.   On the morn he asks for his arms; a carpet is spread on the floor, and he steps thereon.   He is dubbed in a doublet of Tarsic silk, and a well-made hood; they set steel shoes on his feet, lap his legs in steel greaves; put on the steel habergeon, the well-burnished braces, elbow pieces, and gloves of plate: while over all is placed the coat armour. His spurs are then fixed, and his sword is attached to his side by a silken girdle.   Thus attired the knight hears mass, and afterwards takes leave of Arthur and his Court. By that time his horse Gringolet was ready, the harness of which glittered like the gleam of the sun.   Then Sir Gawayne sets his helmet upon his head, and the circle around it was decked with diamonds; and they give him his shield with the "pentangle" of pure gold, devised by King Solomon as a token of truth; for it is called the endless knot, and well becomes the good Sir Gawayne, a knight the truest of speech and the fairest of form.   He was found faultless in his five wits; the image of the Virgin was depicted upon his shield; in courtesy he was never found wanting, and therefore was the endless knot fastened on his shield.

And now Sir Gawayne seizes his lance and bids all "Good-day"; he spurs his horse and goes on his way. All that saw him go, mourned in their hearts, and declared that his equal was not to be found upon earth.   It would have been better for him to have been a leader of men. than to die by the hands of an elvish man.

Meanwhile, many a weary mile goes Sir Gawayne; now rides the knight through the realms of England; he has no companion but his horse, and no men does he see till he approaches North Wales. From Holyhead he passes into Wirral, where he finds but few that love God or man; he inquires after the Green Knight of the Green Chapel, but can gain no tidings of him. His cheer oft changed before he found the chapel; many a cliff he climbed over, many a ford and stream he crossed, and everywhere he found a foe. It were too tedious to tell the tenth part of his adventures with serpents, wolves and wild men; with bulls, bears and boars. Had he not been both brave and good, doubtless he had been dead; the sharp winter was far worse than any war that ever troubled him. Thus in peril he travels till Christmas Eve and on the morn he finds himself in a deep forest, where were old oaks many a hundred; and many sad birds upon bare twigs piped piteously for the cold. Through rough ways and deep mire he goes, that he may celebrate the birth of Christ and blessing himself he says, "Cross of Christ, speed me!"

Scarcely had he blessed himself thrice, than he saw a dwelling in the wood, set on a hill, the comeliest castle that knight ever owned, which shone as the sun through the bright oaks.

Forthwith Sir Gawayne goes to the chief gate, and finds the drawbridge raised, and the gates fast shut; as he abides there on the bank, he observes the high walls of hard hewn stone, with battlements and towers and chalk-white chimneys; and bright and great were its round towers with their well-made capitals. Oh, thinks he, if only he might come within the cloister. Anon he calls, and soon there comes a porter to know the knight's errand.

"Good sir," says Gawayne, "ask the high lord of this house to grant me a lodging."

"You are welcome to dwell here as long as you like," replied the porter. Thereupon is the drawbridge let down, and the gate opened wide to receive him; and he enters and his horse is well stabled, and knights and squires bring Gawayne into the hall. Many a one hastens to take his helmet and sword; the lord of the castle bids him welcome and they embrace each other. Gawayne looks on his host ; a big bold one he seemed ; beaver-hued was his broad beard, and his face as fell as the fire.

The lord then leads Gawayne to a chamber, and assigns a page to wait upon him. In this bright bower was noble bedding ; the curtains were of pure silk with golden hems, and Tarsic tapestries covered the walls and floor. Here the knight doffed his armour, and put on rich robes, which well became him : and in troth a more comely knight than Sir Gawayne was never seen.

Then a chair was placed by the fireplace for him, and a mantle of fine linen, richly embroidered, thrown over him ; a table, too, was brought in, and the knight, having washed, was invited to sit to meat. He was served with numerous dishes, with fish baked and broiled, or boiled and seasoned with spices ; full noble feast, and much mirth did he make, as he ate and drank.

Then Sir Gawayne, in answer to his host, told him he was of Arthur's Court ; and when this was made known, great was the joy in the hall. Each one said softly to his mate : " Now we shall see courteous manners and hear noble speech, for we have amongst us the father of all nurture."

After dinner, the company go to the chapel, to hear the evensong of the great season. The lord of the castle and Sir Gawayne sit together during the service. When his wife, accompanied by her maids, left her seat after the service, she appeared even fairer than Guenever. An older dame led her by the hand, and very unlike they were ; for if the young one was fair, the other was yellow, and had rough and wrinkled cheeks. The younger had a throat fairer than snow ; the elder had black brows and bleared lips. With permission of the lord, Sir Gawayne salutes the elder, and the younger courteously kisses, and begs to be her servant. To the great hall then they go, where spices and wine are served : the lord takes off his hood, and places it on a spear : he who makes most mirth that Christmas-tide is to win it.

On Christmas morn, joy reigns in every dwelling in the world ; so did it in the castle where Sir Gawayne now abode. The lord and the old ancient wife sit together, and Sir Gawayne sits by the wife of his host ; it were too tedious to tell of the meat, the mirth, and the joy that abounded everywhere. Trumpets and horns give forth their merry notes, and great was the joy for three days.

St. John's Day was the last day of the Christmas festival, and on the morrow many of the guests took their departure from the castle. Its lord thanked Sir Gawayne for the honour and pleasure of his visit, and endeavoured to keep him at his court. He desired also to know what had driven Sir Gawayne from Arthur's Court before the end of the Christmas holidays?

Sir Gawayne replied that "a high errand and a hasty one" had forced him to leave the Court. Then he asked his host whether he had ever heard of the Green Chapel? For there he had to be on New Year's Day, and he would as lief die as fail in his errand. The prince tells Sir Gawayne he will teach him the way, and that the Green Chapel is not more than two miles from the castle. Then was Gawayne glad, and he consented to tarry awhile at the castle; and its lord and castellan rejoiced too, and sent to ask the ladies to come and entertain their guest. And he asked Sir Gawayne to grant him one request that he would keep his chamber on the morrow's morn, as he must be tired after his far travel. Meanwhile his host and the other men of the castle were to rise very early, and go a-hunting.

"Whatsoever," said his host, " I win in the wood shall be yours; and whatever hap be yours at home, I will as freely count as mine." And he gave Sir Gawayne in token a ring, which he was not to yield, no, not though it was thrice required of him by the fairest lady under heaven! To all this Sir Gawayne gladly agreed, and so with much cheer, a bargain was made between them; and as night drew on, each went early to his bed.

III

NEXT morn, full early before the day, all the folk of the castle up-rise, and saddle their horses, and truss their saddle-bags. The noble lord of the castle too arrays himself for riding, eats a sop hastily, and goes to mass. Before daylight, he and his men are on their horses; then the hounds are called out and coupled; three short notes

are blown by the bugles, and a hundred hunters join in
the chase.   To their stations the deer-stalkers go, and the
hounds are cast off, and joyously the chase begins.

Roused by the clamour the deer rush to the heights,
but are soon driven back ; the harts and bucks are allowed
to pass, but the hinds and does are driven back to the
shade.   As they fly they are shot by the bowmen : the
hounds and the hunters, with a loud cry, follow in pursuit,
and those that escape the arrows are killed by the hounds.
The lord waxes joyful in the chase, which lasted till the
approach of night.

All this time, Sir Gawayne lay abed,—and woke only to
hear afar the baying of the hounds, and so to doze again.
But at length there befell a knock at his door, and a
damsel entered to bid him rise, and come to meat with her
mistress.   Straightway he arose, attired himself, put the
fair ring on his finger, that his host had given him and
descended to greet the lady of the castle.

"Good-morrow, fair sir," says she, "you are a late
sleeper, I see !"   She tells him, with a laughing glance,
that she doubts if he really be Sir Gawayne that all the
world worships : for he cares better to sleep than to hunt
with the knights in the wood, or talk with the ladies in
their bower.

"In good faith," quoth Sir Gawayne, "save this ring on
my finger, there is nought I would not yield thee in token
of my service and thy courtesy."

The lady told him that if true courtesy were enclosed
in himself, he would keep back nothing,—no, not so much
as a ring !   But Sir Gawayne bethought him of his word
to the lord of the castle ; of his promise also to the Green
Knight.   He may not, he says, yield up his ring ; but he
will be forever her true servant.

We leave now the lady and Sir Gawayne, and turn to
tell how the lord of the land and his men end their hunt
in wood and heath.   Of the killed a "quarry" they make ;
and set about "breaking" the deer, and take away the
"assay" or fat ; and rend off the hide.   When all is
ready, they feed the hounds, and then they make for
home.

Anon Sir Gawayne hearing them approach the castle,
goes out to meet his host.   Then the lord commands all

his household to assemble, and the venison to be brought before him; he calls Gawayne, and asks him whether he does not deserve much praise for his success in the chase. When the knight has said that fairer venison he has not seen in winter,—nay, not this seven year,—his host doth bid him take the whole, according to the agreement between them made last night. Gawayne gives the knight a comely kiss in return, and his host desires to know if he too has gotten much weal at home?

"Nay," says Sir Gawayne, "ask me no more of that!"

Thereupon the lord of the castle laughed, and they went to supper, where were dainties new, enough and to spare. Anon they were sitting by the hearth, while wine is carried round, and again Sir Gawayne and his host renew their compact, as before, and so they take leave of each other and hasten to bed.

Scarce had the cock cackled thrice on the morrow, when the lord was up, and again with his hunters and horns out and abroad, pursuing the chase. The hunters cheer on the hounds, which fall to the scent, forty at once; all come together by the side of a cliff, and look about on all sides, beating the bushes. Out there rushes a fierce wild boar, who fells three to the ground with the first thrust. Full quickly the hunters pursue him; however, he attacks the hounds, causing them to yowl and yell. The bowmen send their arrows after this wild beast, but they glide off, shivered in pieces. Enraged with the blows, he attacks the hunters: then the lord of the land blows his bugle, and pursues the boar.

All this time, Sir Gawayne lies abed, as on the previous day, according to his promise. And again, when he is summoned out of his late slumbers, the lady of the castle twits him with his lack of courtesy.

"Sir," says she, "if ye indeed be Sir Gawayne, me-thinkest you would not have forgotten that which yester-day I taught!"

"What is that?" quoth he.

"That I taught you of giving," says she; "yet, you give not the ring as courtesy requires."

"Poor is the gift," he says, "that is not given of free will!"

But then the lady takes a ring from her own finger, and

bids him to keep it. "And I would hear from you," she says, "some stories of beautiful dames, and of feats of arms and the deeds that become true knights."

Sir Gawayne says he has no sleight in the telling of such tales, and he may not take the ring she would give him, but he would for ever be her servant.

Meanwhile, the lord pursued the wild boar, that bit the backs of his hounds asunder, and caused the stoutest of his hunters to start back. At last the beast was too exhausted to run any more and entered a hole in a rock, by the side of a brook, the froth foaming at his mouth. None durst approach him, so many had he torn with his tusks. The knight, seeing the boar at bay, alights from his horse, and seeks to attack him with his sword; the boar rushes out upon the man, who, aiming well, wounds him in the side, and the wild beast is killed by the hounds.

Then was there blowing of horns and baying of hounds. One, wise in wood-craft, begins to unlace the boar, and hews off the head. Then he feeds his hounds; and the two halves of the carcase are next bound together and hung upon a pole. The boar's head is now borne before the lord of the castle, who hastens home.

Gawayne is called upon, when the hunt returns, to receive the spoil, and the lord of the land is well pleased when he sees him; and shows him the wild boar, and tells him of its length and breadth. "Such brawn of a beast," Sir Gawayne says he never has seen. To Gawayne then the wild boar is given, according to the covenant; and in return he kisses his host, who declares his guest to be the best he knows.

Tables are raised aloft, cloths laid upon them, and waxen torches are lighted. With much mirth and glee, supper is served in the hall. When they had long played in the hall, they went to the upper chamber, where they drank and discoursed. Sir Gawayne at length begs leave of his host to depart on the morrow; but his host swears to him that he must stay, and come to the Green Chapel on New Year's morn long before prime. So Gawayne consents to remain for another night; and full still and softly he sleeps throughout it.

Early in the morning the lord of the castle is up; after

mass, a morsel he takes with his men to break his fast.
Then were they all mounted on their horses before the
hall-gates, and ready for the hunt. It was a clear, frosty
morning when they rode off, and the hunters, dispersed by
a wood's side, came upon the track of a fox, which was
followed up by the hounds. And now they get sight
of the game, and pursue him through many a rough grove.
The fox at last leaps over a spinney, and by a rugged path
seeks to get clear from the hounds; he comes upon one
of the hunting-stations, where he is attacked by the dogs.
However, he slips them, and makes again for the woods.
Then was it fine sport to listen to the hounds, and the
hallooing of the hunters; there the fox was threatened,
and called a thief. But Reynard was wily, and led them
far astray over brake and spinney.

Meanwhile, Sir Gawayne, left at home, soundly sleeps
within his comely curtains. At length the lady of the
castle, clothed in a rich mantle, comes to his chamber,
opens a window, and reproaches him :—

"Ah! man, how canst thou sleep; this morning is so
clear?"

Sir Gawayne was, when she aroused him, dreaming of
his forthcoming adventure at the Green Chapel, but he
started up, and greeted his fair visitor. Again, as she had
done before, she desired some gift by which to remember
him when he was gone.

"Now, sir," she entreats him, "now before thy depart-
ing, do me this courtesy!"

Sir Gawayne tells her that she is worthy of a far better
gift than he can bestow. He has no men laden with
trunks containing precious things.

Thereupon again the lady of the castle offers him a gold
ring, but he refuses to accept it, as he has none that he is
free to give in return. Very sorrowful was she on account
of his refusal; she takes off her green girdle, and beseeches
him to take it. Gawayne again refuses to accept anything,
but promises, "ever in hot and in cold, to be her true
servant."

"Do you refuse it," says the lady, "because it is simple?
Whoso knew the virtues that it possesses would highly
prize it. For he who is girded with this green girdle cannot
be wounded or slain."

Thereupon Sir Gawayne thinks of his adventure at the Green Chapel, and when she again earnestly presses him to take the girdle, he consents not only to take it, but to keep the possession of it a secret. Then she takes her leave; Gawayne hides the girdle, and then hies to the chapel, and asks pardon for any misdeeds he has ever done. When he returns to the hall, he makes himself so merry among the ladies with comely songs and carols, that they said: "This knight was so merry never before, since hither he came to the castle!"

Meanwhile the lord of the castle was still in the field; he had already slain the fox. He had spied Reynard coming through a "rough grove" and tried to strike him with his sword; but the fox was seized by one of the hounds. The rest of the hunters hastened thither, with horns full many, for it was the merriest meet that ever was heard; and carrying the fox's skin and brush they all ride home. The lord at last alights at his dear home, where he finds Sir Gawayne amusing the ladies; the knight comes forward and welcomes his host, and according to covenant kisses him thrice.

"My faith!" says the other, "ye have had much bliss! I have hunted all day and have gotten nothing but the skin of this foul fox, a poor reward for three such kisses." He then tells him how the fox was slain; and with much mirth and minstrelsy they made merry until the time came for them to part. Gawayne takes leave of his host, and thanks him for his happy sojourn. He asks for a man to teach him the way to the Green Chapel. A servant is assigned him, and then he takes leave of the ladies, kissing them sorrowfully. They commend him to Christ. He then departs, thanking each one he meets for his service and solace; he retires to rest, but sleeps little, for much has he to think of on the morrow. Let him lie there, and be still awhile, and I will tell what next befell him.

IV

Now New Year's Day has drawn nigh, and the weather is stormy. Snow falls and the dale is full of deep drift. Gawayne in his bed hears each cock that crows; he calls

for the chamberlain, and bids him bring his armour.
Men knock off the rust from his rich habergeon, and the
knight then calls for his steed. While he clothed himself
in his rich garments, he forgot not the girdle, the lady's
gift, but with it doubly girded his loins; he wore it not for
its rich ornaments, "but to save himself when it behoved
him to suffer." All the people of the castle he thanked
full oft, and then was his steed Gringolet arrayed, full
ready to prick on. Sir Gawayne returns thanks for the
honour and kindness shown to him by all, and then he
steps into the saddle from the mounting-stone, and says,
"This castle to Christ I commend; may He give it ever
good chance!"

Therewith the castle gates are opened, and the knight
rides forth, and goes on his way accompanied by his guide.
They ride by rocky ways and cliffs, where each hill wore a
hat of cloud and a mist-cloak, and when it is full daylight,
they find themselves "on a hill full high." Then his
guide bade Sir Gawayne abide, saying,—

"I have brought you hither, and ye are not now far
from the appointed place. Full perilous is it esteemed,
its lord is fierce and stern, his body is bigger than the
best four in King Arthur's house; none passes by the
Green Chapel that he does not ding to death with dint of
his hand, for be it churl or chaplain, monk, mass-priest or
any man else, he kills them all. He has lived there long,
and against his sore dints ye may not defend you; wherefore, good Sir Gawayne, let this man alone, and go by
some other region, and I swear faithfully that I will never
say that ever ye attempted to flee from any man."

Gawayne replies that to shun this danger would mark
him as a coward knight; to the chapel, therefore, he will
go, though the lord thereof were the cruellest and strongest
of men.

"Full well," says he, "can God devise how to save His
true servants!"

"Marry," quoth the other, "since it pleases thee to lose
thy life, take thy helmet on thy head, and thy spear in thy
hand, and ride down this path by yon rock-side, till thou
come to the bottom of the valley. Look a little to the left,
and thou shalt see the chapel itself and the man that
guards it."

Having thus spoken, the guide takes leave of the knight. "By God's grace," says Sir Gawayne, "I will neither weep nor groan. To God's will I am full ready to bow!" So on he rides, through the dale, and eagerly looks about him. He sees, however, no sign of a resting-place, but only high and steep banks, no chapel can he discern anywhere. At last he sees a hill by the side of a stream; thither he goes, alights, and fastens his horse to the branch of a tree. He walks round the hill, ooking for the chapel, and debating with himself what it might be, and at last he comes upon an old cave in the crag. "Truly," he reflects, "a wild place is here—a fitting place for the Green Knight to make his devotions in evil fashion; if this be the chapel it is the most cursed kirk that ever I saw."

But with that, he hears a loud noise, from beyond the brook. It clattered like the grinding of a scythe on a grindstone, and whirred like a mill-stream.

"Though my life I forego," says Gawayne, "no noise shall terrify me." And he cried aloud, "Who dwells here and will hold discourse with me." Then he heard a loud voice commanding him to abide where he stood, and soon there came out of a hole, with a fell weapon—a Danish axe, quite new—the Green Knight clothed just as Gawayne saw him long before. When he reached the stream, he leapt over it, and striding on, he met Sir Gawayne without the least obeisance.

"God preserve thee!" he says, "as a true knight thou hast timed thy travel. Thou knowest the covenant between us, that on New Year's Day I should return thy blow. Here we are alone; have off thy helmet and take thy pay at once."

"By my faith," quoth Sir Gawayne, "I shall not begrudge thee thy will."

Then he shows his bare neck, and appears undaunted. The Green Knight seizes his grim weapon, and with all his force raises it aloft. As it came gliding down, Sir Gawayne shrank a little with his shoulders, then the other reproved him, saying, "Thou art not that Gawayne that is so good esteemed, for thou fleest for fear before thou feelest harm. I never flinched when thou struckest; my

Here we are alone ; have off thy helmet and take thy pay at once.

c

head flew to my foot, yet I never fled ; wherefore I ought
to be called the better man."

"I flinched once," says Gawayne, "but will no more.
Bring me to the point ; deal me my death-blow at once."

"Have at thee, then," says the other, and with that,
prepares to aim the fatal blow. Gawayne never flinches,
but stands as still as a stone.

"Now," says the Green Knight, "I must strike thee,
since thy heart is whole."

"Strike on," says the other. Then the Green Knight
makes ready to strike, and lets fall his axe on the bare
neck of Sir Gawayne. The sharp weapon pierced the
flesh so that the blood flowed. When Gawayne saw the
blood on the snow, he unsheathed his sword, and thus he
spake,—

"Cease, man, of thy blow. If thou givest me any more,
blow for blow shall I requite thee ! We agreed only upon
one stroke."

The Green Knight rested on his axe, looked at Sir
Gawayne, who appeared bold and fearless, and addressed
him as follows,—

"Bold knight, be not so wroth, I promised thee a stroke,
and thou hast it. Be satisfied ; I could have dealt worse
with thee ; I menaced thee first with one blow for the
covenant between us on the first night. Another I aimed
at thee because of the second night. A true man should
restore truly, and then he need fear no harm. Thou
failed at the third time, and therefore take thee that stroke,
for my girdle (woven by my wife) thou wearest. I know
thy secret, and my wife's gift to thee, for I sent her to try
thee, and faultless I found thee : but yet thou sinnedst a
little, since thou tookest the girdle to save thy skin and for
love of thy life."

Sir Gawayne stands there confounded before the Green
Knight.

"Cursed," he says, "be cowardice and covetousness
both ! "

Then he takes off the girdle, and throws it to the Green
Knight, and confesses himself to have been guilty of
untruth. Then the other, laughing, thus spoke,—

"Thou art confessed so clean, that I hold thee as free,
as if thou hadst never been guilty. I give thee, Sir

Gawayne, the gold-hemmed girdle as a token of thy adventure at the Green Chapel. Come again to my castle, and abide there for the remainder of the New Year's festival."

"Nay, forsooth," says Gawayne, "I have sojourned sadly, but bliss betide thee! Commend me to your comely wife, who beguiled me; but though I be now beguiled, methinks I should be excused! God reward you for your girdle! I will wear it in remembrance of my fault, and when pride shall prick me, one look upon this green band shall abate it. But tell me your right name, and I shall have done."

The Green Knight replies, "I am called Bernlak de Hautdesert, through the might of Morgan le Fay, the pupil of Merlin; she can tame even the haughtiest. It was she who caused me to test the renown of the Round Table, hoping to grieve Queen Guenever, and cause her death through fear. Morgan le Fay is even thine aunt; therefore come to her, and make merry in my house."

But Sir Gawayne refused to return with the Green Knight. He bade him a courteous farewell, and then he turned Gringolet's head again toward Arthur's hall. By wild ways and lonely places did he ride. Sometimes he harboured in a house by night, and sometimes he had to shift under the trees. The wound in his neck became whole, but he still carried about him the belt in token of his fault.

Thus Sir Gawayne comes again at last to the Court of King Arthur, and great was the joy of them all to see him. The king and his knights ask him concerning his journey, and Gawayne tells them of his adventures, and of the Green Knight's castle and the lady, and lastly, of the girdle that he wore. He showed them the cut in his neck, and as he groaned for grief and shame, the blood rushed to his face.

"Lo!" says he, handling the green girdle, "this is the band of blame, a token of my cowardice and covetousness. I must needs wear it as long as I live."

The king comforts the knight, and all the Court too. Each knight of the brotherhood agrees to wear a bright green belt for Gawayne's sake, who evermore honoured it. Thus in Arthur's day this adventure befell. May He who bore the crown of thorns, bring us to His bliss! Amen.

THE GREEN CHILDREN

THAT was a wonderful thing that happened at St. Mary's of the Wolf-pits. A boy and his sister were found by the country folk of that place near the mouth of a pit, who had limbs like those of men; but the colour of their skin wholly differed from that of you and me and the people of our upper world, for it was tinged all of a green colour.

No one could understand the speech of the Green Children. When they were brought to the house of a certain knight, Sir Richard de Calne, they wept bitterly. Bread and honey and milk were set before them, but they would not touch any of these, though they were tormented by great hunger. At length, some beans fresh-cut were brought, stalks and all, into the house, and the children made signs, with great avidity, that the green food should be given to them. Thereupon they seized on it, and opened the bean-stalks instead of the pods, thinking the beans were in the hollow of the stem; and not finding anything of the kind there, they began to weep anew. When the pods were opened and the naked beans offered to them, they fed on these with great delight, and for a long time they would taste no other food.

The people of their country, they said, and all that was to be seen in that country, were of a green colour. Neither did any sun shine there; but instead of it they enjoyed a softer light like that which shines after sunset. Being asked how they came into our upper world, they said that as they were following their green flocks, they came to a great cavern; and on entering it they heard a delightful sound of bells. Ravished by its sweetness, they went for a long time wandering on and on through the cavern until they came to its mouth. When they came out of it, they

37

were struck senseless by the glaring light of the sun, and
the summer warmth of the air ; and they thus lay for a
long time ; then, being awaked, they were terrified by the
noise of those who had come upon them ; they wished to
fly, but they could not find again the entrance of the
cavern, and so were they caught.

.   .   .   .   .   .

If you ask what became of the Green Children, I cannot tell you, for no one seems to know right clearly.   Per-
chance they found their cave, and went back again to the
Green Country, as the mermaid goes back at last to the
sea.

THE STORY OF THE FAIRY HORN

NCE upon a time there was a knight that had a Wyvern [1] on his shield; but he was none the better for that, as you shall hear.

One day as he was riding in the country beyond Gloucester, he came to a forest abounding in boars, stags, and every kind of wild beast. Now in a grovy lawn of this forest there was a little mount, rising in a point to the height of a man, on which knights and other hunters were used to ascend when fatigued with heat and thirst, to seek some relief. The nature of the place—for it is a fairy place—is, however, such that whoever ascends the mount must leave his companions, and go quite alone.

As the knight rode in the wood, and came nigh this fairy-knoll, he met with a wood-cutter and questioned him about it. He must go thither alone, the wood-cutter told him, and say, as if speaking to some other person,—

"I thirst!"

Immediately there would appear a cup-bearer in a rich crimson dress, with a shining face, bearing in his stretched-out hand a large horn, adorned with gold and gems, such as was the custom among the most ancient English. The cup was full of nectar, of an unknown but most delicious flavour, and when it was drunk, all heat and weariness fled from those who drank of it, so that they became ready to toil anew, instead of being tired from having toiled. Moreover, when the nectar was drunk, the cup-bearer offered a towel to the drinker, to wipe his mouth with, and then having done this courtesy, he waited neither for a silver penny for his services, nor for any question to be asked.

[1] A Wyvern was a kind of dragon with two legs and a curled, or rather coiled, tail.

Now the knight with the Wyvern laughed to himself when he heard this.

"Who," thought he, "would be fool enough, having within his grasp such a drinking-horn, ever to let it go again from him!"

Later, that very same day, as he rode back hot and tired and thirsty from his hunting, he bethought him of the fairy-knoll and the fairy-horn. Sending away his followers, he repaired thither all alone, and did as the wood-cutter had told him. He ascended the little hill, and said in a bold voice,—

"I thirst!"

Instantly there appeared, as the wood-cutter had fore-told, a cup-bearer in a crimson dress, bearing in his hand a drinking-horn. The horn was richly beset with precious gems; and the knight was filled with envy at sight of it. No sooner had he seized upon it, and tasted of its delicious nectar, which glowed in his veins, than he determined when he had drained it to make off with the horn. So, having gotten the horn, and drunk of it every drop, instead of returning it to the cup-bearer, as in good manners he should have done, he stepped down from the knoll, and rudely made off with it in his hand.

But, learn ye then what fate overtook this knight that bore the Wyvern on his shield, but was without true knighthood, and robbed the Fairy Horn. For the good Earl of Gloucester, who had often quenched his thirst, and restored his strength, standing on the fairy-knoll, when he heard that the wicked knight had destroyed the kind custom of the horn, attacked the robber in his stronghold, and forthright slew him, and carried off the horn. But alas! the earl did not return it to the fairy-cupbearer, but gave it to his master and lord, King Henry the Elder. Since then you may stand all day at the fairy-knoll, and many times cry "I thirst!" but you may not taste of the Fairy Horn.

THE LADY MOLE

 LONELY life for the dark and silent mole! Day is to her night. She glides along her narrow vaults, unconscious of the glad and glorious scenes of earth and air and sea. She was born, as it were, in a grave; and in one long, living sepulchre she dwells and dies. Is not existence to her a kind of doom? Wherefore is she thus a dark, sad exile from the blessed light of day? Hearken!

Here, in our bleak old Cornwall, the first mole was once a lady of the land. Her abode was in the far west, among the hills of Morwenna, beside the Severn Sea. She was the daughter of a lordly race, the only child of her mother, and the father of the house was dead: her name was Alice of the Combe. Fair was she and comely, tender and tall; and she stood upon the threshold of her youth. But most of all did men marvel at the glory of her large blue eyes. They were, to look upon, like the summer waters, when the sea is soft with light. They were to her mother a joy, and to the maiden herself, ah, benedicite! a pride. She trusted in the loveliness of those eyes, and in her face and features and form; and so it was that the damsel was wont to pass the whole summer day in the choice of rich apparel and precious stones and gold. Howbeit this was one of the ancient and common usages of those old departed days. Now, in the fashion of her stateliness and in the hue and texture of her garments, there was none among the maidens of old Cornwall like Alice of the Combe. Men sought her far and near, but she was to them all, like a form of graven stone, careless and cold. Her soul was set upon a Granville's love, fair Sir Beville of Stowe—the flower of the Cornish chivalry—that noble gentleman! That valorous knight!

he was her star. And well might she wait upon his eyes; for he was the garland of the west. The loyal soldier of a Stuart king—he was that stately Granville who lived a hero's life and died a warrior's death! He was her star. Now there was a signal made of banquet in the halls of Stowe, of wassail and dance. The messenger had sped, and Alice of the Combe would be there. Robes, precious and many, were unfolded from their rest, and the casket poured forth jewel and gem, that the maiden might stand before the knight victorious. It was the day—the hour—the time—her mother sat at her wheel by the hearth—the page waited in the hall—she came down in her loveliness, into the old oak room, and stood before the mirrored glass—her robe was of woven velvet, rich and glossy and soft; jewels shone like stars in the midnight of her raven hair, and on her hand there gleamed afar off a bright and glorious ring! She stood—she gazed upon her own fair countenance and form, and worshipped! "Now all good angels succour thee, my Alice, and bend Sir Beville's soul! Fain am I to greet thee wedded wife before I die! I do yearn to hold thy children on my knee! Often shall I pray to-night that the Granville heart may yield! Ay, thy victory shall be thy mother's prayer." "Prayer!" was the haughty answer, "now, with the eyes that I see in that glass, and with this vesture meet for a queen, I lack no trusting prayer!" Saint Juliet shield us! Ah! words of fatal sound—there was a sudden shriek, a sob, a cry, and where was Alice of the Combe? Vanished, silent, gone! They had heard wild tones of mystic music in the air, there was a rush, a beam of light, and she was gone, and that for ever! East sought they her, and west, in northern parts and south; but she was never more seen in the land. Her mother wept till she had not a tear left; none sought to comfort her, for it was vain. Moons waxed and waned, and the crones by the cottage hearth had whiled away many a shadowy night with tales of Alice of the Combe. But at the last, as the gardener in the pleasaunce leaned one day on his spade, he saw among the roses a small round hillock of earth, such as he had never seen before, and upon it something which shone. It was her ring! It was the very jewel she had worn the day she vanished out of sight! They looked earnestly upon it, and they saw within the border, for it was wide, the tracery of certain small fine runes, in the ancient Cornish tongue, which said,—

> "Beryan erde
> Ayn und perde!"

Then came the priest of the place of Morwenna, a grey and silent man. He had served long years at his lonely

altar, a worn and solitary form. But he had been wise in language in his youth, and men said that he heard and understood voices in the air when spirits speak and glide. He read and he interpreted thus the legend on the ring,—

> " 'The earth must hide
> Both eyes and pride!"

Now as on a day he uttered these words, in the pleasaunce, by the mound, on a sudden there was among the grass a low faint cry. They beheld, and oh, wondrous and strange! There was a small dark creature, clothed in a soft velvet skin in texture and in hue like the Lady Alice

her robe, and they saw, as it groped into the earth, that
it moved along without eyes, in everlasting night! Then
the ancient man wept, for he called to mind many things
and saw what they meant; and he showed them how that
this was the maiden, who had been visited with a doom
for her pride! Therefore her rich array had been changed
into the skin of a creeping thing, and her large proud eyes
were sealed up, and she herself had become—

THE FIRST MOLE OF THE HILLOCKS OF CORNWALL!

Ah, woe is me and well-a-day! that damsel so stately
and fair, sweet Lady Alice of the Combe, should become,
for a judgment, the dark mother of the moles! Now take
ye good heed, Cornish maidens, how ye put on vain
apparel to win love! And cast down your eyes, all ye
damsels of the west, and look meekly on the ground! Be
ye ever good and gentle, tender and true; and when ye
see your own image in the glass, and ye begin to be lifted
up with the loveliness of that shadowy thing, call to mind
the maiden of the vale of Morwenna, her noble eyes and
comely countenance, her vesture of price, and the glittering ring! Sit ye by the wheel as of old they sate, and
when ye draw forth the lengthening wool, sing ye ever
more and say,—

> " Beryan erde
> Ayn und perde ! "

CATSKIN

I

NCE upon a time there was a little girl who, when she came into the world, found she was not wanted there, for her father had long wished for a son and heir, and when a daughter was born instead, he fell into a blind rage and said, "She sha'n't stay long in my house!"

Her mother became very sad at this, and fearing her father's hatred, sent away the poor little babe to a foster-nurse, who lived in a house by a great oak wood. There the child lived till she was fifteen summers old. Then her old foster-mother died, but before she died, she told the poor child at her bedside, to hide all her pretty white frocks in the wood by the crystal waterfall that sounded there all day long among the oak leaves. Then she was to put on a dress of catskin the old dame gave her, and go and seek a place as a servant-maid far away in the town.

Catskin (for so she must now be called) did as the old dame had told her, and presently set off all alone in her travels. She wandered a long way, and at last came to the town, and to a great house. There she knocked at the gate, and begged the porter for a place as a servant. He sent her upstairs then to speak to the lady of the house, who looked hard at poor Catskin, and patted her on the head, and ended by saying,—

"I'm sorry I've no better place for you, my dear, but you can be a scullion under the cook, if you like!"

So Catskin was put under the cook, and a very sad life she led with her, for as often as the cook got out of temper she took a ladle and broke it over poor Catskin's head. Well, time went on and there was to be a grand ball in the town.

45

"Oh, Mrs. Cook," said Catskin, "how much I should like to go!"

"You go, with your catskin robe, among the fine ladies and lords, you dirty slut, a very fine figure you'd make!" And with that she took a basin of water and dashed it in poor Catskin's face.

But Catskin briskly shook her ears and went off to her hiding-place in the wood; and there, as the old song says,—

> "She washed every stain from her skin,
> In some crystal waterfall;
> Then put on a beautiful dress,
> And hasted away to the ball."

II

WHEN she entered the ladies were mute, overcome by her beauty; but the lord, her young master, at once fell in love with her. He prayed her to be his partner in the dance. To this Catskin said "Yes," with a sweet smile. All that evening with no other partner but Catskin would he dance.

"Pray tell me, fair maid," he said at last, "where you live?" For now was the sad parting time; but no other answer would she give him than this distich,—

> *Kind sir, if the truth I must tell,*
> *At the sign of the Basin of Water I dwell."*

Then Catskin flew from the ballroom and put on her furry robe again, and slipt into the kitchen unseen by the cook, who little thought where her scullion had been. The very next day the young squire told his mother he would never rest till he'd found out this beautiful maid, and who she was, and where she lived.

Well, time went on, and another grand ball was to be given in the town. When Catskin heard of it,—"Mrs. Cook, oh, Mrs. Cook," she cried, "how much I should like to go!"

"You go with your catskin robe among the fine lords and ladies, you dirty slut! a very fine figure you'd make!" And in a great rage she took the ladle and struck poor Catskin's head a terrible blow.

But off went Catskin, none the worse, shaking her ears, and swift to her forest she fled.   And there, as the old song says,—

> " She washed every blood-stain off,
> In some crystal waterfall ;
> Put on a more beautiful dress,
> And hasted away to the ball."

III

Now at the ballroom door the young squire was in waiting ; he longed to see nothing so much as the beautiful Catskin again.   When she arrived he asked her to dance, and again she said " Yes " with the same smiling look as before.

And again all the night he would have none but pretty Catskin for his partner.

" Pray tell me," said he, presently, " where you live ? " for now the time came for parting.

But Catskin no other answer would give than this distich,—

> " Kind sir, if the truth I must tell,
> At the sign of the Broken-Ladle I dwell."

Then she flew from the ball, put on her catskin robe under the dark oak trees, and slipt back into the kitchen unseen by the cook, who little thought where she had been.

But now the grandest ball of the whole year was to be held in the town.   And just as she had done before, when Catskin heard of it, she resolved that go she must, Mrs. Cook or no Mrs. Cook.

" Mrs. Cook," said Catskin to her one evening, " have you heard of the grand ball ?   How much I should like to go ! "

" You go ? " said Mistress Cook as before, " with your catskin robe, you impudent girl ! among the fine ladies and lords, a very fine figure you'd cut."

In a fury she snatched up the skimmer, and broke it on Catskin's head ; but heart-whole and as lively as ever.

away to the oakwood Catskin flew ; and there, as the old
song says,—

> " She washed the stains of blood,
>   In the crystal waterfall ;
>   Then put on her most beautiful dress,
>   And hastened away to the ball."

IV

AT the ballroom door the young squire stood waiting,
dressed in a velvet coat.   He longed to see nothing so
much as the beautiful Catskin again.   When he asked her
to dance, she agreed with a smile, and again all the night
long, with none but fair Catskin would he dance.
  " Pray tell me, fair maid, where you live ? " he asked
her when the parting-time came ; but she had no other
answer for him than this distich,—

> " *Kind sir, if the truth I must tell,*
>   *At the sign of the Broken-Skimmer I dwell.*"

V

THEN she flew from the ball to the oakwood, and threw on
her catskin cloak again.   She slipt into the house unseen
by the cook, but not unseen by the young squire ; for
this time he had followed too fast, and hid himself in the
forest, and saw the strange disguise she put on there.
  Next day he took to his bed and sent for the doctor to
come, and said he should die if Catskin did not come to
see him.   Well, Catskin was sent for, and he told her how
dearly he loved her ; indeed, if she did not love him, his
heart would break.
  Then the doctor, who knew how proud the old lady his
mother was, promised to ask her consent to their wedding.
Had she not feared her son would die, her pride would
never have yielded ; but after a hard struggle she said
" Yes ! "
  The sick young squire got quickly well, when he heard
this good tidings.   And so it was Catskin, before a twelvemonth was gone, when the oakwood grew green again, was
married to him, and they lived happily for ever after.

MR. FOX

" Like the old tale, my Lord : it is not so, nor 'twas not so ; but indeed, God forbid it should be so." *Much Ado About Nothing.*

NCE upon a time there was a young lady called Lady Mary, who had two brothers. One summer they all three went to a country seat of theirs, which they had not before visited. Among the other gentry in the neighbourhood who came to see them was a Mr. Fox, a bachelor, with whom they, and the young lady particularly, were much pleased. He used often to dine with them, and frequently invited Lady Mary to come and see his house. One day that her brothers were absent elsewhere, and she had nothing better to do, she determined to go thither, and accordingly set out unattended. When she arrived at the house and knocked at the door, no one answered.

At length she opened it and went in ; over the portal of the door was written,—

" Be bold, be bold, but not too bold. "

She went on ; over the staircase was the same inscription,—

" Be bold, be bold, but not too bold."

She went up ; over the entrance of a gallery was the same again,—

" Be bold, be bold, but not too bold. "

Still she went on, and over the door of a chamber found written,—

" Be bold, be bold, but not too bold,
Lest that your heart's blood should run cold !"

Lady Mary opened it ; it was full of skeletons. She retreated in haste, and, coming downstairs, saw from a window Mr. Fox advancing towards the house with a drawn

D

sword in one hand, while with the other he dragged along a young lady by her hair. She had just time to slip down and hide herself under the stairs before Mr. Fox and his victim arrived at the foot of them. As he pulled the young lady upstairs, she caught hold of one of the banisters with her hand, on which was a rich bracelet. Mr. Fox cut it off with his sword. The hand and bracelet fell into Lady Mary's lap, who then contrived to escape unobserved, and got safe home to her brothers' house.

A few days afterwards Mr. Fox came to dine with them as usual. After dinner the guests began to amuse each other with stories and strange anecdotes, and Lady Mary said she would relate to them a remarkable dream she had lately had.

"I dreamt," said she, "that as you, Mr. Fox, had often invited me to your house, I would go there one morning. When I came to the house I knocked at the door, but no one answered. When I opened the door, over the hall I saw written,—

"'Be bold, be bold, but not too bold.'

"But," said she, turning to Mr. Fox, and smiling, "it is not so, nor it was not so."

She pursued the rest of the story in the same way, concluding at every turn with, "it is not so, nor it was not so," till she came to the room full of skeletons, when Mr. Fox took up the burden of the tale, and said,—

"It is not so, nor it was not so,
And God forbid it should be so!"—

He continued to repeat this at every further turn of the dreadful tale, till she came to the cutting-off the young lady's hand, when, upon his saying, as usual,—

"It is not so, nor it was not so,
And God forbid it should be so!"—

Lady Mary retorts by saying,—

"But it is so, and it was so,
And here the hand I have to show!"—

at the same moment producing the hand and bracelet from her lap, whereupon the guests drew their swords and instantly cut Mr. Fox into a thousand pieces.

"TOM TIT TOT"

NCE upon a time there were a woman, and she baked five pies. And when they come out of the oven, they was that overbaked the crust were too hard to eat. So she says to her darter,—

"Maw'r,"[1] says she, "put you them there pies on the shelf, an' leave 'em there a little, an' they'll come again."
—She meant, you know, the crust would get soft.

But the gal, she says to herself: "Well, if they'll come agin, I'll ate 'em now." And she set to work and ate 'em all, first and last.

Well, come supper-time, the woman she said: "Goo you, and git one o' them there pies. I dare say they've come agin now."

The gal she went an' she looked, and there warn't nothin' but the dishes. So back she come and says she: "Noo, they ain't come again."

"Not none on 'em?" says the mother.

"Not none on 'em," says she.

"Well, come agin, or not come agin," says the woman, "I'll ha' one for supper."

"But you can't, if they ain't come," says the gal.

"But I can," says she. "Goo you and bring the best of em."

"Best or worst," says the gal, "I've ate 'em all, and you can't ha' one till that's come agin."

Well, the woman she were wholly bate,[2] and she took her spinnin' to the door to spin, and as she span she sang,—

> "My darter ha' ate five, five pies to-day.
> My darter ha' ate five, five pies to-day."

The king he were a-comin' down the street, an' he heard

---

[1] Lass, girl.   [2] Beaten.

her sing, but what she sang he couldn't hear, so he stopped and said,—

"What were that you was a-singing of, maw'r?"

The woman she were ashamed to let him hear what her darter had been a-doin', so she sang, 'stids ¹ o' that,—

> "My darter ha' spun five, five skeins to-day.
> My darter ha' spun five, five skeins to-day."

"S'ars o' mine!" said the king, "I never heerd tell of any one as could do that."

Then he said: "Look you here, I want a wife, and I'll marry your darter. But look you here," says he, "'leven months out o' the year she shall have all the vittles she likes to eat, and all the gowns she likes to get, and all the company she likes to have; but the last month o' the year she'll ha' to spin five skeins every day, an' if she doon't, I shall kill her."

"All right," says the woman; for she thought what a grand marriage that was. And as for them five skeins, when it came to the time, there'd be plenty o' ways of getting out of it, and likeliest, he'd ha' forgot about it.

Well, so they was married. An' for 'leven months the gal had all the vittles she liked to ate, and all the gowns she liked to get, and all the company she liked to have.

But when the time was gettin' oover, she began to think about them there skeins an' to wonder if he had 'em in mind. But not one word did he say about 'em, an' she wholly thought he'd forgot 'em.

But the last day o' the last month he takes her to a room she'd never sets eyes on afore. There worn't nothing in it but a spinnin'-wheel and a stool. An' says he: "Now, my dear, here yow'll be shut in to-morrow with some vittles and some flax, and if you hain't spun five skeins by the night, your head will goo off."

An' awa' he went about his business.

Well, she were that frightened, she'd allus been such a useless mawther, that she didn't so much as know how to spin, an' what were she to do to-morrow, with no one to come nigh her to help her. She sat down on a stool in the kitchen, and lawk! how she did cry!

However, all on a sudden she heard a sort of a knockin'

¹ Instead.

low down on the door. She upped and oped it, an' what should she see but a small little black thing with a long tail. That looked up at her right c rious, an' that said,—

" What are you a-cryin' for ? "

" Wha's that to you ? " says she

" Never you mind," that said, ' but tell me what you're a-cryin' for."

" That won't do me no good if I do," says she.

" You don't know that," that said, an' twirled that's tail round.

" Well," says she, " that won't do no harm, if that don't do no good," and she upped and told about the pies and the skeins, and everything.

" This is what I'll do," says the little black thing, " I'll come to your window every morning and take the flax and bring it spun at night."

" What's your pay ? " says she.

That looked out o' the corner o' that's eyes, and that said : " I'll give you three guesses every night to guess my name, an' if you hain't guessed it afore the month's up, you shall be mine."

Well, she thought she'd be sure to guess that's name afore the month was up. ." All right," says she, " I agree."

" All right," that says, an' lawk ! how that twirled that's tail.

Well, the next day, the king he took her into the room, an' there was the flax an' the day's vittles.

" Now there's the flax," says he, " an' if that ain't spun up this night, off goes your head." An' then he went out an' locked the door.

He'd hardly gone when there was a knockin' on the window.

She upped and she oped it, and there sure enough was the little old thing a-settin' on the ledge.

" Where's the flax ? " says he.

" Here it be," says she. And she gonned [1] it to him.

Well, in the evening a knockin' came again to the window. She upped and she oped it, and there were the little old thing with five skeins of flax on his arm.

" Here te be," says he, and he gonned it to her.

" Now, what's my name ? " says he.

Gave.

"What, is that Bill?" says she.

"Noo, that ain't," says he, an' he twirled his tail.

"Is that Ned?" says she.

"Noo, that ain't," says he, an' he twirled his tail.

"Well, is that Mark?" says she.

"Noo, that ain't," says he, an' he twirled his tail harder an' away he flew.

Well, when her husband he come in, there was the five skeins ready for him. "I see I sha'n't have for.to kill you to-night, my dear," says he; "you'll have your vittles and your flax in the mornin'," says he, an' away he goes.

Well, every day the flax an' the vittles they was brought, an' every day that there little black impet used for to come mornings and evenings. An' all the day the mawther she set a-trying for to think of names to say to it when it come at night. But she never hit on the right one. An' as it got towards the end o' the month, the impet that began for to look so maliceful, an' that twirled that's tail faster an' faster each time she gave a guess.

At last it came to the last day but one. The impet, that came at night along o' the five skeins, and that said,—

"What, ain't you got my name yet?"

"Is that Nicodemus?" says she.

"Noo, t'ain't," that says.

"Is that Sammle?" says she.

"Noo, t'ain't," that says.

"A-well, is that Methusalem?" says she.

"Noo, t'ain't that neither," that says.

Then that looks at her with that's eyes like a coal 'o fire, an' that says: "Woman, there's only to-morrow night, an' then you'll be mine!" An' away it flew.

Well, she felt that horrid. Howsomeover, she heard the king a-comin' along the passage. In he came, an' when he see the five skeins, he says, says he,—

"Well, my dear," says he, "I don't see but what you'll have your skeins ready to-morrow night as well, an' as I reckon I sha'n't have to kill you, I'll have supper in here to-night." So they brought supper an' another stool for him, and down the two they sat.

Well, he hadn't eat but a mouthful or so, when he stops an' begins to laugh.

"THE FUNNIEST LITTLE BLACK THING YOU EVER SET
EYES ON."

"What is it?" says she.

"A-why," says he, "I was out a huntin' to-day, an' I got away to a place in the wood I'd never seen afore. An' there was an old chalk-pit. An' I heard a sort of a hummin', kind o'. So I got off my hobby,[1] an' I went right quiet to the pit, an' I looked down. Well, what should there be but the funniest little black thing you ever set eyes on. An' what was that a-doing on, but that had a little spinnin'-wheel, an' that were a-spinnin' wonderful fast, an' a-twirlin' that's tail. An' as that span, that sang:

> "'Nimmy Nimmy Not
> My name's TOM TIT TOT.'"

Well, when the mawther heard this, she fared as if she could ha' jumped out of her skin for joy, but she didn't say a word.

Next day that there little thing looked so maliceful when he came for the flax. And when night came, she heard that a-knockin' on the window panes. She oped the window, an' that come right in on the ledge. That were grinnin' from ear to ear an' Oo! that's tail were twirlin' round so fast.

"What's my name?" that says, as that gonned her the skeins.

"Is that Solomon?" she says, pretendin' to be afeard.

"Noo, t'ain't," that says, and that come further into the room.

"Well, is that Zebedee?" says she again.

"Noo, t'ain't," says the impet. An' then that laughed an' twirled that's tail till you couldn't hardly see it.

"Take time, woman," that says; "next guess, and you're mine." An' that stretched out that's black hands at her.

Well, she backed a step or two, an' she looked at it, and then she laughed out, and says she, a-pointin' of her finger at it,—

> "Nimmy Nimmy Not
> Yar name's TOM TIT TOT."

Well, when that heard her, that shrieked awful and away that flew into the dark, and she never saw it no more.

[1] Horse.

THE FAIRY BEGGAR

PLEASE, your grace, from out your store
  Give an alms to one that's poor,
That your mickle may have more.
Black I'm grown for want of meat;
Give me then an ant to eat,
Or the cleft ear of a mouse
Over-soured in drink of souce;
Or, sweet lady, reach to me
The abdomen of a bee;
Flour of fuz-balls, that's too good
For a man in needy-hood:
But the meal of mill-dust can
Well content a craving man;
Any arts the elves refuse
Well will serve the beggar's use.
But if this may seem too much
For an alms, then give me such
Little bits that nestle there
In the pris'ner's pannier.
So a blessing light upon
You and mighty Oberon:
That your plenty last till when
I return your alms again.

THE CAULD LAD OF HILTON

AT Hilton Hall, in the pleasant vale of the Wear, there used to be in the old days, a Brownie called The Cauld Lad. Every night the menservants who slept in the great hall heard him at work in the kitchen, knocking the things about if they had been set in order, or putting them straight, if the place was untidy. The servant-folk soon resolved to banish him if they could, and The Cauld Lad, who seemed to know of their design, was often heard singing in a melancholy tone,—

> "Wae's me! wae's me!
> The acorn is not yet
> Fallen from the tree,
> That's to grow the wood,
> That's to make the cradle,
> That's to rock the bairn,
> That's to grow to a man,
> That's to lay me."

The maidservants, however, knew the old way of banishing a Brownie; one night they left a green cloak and hood for The Cauld Lad by the kitchen fire, and remained on the watch. At midnight they saw him come in, gaze at the new clothes, try them on, and, apparently in great delight, go jumping and frisking about the kitchen. But at the first crow of the cock he vanished crying,—

> "Here's a cloak, and here's a hood!
> The Cauld Lad of Hilton will do no more good;"

and he never again returned to the kitchen; yet it was said that he might still be heard at midnight singing those lines in a tone of melancholy.

There was one room at Hilton Hall long called The
Cauld Lad's Room, and it was never occupied unless
the house was full of company; and many folk heard,
late and early, The Cauld Lad wailing in the night :—

"Here's a cloak, and here's a hood!
The Cauld Lad of Hilton will do no more good!"

H . C

THE FAIRY'S DINNER

A LITTLE mushroom-table spread,
　　After short prayers they set on bread,
A moon-parched grain of purest wheat
With some small glitt'ring grit, to eat
His choice bits with ; then in a trice
They make a feast less great than nice.
But all this while his eye is served,
We must not think his ear was starved ;
But that there was in place to stir
His spleen, the chirring grasshopper,
The merry cricket, puling fly,
The piping gnat for minstrelsy.
And now, we must imagine first,
The elves present, to quench his thirst,
A pure seed-pearl of infant dew,
Brought and besweetened in a blue
And fragrant violet ; which done,
His kitling eyes begin to run
Quite through the table, where he spies
The horns of papery butterflies,
Of which he eats ; and tastes a little
Of that we call the cuckoo's spittle.
A little fuz-ball pudding stands
By, yet not blessed by his hands,
That was too coarse ; but then forthwith
He ventures boldly on the pith
Of sugared rush, and eats the sagg
And well bestrutted bee's sweet bag ;
Gladding his palate with some store
Of emmets' eggs ; what would he more,
But beards of mice, a newt's stewed thigh,
A bloated earwig, and a fly ;
With the red-capped worm, that's shut
Within the concave of a nut,

Brown as his tooth. A little moth,
Late fattened in a piece of cloth;
With withered cherries, mandrake's ears,
Mole's eyes; to these the slain stag's tears;
The unctuous dewlaps of a snail,
The broke-heart of a nightingale
O'ercome in music; with a wine
Ne'er ravished from the flattering vine,
Brought in a dainty daisy, which
He fully quaffs up to bewitch
His blood to height; this done, commended
Grace by his priest; the feast is ended.

THE GIANT THAT WAS A MILLER

NCE upon a time there was a Giant that was a miller. He lived in Yorkshire at a place called Dalton. His mill has been rebuilt; but when I was a boy there, the great old building still stood. In front of the house was a long mound, which went by the name of "the Giant's grave," and in the mill was shown a long blade of iron something like a scythe-blade, but not curved, which was the Giant's knife. Now, the Giant who lived at Dalton mill, ground men's bones to make his bread.

One day he captured a lad called Jack, on Pilmoor, and instead of grinding him body and bones in the mill he kept him as his servant, and never let him get away. Jack served the Giant many years, and never was allowed a holiday. At last he could bear it no longer. Topcliffe fair was coming on, and very hard Jack entreated that he might be allowed to go there to see the lasses and buy some fairings. The Giant surlily refused leave; but Jack resolved to take it.

The day was hot, and after dinner the Giant lay down in the mill with his head on a sack and dozed. He had been eating in the mill, and had laid down a great loaf of bone bread by his side, and the knife was in his hand, but his fingers relaxed their hold of it in sleep. Jack seized the moment, drew the knife away, and holding it with both his hands drove the blade into the single eye of the giant, who woke with a howl of agony, and starting up barred the door. Jack thought he was dead and done for, then; but he soon found a way out. The Giant had a favourite dog, which lay sleeping in the corner by the fire; but sprang up when

63

his master was blinded. Jack killed the dog with the fire-tongs, skinned it while his master was getting the knife out of his eye, and throwing the hide over his back ran on all-fours barking between the legs of the Giant, and so escaped.

H . C .

THE PRINCESS OF COLCHESTER

LONG before Arthur and the Knights of the Round Table, there reigned in the eastern part of England a king who kept his Court at Colchester. He was witty, strong, and valiant, by which means he subdued his enemies abroad, and planted peace among his subjects at home. Nevertheless, in the midst of all his glory, his queen died, leaving behind her an only daughter, about fifteen years of age. This little lady, from her courtly carriage, beauty and affability, was the wonder of all that knew her.

But as covetousness is the root of all evil, so it happened here. The king, hearing of a rich dame, who had an only daughter, for the sake of her riches had a mind to marry her; and though she was old, ugly, hook-nosed, and hump-backed, yet all this could not deter him from doing so. Her daughter was a yellow dowdy, full of envy and ill-nature; and, in short, was much of the same mould as her mother. This signified nothing, for in a few weeks the king, attended by the nobility and gentry brought his new queen home to his palace. She had not been long in the Court before she set the king against his own beautiful daughter, by false reports and evil tales.

The young princess, having lost her father's love, grew weary of the Court, and one day, meeting with her father in the garden, she desired him, with tears in her eyes, to give her a small pittance, and she would go and seek her fortune; to which the king consented, and ordered her mother-in-law to make up a small sum according to her discretion. She went to the queen, who gave her a canvas bag of brown bread and hard cheese, with a bottle of beer; though this was but a very pitiful dowry for a king's daughter.

She took it, returned thanks, and proceeded on her journey, passing through groves, woods, and valleys, till at length she saw an old man sitting on a stone at the mouth of a cave.

"Good morrow, fair maiden," he said, "whither away so fast?"

"Aged father," says she, "I am going to seek my fortune."

"What hast thou in thy bag and bottle?"

"In my bag I have got bread and cheese, and in my bottle good small beer. Will you please to partake of either?"

"Yes," said he, "with all my heart."

With that the lady pulled out her provisions, and bade him eat and welcome.

He did so, and gave her many thanks, and then he said to her: "There is a thick thorny hedge before you, which will appear impassable, but take this wand in your hand, strike three times, and say, 'Pray, hedge, let me come through,' and it will open immediately; then, a little further, you will find a well; sit down on the brink of it, and there will come up three golden heads, which will speak; and whatever they require, that do!"

Promising she would, she took her leave of him. Coming to the hedge, she pursued the old man's directions; it opened, and gave her a passage; then, coming to the well, she had no sooner sat down than a golden head came up singing, —

> "Wash me, and comb me,
> And lay me down softly."

"Yes," said she, and putting forth ner hand, with a silver comb performed the office, placing it upon a primrose bank.

Then came up a second and a third head, saying the same as the former. And again she complied, and then pulling out her provisions ate her dinner.

Then said the heads one to another, "What shall we do for this lady who hath used us so kindly?"

The first said, "I will add such grace to her beauty as shall charm the most powerful prince in the world."

The second said, "I will endow her with fragrance such as shall far exceed the sweetest flowers."

The third said, "My gift shall be none of the least, for, as she is a king's daughter, I'll make her so fortunate that she shall become queen to the greatest prince that reigns."

This done, at their request she let them down into the well again, and so proceeded on her journey.

She had not travelled long before she saw a king hunting in the park with his nobles. She would have shunned him, but the king, having caught a sight of her, approached, and what with her beauty and grace, was so powerfully charmed that he fell in love with her at sight. Forthwith he offered her the finest horse in his train to ride upon; and so, bringing her to his palace, he there caused her to be clothed in the most magnificent manner with white and gold raiment.

This being ended, when the king heard that she was the King of Colchester's daughter he ordered some chariots to be got ready, that he might pay her father a visit. The chariot in which the king and queen rode was adorned with rich ornamental gems of gold. Her father was at first astonished that his daughter had been so fortunate as she was, till the young king made him sensible of all that happened. Great was the joy at Court amongst all, with the exception of the queen and her club-footed daughter, who were ready to burst with malice and envy of her happiness; and the greater was their madness because she was now above them all. Great rejoicings, with feasting and dancing, continued many days. Then at length, with the dowry her father gave her, they returned home.

The hump-backed sister-in-law, perceiving that her sister was so happy in seeking her fortune, would needs do the same; so, disclosing her mind to her mother, all preparations were made, and she was furnished not only with rich apparel, but sugar, almonds, and sweet-meats, in great quantities, and a large bottle of Malaga sack.

Thus provided, she went the same road as her sister; and coming near the cave, the old man said, "Young woman, whither so fast?"

"What is that to you?" said she.

"Then," said he, "what have you in your bag and bottle?"

She answered, "Good things, which you shall not be troubled with."

"Won't you give me some?" said he.

"No, not a bit, nor a drop, unless it would choke you."

The old man frowned, saying, "Evil fortune attend thee!"

Going on, she came to the hedge, through which she espied a gap, and thought to pass through it; but, going in, the hedge closed, and the thorns ran into her flesh, so that it was with great difficulty that she got out. Being now in a most sad condition, she searched for water to wash herself, and looking round, she saw the well.

She sat down on the brink of it, and one of the heads came up, saying, "Wash me, comb me, and lay me down softly." But she banged it with her bottle, saying, "Take this for your washing."

Then the second and third heads came up, and met with no better treatment than the first; whereupon the heads consulted among themselves what evils to plague her with for such usage!

The first said, "Let her be struck with leprosy!"

The second, "Let her hair turn into packthread!"

The third bestowed on her for a husband but a poor country cobbler.

This done, she went on till she came to a town, and it being market-day, the people looked at her. and seeing such a leper's face, all fled but a poor country cobbler. Now, not long before he had mended the shoes of an old hermit, who, having no money, gave him a box of ointment for the cure of the leprosy. So the cobbler, having a mind to do an act of charity, went up to her and asked her who she was?

"I am," said she, "the King of Colchester's daughter-in-law."

"Well," said the cobbler, "if I restore you to your natural complexion, and make a sound cure of you, will you take me for a husband?"

"Yes, friend," replied she; "with all my heart!"

With this the cobbler applied his ointment, and it worked a cure in a few weeks; after which they were married, and so set forth for the Court at Colchester.

When the queen understood her dear daughter had married nothing but a poor cobbler, she fell into fits of rage, and hanged herself in wrath. The death of the ugly old queen pleased the king, who was glad to be rid of her so soon, and he gave the cobbler a hundred pounds to quit the Court with his lady, and take her to a remote part of the kingdom. There he lived many years mending shoes, his wife spinning thread, and I hope she made him happy.

H. C.

LAZY JACK

A STORY WITHOUT A MORAL

NCE upon a time there was a boy whose name was Jack, and he lived with his mother upon a dreary common. They were very poor, and the old woman got her living by spinning; but Jack was so lazy that he would do nothing but bask in the sun in the hot weather, and sit by the corner of the hearth in the winter-time. His mother could not persuade him to do anything for her, and was obliged at last to tell him that if he did not begin to work for his porridge, she would turn him out to get his living as he could.

This threat at length roused Jack, and he went out and hired himself for the day to a farmer for a penny; but as he was coming home, never having had any money before, he lost it in passing over a brook. "You stupid boy," said his mother, "you should have put it in your pocket." "I'll do so another time," replied Jack.

The next day Jack went out again, and hired himself to a cowkeeper, who gave him a jar of milk for his day's work. Jack took the jar and put it into the large pocket of his jacket, spilling it all long before he got home. "Dear me!" said the old woman, "you should have carried it on your head." "I'll do so another time," replied Jack.

The following day Jack hired himself again to a farmer, who agreed to give him a cream cheese for his services. In the evening Jack took the cheese and went home with it on his head. By the time he got home the cheese was completely spoilt, part of it being lost and part melted in his hair. "You stupid lout," said his mother, "you should have carried it very carefully in your hands." "I'll do so another time," replied Jack.

The day after this Jack again went out, and hired himself to a baker, who would give him nothing for his work but a large tom cat. Jack took the cat, and began carrying it very carefully in his hands, but in a short time Pussy scratched him so much that he was compelled to let it go. When he got home his mother said to him, "You silly fellow, you should have tied it with a string and dragged it along after you." "I'll do so another time," said Jack.

The next day Jack hired himself to a butcher, who rewarded his labours with a handsome present of a shoulder of mutton. Jack took the mutton, tied it to a string, and trailed it along after him in the dirt, so that by the time he got home the meat was completely spoilt. His mother was this time quite out of patience with him, for the next day was Sunday, and she was obliged to content herself with cabbage for her dinner. "You ninny-hammer," said she to her son, "you should have carried it on your shoulder." "I'll do so another time," replied Jack.

On the Monday Jack went once more, and hired himself to a cattle-keeper, who gave him a donkey for his trouble. Although Jack was very strong, he found some difficulty in hoisting the donkey on his shoulders, but at last he managed it, and began walking home with his prize. Now, it happened that in the course of his journey there lived a rich man with his only daughter, a beautiful girl, but unfortunately deaf and dumb. She had never laughed in her life, and the doctors said she would never recover till somebody made her laugh. Many tried without success, and at last the father, in despair, offered to marry her to the first man who could make her laugh. This young lady happened to be looking out of the window when Jack was passing with the donkey on his shoulders, the legs sticking up in the air, and the sight was so comical and strange, that she burst out into a great fit of laughter, and immediately recovered her speech and hearing. Her father was overjoyed, and fulfilled his promise by marrying her to Jack, who was thus made a rich man for life. They lived in a large house, and Jack's mother lived with them in great happiness until she died.

ROBIN GOODFELLOW

I

NCE upon a time, a great while ago, when men did eat and drink less, and were more honest, and knew no knavery, there was wont to walk many harmless spirits called fairies, dancing in brave order in fairy rings on green hills with sweet music. Sometimes they were invisible, and sometimes took divers shapes. Many mad pranks would they play, as pinching of untidy damsels black and blue, and misplacing things in ill-ordered houses ; but lovingly would they use good girls, giving them silver and other pretty toys, which they would leave for them, sometimes in their shoes, other times in their pockets, sometimes in bright basons and other clean vessels.

Now it chanced that in those happy days, a babe was born in a house to which the fairies did like well to repair. This babe was a boy, and the fairies, to show their pleasure, brought many pretty things thither, coverlets and delicate linen for his cradle ; and capons, woodcock and quail for the christening, at which there was so much good cheer that the clerk had almost forgot to say the babe's name, —Robin Goodfellow. So much for the birth and christening of little Robin.

II

WHEN Robin was grown to six years of age, he was so knavish that all the neighbours did complain of him ; for no sooner was his mother's back turned, but he was in one knavish action or other, so that his mother was constrained (to avoid the complaints) to take him with her to market, or wheresoever she went or rode. But this helped little or nothing, for if he rode before her, then would he make mouths and ill-favoured faces at those he met: if he rode behind her, then would he clap his hand on the tail; so that his mother was weary of the many complaints that came against him. Yet knew she not how to beat him justly for it, because she never saw him do that which was worthy blows. The complaints were daily so renewed that his mother promised him a whipping. Robin did not like that cheer, and therefore, to avoid it, he ran away, and left his mother a-sorrowing for him.

After Robin had travelled a good day's journey from his mother's house he sat down, and being weary he fell asleep. No sooner had slumber closed his eyelids, but he thought he saw many goodly proper little personages in antic measures tripping about him, and withal he heard such music, as he thought that Orpheus, that famous Greek fiddler (had he been alive), compared to one of these had been but a poor musician. As delights commonly last not long, so did those end sooner than Robin would willingly they should have done; and for very grief he awaked, and found by him lying a scroll wherein was written these lines following in golden letters,—

> "Robin, my only son and heir,
> How to live take thou no care:
> By nature thou hast cunning shifts,
> Which I'll increase with other gifts.
> Wish what thou wilt, thou shall it have;
> And for to fetch both fool and knave,
> Thou hast the power to change thy shape,
> To horse, to hog, to dog, to ape.
> Transformed thus, by any means
> See none thou harm'st but knaves and queanes:
> But love thou those that honest be,
> And help them in necessity.
> Do thus and all the world shall know
> The pranks of Robin Goodfellow,
> For by that name thou called shall be
> To age's last posterity;
> And if thou keep my just command,
> One day thou shall see Fairy Land!"

Robin, having read this, was very joyful, yet longed he to know whether he had the power or not, and to try it he wished for some meat; presently a fine dish of roast veal was before him. Then wished he for plum-pudding; he straightway had it. This liked him well, and because he was weary, he wished himself a horse: no sooner was his wish ended, but he was changed into as fine a nag as you need see, and leaped and curveted as nimbly as if he had been in stable at rack and manger a full month. Then he wished himself a black dog, and he was so; then a green tree, and he was so. So from one thing to another, till he was quite sure that he could change himself to anything whatsoever he liked.

Thereupon full of delight at his new powers, Robin Goodfellow set out, eager to put them to the test.

As he was crossing a field, he met with a red-faced carter's clown, and called to him to stop.

"Friend," quoth he, "what is a clock?"

"A thing," answered the clown, "that shows the time of the day."

"Why then," said Robin Goodfellow, "be thou a clock and tell me what time of the day it is."

"I owe thee not so much service," answered the clown again, "but because thou shalt think thyself beholden to me, know that it is the same time of the day as it was yesterday at this time!"

These shrewd answers vexed Robin Goodfellow, so that in himself he vowed to be revenged of the clown, which he did in this manner.

Robin Goodfellow turned himself into a bird, and followed this fellow who was going into a field a little from that place to catch a horse that was at grass. The horse being wild ran over dyke and hedge, and the fellow after, but to little purpose, for the horse was too swift for him. Robin was glad of this occasion, for now or never was the time to have his revenge.

Presently Robin shaped himself exactly like the horse that the clown followed, and so stood right before him. Then the clown took hold of the horse's mane and got on his back, but he had not ridden far when, with a stumble, Robin hurled his rider over his head, so that he almost broke his neck. But then again he stood still, and let the clown mount him once more.

By the way which the clown now would ride was a great pond of water of a good depth, which covered the road. No sooner did he ride into the very middle of the pond,

than Robin Goodfellow turned himself into a fish, and so
left him with nothing but the pack-saddle on which he was
riding betwixt his legs. Meanwhile the fish swiftly swam
to the bank. And then Robin, changed to a naughty boy

again, ran away laughing, " *Ho, ho, hoh,*" leaving the poor
clown half drowned and covered with mud.

III

As Robin took his way then along a green hedge-side he
fell to singing,—

> " And can the doctor make sick men well?
> And can the gipsy a fortune tell
> Without lily, germander, and cockle-shell?
>   With sweet-brier,
>   And bon-fire
>   And straw-berry wine,
>   And columbine.

When Saturn did live, the sun did shine,
The king and the beggar on roots did dine
With lily, germander, and sops in wine.
    With sweet-brier,
    And bon-fire,
    And straw-berry wine,
    And columbine."

And when he had sung this over, he fell to wondering
what he should next turn himself into.   Then as he saw
the smoke rise from the chimneys of the next town, he
thought to himself, it would be to him great sport to walk
the streets with a broom on his shoulder, and cry
" Chimney sweep."

But when presently Robin did this, and one did call
him, then did Robin run away laughing, " *Ho, ho, hoh !* "

Next he set about to counterfeit a lame beggar,—
begging very pitifully, but when a stout chandler came out
of his shop to give Robin an alms, again he skipped off
nimbly, laughing, as his naughty manner was.

That same night, he did knock at many men's doors,
and when the servants came out, he blew out their candle
and straightway vanished in the dark street, with his
' *Ho, ho, hoh !* "

All these mirthful tricks did Robin play, that day and
night, and in these humours of his he had many pretty
songs, one of which I will sing as perfect as I can.   He
sang it in his chimney-sweeper's humour to the tune of,
" *I have been a fiddler these fifteen years.*"

    " Black I am from head to foot,
    And all doth come by chimney soot.
    Then, maidens, come and cherish him
    That makes your chimneys neat and trim."

But it befell that, on the very next night to his playing
the chimney-sweep, Robin had a summons from the land
where there are no chimneys.

For King Oberon, seeing Robin Goodfellow do so many
merry tricks, called him out of his bed with these words,
saying,—

    " Robin, my son, come quickly rise :
    First stretch, then yawn, and rub your eyes ;
    For thou must go with me to-night,
    And taste of Fairy-land's delight."

Robin, hearing this, rose and went to him. There were with King Oberon many fairies, all attired in green. All these, with King Oberon, did welcome Robin Goodfellow into their company. Oberon took Robin by the hand and led him a fair dance : their musician had an excellent bagpipe made of a wren's quill and the skin of a Greenland fly. This pipe was so shrill, and so sweet, that a Scottish pipe compared to it, it would no more come near it than a Jew's-harp doth to an Irish harp. After they had danced, King Oberon said to Robin,—

> " Whene'er you hear the piper blow,
> Round and round the fairies go !
> And nightly you must with us dance,
> In meadows where the moonbeams glance,
> And make the circle, hand in hand—
> That is the law of Fairy-land !
> There thou shalt see what no man knows ;
> While sleep the eyes of men doth close !

So marched they, with their piper before, to the Fairy Land. There did King Oberon show Robin Goodfellow many secrets, which he never did open to the world. And there, in Fairy Land, doth Robin Goodfellow abide now this many a long year.

TOM HICKATHRIFT

LONG before William the Conqueror, there dwelt a man in the Isle of Ely, named Thomas Hickathrift, a poor labouring man, but so strong that he was able to do in one day the ordinary work of two. He had an only son, whom he christened Thomas, after his own name. The old man put his son to good learning, but he would take none, for he was none of the wisest, but something soft, and had no docility at all in him. God calling this good man, the father, to his rest, his mother, being tender of him, kept him by her hard labour as well as she could; but this was no easy matter, for Tom would sit all day in the chimney-corner, instead of doing anything to help her, and although at the time we are speaking of he was only ten years old, he would eat more than four or five ordinary men, and was five feet and a half in height, and two feet and a half broad. His hand was more like a shoulder of mutton than a boy's hand, and he was altogether like a little monster; but yet his great strength was not known.

Tom's strength came to be known in this manner: his mother, it seems, as well as himself, for they lived in the days of merry old England, slept upon straw. Now, being a tidy old creature, she must every now and then have a new bed, and one day having been promised a bottle of straw by a neighbouring farmer, after much begging, she got her son to fetch it. Tom, however, made her borrow a cart-rope first, before he would budge a step, without saying what he wanted it for; but the poor woman, too glad to gain his help upon any terms, let him have it at once. Tom, swinging the rope round his shoulders, went to the farmer's, and found him with two men threshing in a barn. Having told what he wanted, the farmer said he might take as much straw as he could carry. Tom at

78

once took him at his word, and, placing the rope in a right position, rapidly made up a bundle, containing at least a cartload, the men jeering at him all the while. Their merriment, however, did not last long, for Tom flung the enormous bundle over his shoulders, and walked away with it without any difficulty, and left them all gaping after him.

After this exploit Tom was no longer allowed to be idle. Every one tried to secure his services, and we are told many tales of his mighty strength. On one occasion, having been offered as great a bundle of firewood as he could carry, he marched off with one of the largest trees in the forest. Tom was also extremely fond of attending fairs; and in cudgelling, wrestling, or throwing the hammer, there was no one who could compete with him. He thought nothing of flinging a huge hammer into the middle of a river a mile off, and, in fact, performed such extraordinary feats, that the folk began to have a fear of him.

At length a brewer at Lynn, who required a strong lusty fellow to carry his beer to the Marsh and to Wisbeach, after much persuasion, and promising him a new suit of clothes and as much as he liked to eat and drink, secured Tom for his business. The distance he daily travelled with the beer was upwards of twenty miles, for although there was a shorter cut through the Marsh, no one durst go that way for fear of a monstrous giant, who was lord of a portion of the district, and who killed or made slaves of every one he could lay his hands upon.

Now, in the course of time, Tom was thoroughly tired of going such a roundabout way, and without telling his plans to any one, he resolved to pass through the giant's domain, or lose his life in the attempt. This was a bold undertaking, but good living had so increased Tom's strength and courage, that venturesome as he was before, his hardiness was so much increased that he would have faced a still greater danger. He accordingly drove his cart in the forbidden direction, flinging the gates wide open, as if for the purpose of making his daring more plain to be seen.

At length he was espied by the giant, who was in a rage at his boldness, but consoled himself by thinking that

Tom and the beer would soon become his prey. "Sirrah," said the monster, "who gave you permission to come this way? Do you not know how I make all stand in fear of me? and you, like an impudent rogue, must come and fling my gates open at your pleasure! Are you careless of your life? Do not you care what you do? But I will make you an example for all rogues under the sun! Dost thou not see how many thousand heads hang upon yonder tree—heads of those who have offended against my laws? But thy head shall hang higher than all the rest for an example!" But Tom made him answer: "A dishclout in your teeth for your news, for you shall not find me to be one of them." "No!" said the giant, in astonishment and indignation; "and what a fool you must be if you come to fight with such a one as I am, and bring never a weapon to defend yourself!" Quoth Tom, "I have a weapon here that will make you know you are a traitorly rogue." This speech highly incensed the giant, who immediately ran to his cave for his club, intending to dash out Tom's brains at one blow. Tom was now much distressed for a weapon, as by some chance he had forgot one, and he began to reflect how very little his whip would help him against a monster twelve feet in height and six feet round the waist. But while the giant was gone for his club, Tom bethought himself, and turning his cart upside down, adroitly takes out the axletree, which would serve him for a staff, and removing a wheel, fits it to his arm instead of a shield—very good weapons indeed in time of trouble, and worthy of Tom's wit. When the monster returned with his club, he was amazed to see the weapons with which Tom had armed himself; but uttering a word of defiance, he bore down upon the poor fellow with such heavy strokes that it was as much as Tom could do to defend himself with his wheel. Tom, however, at length cut the giant a heavy blow with the axletree on the side of his head, that he nearly reeled over. "What!" said Tom, "have you drunk of my strong beer already?" This inquiry did not, as we may suppose, mollify the giant, who laid on his blows so sharply and heavily that Tom was obliged to defend himself. By-and-bye, not making any impression on the wheel, he got almost tired out, and was obliged to ask Tom if he would let him drink a little, and then he would fight again. "No," said Tom, "my mother did not teach me that wit : who would be fool then ? " The end may readily be imagined ; Tom having beaten the giant, cut off his head, and entered the cave, which he found completely filled with gold and silver.

The news of this victory rapidly spread throughout the country, for the giant had been a common enemy to the people about. They made bonfires for joy, and showed their respect to Tom by every means in their power. A few days afterwards Tom took possession of the cave and all the giant's treasure. He pulled down the former, and built a magnificent house on the spot ; but as for the land stolen by the giant, part of it he gave to the poor for their common, merely keeping enough for himself and his good old mother, Jane Hickathrift.

Tom was now a great man and a hero with all the country folk, so that when any one was in danger or difficulty, it was to Tom Hickathrift he must turn. It chanced that about this time many idle and rebellious persons drew themselves together in and about the Isle of Ely, and set themselves to defy the King and all his men.

By this time, you must know, Tom Hickathrift had secured to himself a trusty friend and comrade, almost his equal in strength and courage, for though he was but a tinker, yet he was a great and lusty one. Now the sheriff of the county came to Tom, under cover of night, full of fear and trembling, and begged his aid and protection against the rebels, "else," said he, "we be all dead men ! " Tom, nothing loth, called his friend the tinker, and as soon as it was day, led by the sheriff, they went out armed with their clubs to the place where the rebels were gathered together. When they were got thither, Tom and the tinker marched up to the leaders of the band, and asked them why they were set upon breaking the King's peace. To this they answered loudly, " Our will is our law, and by that alone we will be governed ! " " Nay," quoth Tom, "if it be so, these trusty clubs are our weapons, and by them alone you shall be chastised." These words were no sooner uttered than they madly rushed on the throng of men, bearing all before them, and laying twenty or thirty sprawling with every blow. The

F

tinker struck off heads with such violence that they flew
like balls for miles about, and when Tom had slain
hundreds and so broken his trusty club, he laid hold of a
lusty raw-boned miller and made use of him as a weapon
till he had quite cleared the field.

If Tom Hickathrift had been a hero before, he was
twice a hero now.　When the King heard of it all, he sent
for him to be knighted, and when he was Sir Thomas
Hickathrift nothing would serve him but that he must be
married to a great lady of the county.

So married he was, and a fine wedding they had of it.
There was a great-feast given, to which all the poor widows
for miles round were invited, because of Tom's mother,
and rich and poor feasted together.　Among the poor
widows who came was an old woman called Stumbelup,
who with much ingratitude stole from the great table a
silver tankard.　But she had not got safe away before she
was caught and the people were so enraged at her
wickedness that they had nearly hanged her.　However,
Sir Tom had her rescued, and commanded that she should
be drawn on a wheel-barrow through the streets and lanes
of Cambridge, holding a placard in her hand on which was
written—

> " I am the naughty Stumbelup,
> Who tried to steal the silver cup."

THE THREE BEARS

 NCE upon a time there were Three Bears, who lived together in a house of their own, in a wood. One of them was a Little, Small, Wee Bear; and one was a Middle-sized Bear, and the other was a Great, Huge Bear. They had each a pot for their porridge; a little pot for the Little, Small, Wee Bear; and a middle-sized pot for the Middle Bear; and a great pot for the Great, Huge Bear. And they had each a chair to sit in; a little chair for the Little, Small Wee Bear; and a middle-sized chair for the Middle Bear and a great chair for the Great, Huge Bear. And they had each a bed to sleep in; a little bed for the Little, Small, Wee Bear; and a middle-sized bed for the Middle Bear; and a great bed for the Great, Huge Bear.

One day, after they had made the porridge for their breakfast, and poured it into their porridge-pots, they walked out into the wood while the porridge was cooling, that they might not burn their mouths, by beginning too soon to eat it. And while they were walking, a little old Woman came to the house. She could not have been a good, honest old Woman; for first she looked in at the window, and then she peeped in at the keyhole; and seeing nobody in the house, she lifted the latch. The door was not fastened, because the Bears were good Bears, who did nobody any harm, and never suspected that anybody would harm them. So the little old Woman opened the door, and went in; and well pleased she was when she saw the porridge on the table. If she had been a good little old Woman, she would have waited till the Bears came home; and then, perhaps, they would have asked her to breakfast; for they were good Bears,—a little rough or so, as the manners of Bears are, but for all that very good-natured and hospitable.   But she was an impudent, bad old Woman, and set about helping herself.

So first she tasted the porridge of the Great, Huge Bear, and that was too hot for her; and she said a bad word about that.   And then she tasted the porridge of the Middle Bear, and that was too cold for her; and she said a bad word about that too.   And then she went to the porridge of the Little, Small, Wee Bear, and tasted that; and that was neither too hot, nor too cold, but just right; and she liked it so well, that she ate it all up: but the naughty old Woman said a bad word about the little porridge-pot, because it did not hold enough for her.

Then the little old Woman sate down in the chair of the Great, Huge Bear, and that was too hard for her.   And then she sate down in the chair of the Middle Bear, and that was too soft for her.   And then she sate down in the chair of the Little, Small, Wee Bear, and that was neither too hard, nor too soft, but just right.   So she seated herself in it, and there she sate till the bottom of the chair came out, and down came she plump upon the ground. And the naughty old Woman said a wicked word about that too.

Then the little old Woman went upstairs into the bed-chamber in which the three Bears slept.   And first she lay down upon the bed of the Great, Huge Bear; but that was too high at the head for her.   And next she lay down upon the bed of the Middle Bear; and that was too high at the foot for her.   And then she lay down upon the bed of the Little, Small, Wee Bear; and that was neither too high at the head, nor at the foot, but just right.   So she covered herself up comfortably, and lay there till she fell fast asleep.

By this time the Three Bears thought their porridge would be cool enough; so they came home to breakfast. Now the little old Woman had left the spoon of the Great, Huge Bear standing in his porridge.

"Somebody has been at my porridge!"

said the Great, Huge Bear, in his great, rough, gruff voice. And when the Middle Bear looked at his, he saw that the spoon was standing in it too.   They were wooden spoons;

if they had been silver ones, the naughty old Woman would have put them in her pocket.

"SOMEBODY HAS BEEN AT MY PORRIDGE!"
said the Middle Bear, in his middle voice.

THE LITTLE OLD WOMAN SITS DOWN IN THE LITTLE BEAR'S CHAIR

Then the Little, Small, Wee Bear looked at his, and there was the spoon in the porridge-pot, but the porridge was all gone.

"*Somebody has been at my porridge, and has eaten it all up!*"

said the Little, Small, Wee Bear, in his little, small, wee voice.

Upon this the Three Bears, seeing that some one had entered their house, and eaten up the Little, Small, Wee Bear's breakfast, began to look about them. Now the little old Woman had not put the hard cushion straight when she rose from the chair of the Great, Huge Bear.

"Somebody has been sitting in my chair!"

said the Great, Huge Bear, in his great rough, gruff voice.

And the little old Woman had squatted down the soft cushion of the Middle Bear.

"SOMEBODY HAS BEEN SITTING IN MY CHAIR!"

said the Middle Bear in his middle voice.

And you know what the little old Woman had done to the third chair.

"Somebody has been sitting in my chair, and has sate the bottom of it out!"

said the Little, Small, Wee Bear, in his little, small, wee voice.

Then the Three Bears thought it necessary that they should make farther search; so they went upstairs into their bed-chamber.   Now the little old Woman had pulled the pillow of the Great, Huge Bear out of its place.

"Somebody has been lying in my bed!"

said the Great, Huge Bear, in his great, rough, gruff voice.

And the little old Woman had pulled the bolster of the Middle Bear out of its place.

"SOMEBODY HAS BEEN LYING IN MY BED!"

said the Middle Bear, in his middle voice.

And when the Little, Small, Wee Bear came to look at his bed, there was the bolster in its place; and the pillow in its place upon the bolster; and upon the pillow was the little old Woman's ugly, dirty head,—which was not in its place, for she had no business there.

"Somebody has been lying in my bed and here she is!"

said the Little, Small, Wee Bear, in his little, small, wee voice.

The little old Woman had heard in her sleep the great, rough, gruff voice of the Great, Huge Bear; but she was so fast asleep that it was no more to her than the roaring of wind, or the rumbling of thunder.   And she had heard

the middle voice of the Middle Bear, but it was only as if
she had heard some one speaking in a dream. But when
she heard the Little, Small, Wee Bear, it was so sharp,
and so shrill, that it awakened her at once. Up she
started ; and when she saw the Three Bears on one side of
the bed, she tumbled herself out at the other, and ran to
the window. Now the window was open, because the
Bears, like good, tidy Bears, as they were, always opened
their bed-chamber window when they got up in the morning. Out the little old Woman jumped ; and whether she
broke her neck in the fall ; or ran into the wood and was
lost there ; or found her way out of the wood, and was
taken up by the constable and sent to the House of
Correction for a vagrant as she was, I cannot tell. But
the Three Bears never saw anything more of her.

THE HISTORY OF TOM THUMB

I T is said that in the days of the famed Prince Arthur, who was king of Britain, in the year 516 there lived a great magician, called Merlin, the most learned and skilful enchanter in the world at that time.

This great magician, who could assume any form he pleased, was travelling in the disguise of a poor beggar, and being very much fatigued, he stopped at the cottage of an honest ploughman to rest himself, and asked for some refreshment.

The countryman gave him a hearty welcome, and his wife, who was a very good-hearted, hospitable woman, soon brought him some milk in a wooden bowl, and some coarse brown bread on a platter.

Merlin was much pleased with this homely repast and the kindness of the ploughman and his wife; but he could not help seeing that though everything was neat and comfortable in the cottage, they seemed both to be sad and much cast down. He therefore questioned them on the cause of their sadness, and learned that they were miserable because they had no children.

The poor woman declared, with tears in her eyes, that she should be the happiest creature in the world if she had a son; and although he was no bigger than her husband's thumb, she would be satisfied.

Merlin was so much amused with the idea of a boy no bigger than a man's thumb, that he made up his mind to pay a visit to the queen of the fairies, and ask her to grant the poor woman's wish. The droll fancy of such a little person among the human race pleased the fairy queen too, greatly, and she promised Merlin that the wish should be granted. Accordingly, in a short time after, the ploughman's wife had a son, who, wonderful to relate, was not a bit bigger than his father's thumb.

The fairy queen, wishing to see the little fellow thus born into the world, came in at the window while the mother was sitting up in bed admiring him. The queen kissed the child, and giving it the name of Tom Thumb, sent for some of the fairies, who dressed her little favourite as she bade them.

> " An oak-leaf hat he had for his crown ;
> His shirt of web by spiders spun ;
> With jacket wove of thistle's down ;
> His trowsers were of feather's done.
> His stockings, of apple-rind, they tie
> With eyelash from his mother's eye :
> His shoes were made of mouse's skin,
> Tann'd with the downy hair within."

It is remarkable that Tom never grew any larger than his father's thumb, which was only of an ordinary size; but as he got older he became very cunning and full of tricks. When he was old enough to play with the boys, and had lost all his own cherry-stones, he used to creep into the bags of his playfellows, fill his pockets, and, getting out unseen, would again join in the game.

One day, however, as he was coming out of a bag of cherry-stones, where he had been pilfering as usual, the boy to whom it belonged chanced to see him. "Ah, ha ! my little Tommy," said the boy, "so I have caught you stealing my cherry-stones at last, and you shall be rewarded for your thievish tricks." On saying this, he drew the string tight round his neck, and gave the bag such a hearty shake, that poor little Tom's legs, thighs, and body were sadly bruised. He roared out with pain, and begged to be let out, promising never to be guilty of such bad practices again.

A short time afterwards his mother was making a batter-pudding, and Tom being very anxious to see how it was made, climbed up to the edge of the bowl ; but unfortunately his foot slipped and he plumped over head and ears into the batter, unseen by his mother, who stirred him into the pudding-bag, and put him in the pot to boil.

The batter had filled Tom's mouth, and prevented him from crying ; but, on feeling the hot water, he kicked and struggled so much in the pot, that his mother thought that the pudding was bewitched, and, instantly pulling it out of the pot, she threw it to the door. A poor tinker, who was passing by, lifted up the pudding, and, putting it into his budget, he then walked off. As Tom had now got his mouth cleared of the batter, he then began to cry aloud, which so frightened the tinker that he flung down the pudding and ran away. The pudding being broke to pieces by the fall, Tom crept out covered over with the batter, and with difficulty walked home. His mother, who was very sorry to see her darling in such a woful state, put him into a tea-cup, and soon washed off the batter; after which she kissed him, and laid him in bed.

Soon after the adventure of the pudding, Tom's mother went to milk her cow in the meadow, and she took him along with her. As the wind was very high, fearing lest he should be blown away, she tied him to a thistle with a piece of fine thread. The cow soon saw the oak-leaf hat, and, liking the look of it, took poor Tom and the thistle at one mouthful. While the cow was chewing the thistle Tom was afraid of her great teeth, which threatened to crush him in pieces, and he roared out as loud as he could : " Mother, mother ! "

" Where are you, Tommy, my dear Tommy ? " said his mother.

" Here, mother," replied he, " in the cow's mouth."

His mother began to cry and wring her hands ; but the cow, surprised at the odd noise in her throat, opened her mouth and let Tom drop out. Fortunately his mother caught him in her apron as he was falling to the ground, or he would have been dreadfully hurt. She then put Tom in her bosom and ran home with him.

Tom's father made him a whip of a barley straw to drive the cattle with, and having one day gone into the fields, he slipped a foot and rolled into the furrow. A raven, which was flying over, picked him up, and flew with him to the top of a giant's castle that was near the sea-side, and there left him.

Tom was in a dreadful state, and did not know what to do ; but he was soon more dreadfully frightened ; for old Grumbo the giant came up to walk on the terrace, and seeing Tom, he took him up and swallowed him like a pill.

The giant had no sooner swallowed Tom than he began to repent what he had done ; for Tom began to kick and jump about so much that he felt very uncomfortable, and at last threw him up again into the sea. A large fish swallowed Tom the moment he fell into the sea, which was soon after caught, and bought for the table of King Arthur. When they opened the fish in order to cook it, everyone was astonished at finding such a little boy, and Tom was quite delighted to be out again. They carried him to the king, who made Tom his dwarf, and he soon grew a great favourite at Court; for by his tricks and gambols he not only amused the king and queen, but also all the knights of the Round Table.

It is said that when the king rode out on horseback, he often took Tom along with him, and if a shower came on, he used to creep into his majesty's waistcoat pocket, where he slept till the rain was over.

King Arthur one day asked Tom about his parents, wishing to know if they were as small as he was, and whether rich or poor. Tom told the king that his father and mother were as tall as any of the sons about Court, but rather poor. On hearing this, the king carried Tom to his treasury, the place where he kept all his money, and told him to take as much money as he could carry home to his parents, which made the poor little fellow caper with joy. Tom went immediately to fetch a purse, which was made of a water-bubble, and then returned to the treasury, where he got a silver threepenny-piece to put into it.

Our little hero had some trouble in lifting the burden upon his back; but he at last succeeded in getting it placed to his mind, and set forward on his journey. However, without meeting with any accident and after resting himself more than a hundred times by the way, in two days and two nights he reached his father's house in safety.

Tom had travelled forty-eight hours with a huge silver-piece on his back, and was almost tired to death, when his mother ran out to meet him, and carried him into the house.

Tom's parents were both happy to see him, and the more so as he had brought such an amazing sum of money with him; but the poor little fellow was excessively wearied, having travelled half a mile in forty-eight hours, with a huge silver threepenny-piece on his back. His mother, in order to recover him, placed him in a walnut shell by the fireside, and feasted him for three days on a hazel-nut, which made him very sick; for a whole nut used to serve him a month.

Tom was soon well again; but as there had been a fall of rain, and the ground was very wet, he could not travel back to King Arthur's Court; therefore his mother, one day when the wind was blowing in that direction, made a little parasol of cambric paper, and tying Tom to it, she gave him a puff into the air with her mouth, which soon carried him to the king's palace.

Just at the time when Tom came flying across the court-yard, the cook happened to be passing with the king's great bowl of furmenty, which was a dish his majesty was very fond of; but unfortunately the poor little fellow fell plump into the middle of it, and splashed the hot furmenty about the cook's face.

The cook, who was an ill-natured fellow, being in a terrible rage at Tom for frightening and scalding him with the furmenty, went straight to the king, and said that Tom had jumped into the royal furmenty, and thrown it down out of mere mischief. The king was so enraged when he heard this, that he ordered Tom to be seized and tried for high treason; and there being no person who dared to plead for him, he was condemned to be beheaded immediately.

On hearing this dreadful sentence pronounced, poor Tom fell a-trembling with fear, but, seeing no means of escape, and observing a miller close to him gaping with his great mouth, as country boobies do at a fair, he took a leap, and fairly jumped down his throat. This exploit was done with such activity that not one person present saw it, and even the miller did not know the trick which Tom had played upon him. Now, as Tom had disap-peared, the court broke up, and the miller went home to his mill.

When Tom heard the mill at work he knew he was clear of the court, and therefore he began to roll and tumble about, so that the poor miller could get no rest, thinking he was bewitched; so he sent for a doctor. When the doctor came, Tom began to dance and sing; and the doctor, being as much frightened as the miller, sent in haste for five other doctors and twenty learned men.

When they were debating about this extraordinary case, the miller happened to yawn, when Tom, seizing the chance, made another jump, and alighted safely upon his feet on the middle of the table.

The miller, who was very much provoked at being tormented by such a little pigmy creature, fell into a terrible rage, and, laying hold of Tom, ran to the king with him ; but his majesty, being engaged with state affairs, ordered him to be taken away, and kept in custody till he sent for him.

The cook was determined that Tom should not slip out of his hands this time, so he put him into a mouse-trap, and left him to peep through the wires. Tom had remained in the trap a whole week, when he was sent for by King Arthur, who pardoned him for throwing down the furmenty, and took him again into favour. On account of his wonderful feats of activity, Tom was knighted by the king, and went under the name of the renowned Sir Thomas Thumb. As Tom's clothes had suffered much in the batter-pudding, the furmenty, and the insides of the giant, miller, and fishes, his majesty ordered him a new suit of clothes, and to be mounted as a knight.

> " Of Butterfly's wings his shirt was made,
>   His boots of chicken's hide ;
> And by a nimble fairy blade,
>   Well learned in the tailoring trade,
>   His clothing was supplied.—
> A needle dangled by his side ;
> A dapper mouse he used to ride,
> Thus strutted Tom in stately pride ! "

It was certainly very diverting to see Tom in this dress, and mounted on the mouse, as he rode out a-hunting with the king and nobility, who were all ready to expire with laughter at Tom and his fine prancing charger.

One day, as they were riding by a farmhouse, a large cat, which was lurking about the door, made a spring, and seized both Tom and his mouse. She then ran up a tree with them, and was beginning to devour the mouse ; but Tom boldly drew his sword, and attacked the cat so fiercely that she let them both fall, when one of the nobles caught him in his hat, and laid him on a bed of down, in a little ivory cabinet.

The queen of the fairies came soon after to pay Ton
a visit, and carried him back to Fairy-land, where he lived
several years.   During his residence there, King Arthur,
and all the persons who knew Tom, had died; and as he
was desirous of being again at Court, the fairy queen, after
dressing him in a suit of clothes, sent him flying through
the air to the palace, in the days of King Thunstone, the
successor of Arthur.   Every one flocked round to see him,
and being carried to the king, he was asked who he
was — whence he came — and where he lived? Tom
answered, —

> " My name is Tom Thumb,
> From the fairies I've come.
> When King Arthur shone,
> His Court was my home.
> In me he delighted,
> By him I was knighted :
> Did you never hear of Sir Thomas Thumb ? "

The king was so charmed with this address that he
ordered a little chair to be made, in order that Tom might
sit upon his table, and also a palace of gold, a span high,
with a door an inch wide, to live in.   He also gave him a
coach, drawn by six small mice.

The queen was so enraged at the honour paid to Sir
Thomas that she resolved to ruin him, and told the king
that the little knight had been saucy to her.

The king sent for Tom in great haste, but being fully
aware of the danger of royal anger, he crept into an empty
snail-shell, where he lay for a long time, until he was
almost starved with hunger; but at last he ventured to
peep out, and seeing a fine large butterfly on the ground,
near his hiding-place, he approached very cautiously, and
getting himself placed astride on it, was immediately
carried up into the air.   The butterfly flew with him from
tree to tree and from field to field, and at last returned to
the Court, where the king and nobility all strove to catch
him; but at last poor Tom fell from his seat into a watering-pot, in which he was almost drowned.

When the queen saw him she was in a rage, and said
he should be beheaded; and he was again put into a
mouse-trap until the time of his execution.

However, a cat, observing something alive in the trap,

patted .t about till the wires broke, and set Thomas at liberty.

The king received Tom again into favour, which he did not live to enjoy, for a large spider one day attacked him ; and although he drew his sword and fought well, yet the spider's poisonous breath at last overcame him ;

> " He fell dead on the ground where he stood,
> And the spider suck'd every drop of his blood."

King Thunstone and his whole Court were so sorry at the loss of their little favourite, that they went into mourning, and raised a fine white marble monument over his grave, with the following epitaph :—

> " Here lyes Tom Thumb, King Arthur's knight,
> Who died by a spider's cruel bite,
> He was well known in Arthur's Court,
> Where he afforded gallant sport ;
> He rode at tilt and tournament,
> And on a mouse a-hunting went.
> Alive he filled the Court with mirth ;
> His death to sorrow soon gave birth.
> Wipe, wipe your eyes, and shake your head
> And cry,—Alas ! Tom Thumb is dead ! "

THE GIANT OF SAINT MICHAEL'S

WHEN King Arthur was king of this realm, it befell at one time that he departed and entered into the sea at Sandwich with all his army, with a great multitude of ships, galleys, and dromons,[1] sailing on the sea.

And as the king lay in his cabin in the ship, he fell in a slumbering, and dreamed a marvellous dream: him seemed that a dreadful dragon did drown much of his people, and he came flying out of the west, and his head was enamelled with azure, and his shoulders shone as gold, his body like mails[2] of a marvellous hue, his tail full of tatters, his feet full of fine sable, and his claws like fine gold; and an hideous flame of fire flew out of his mouth, like as the land and water had flamed all of fire. After him, there came out of the Orient a grimly boar, all black, sailing in a cloud, and his paws as big as a post. He was rugged looking, roughly; he was the foulest beast that ever man saw, he roared and romed[3] so hideously that it was marvel to hear. Then the dreadful dragon advanced him, and came in the wind like a falcon, giving great strokes on the boar, and the boar hit him again with his grisly tusks that his breast was all bloody, and that the hot blood made all the sea red of his blood. Then the dragon flew away all on an height, and came down with such a swough, and smote the boar on the ridge, which was ten foot large from the foot to the tail, and smote the boar all to powder, both flesh and bones, that it flittered all abroad on the sea. And therewith the king awoke anon and was sore abashed of this dream; and sent anon for a wise man commanding to tell him the meaning of his dream.

"Sir," said the wise man, "the dragon that thou

[1] War-vessels, with high prows.
[2] A coat of mail.   [3] Growled.

96

dreamedst of betokeneth thine own person that sailest here, and the colour of his wings be thy realms that thou hast won, and his tail which is all to-tattered signifieth the noble knights of the Round Table. And the boar that the dragon slew coming from the clouds, either betokeneth some tyrant that tormenteth the people, or else that thou art like to fight with some giant thyself, being horrible and abominable, whose peer ye saw never in your days. Wherefore of this dreadful dream doubt thee nothing, but as a conqueror come forth thyself."

Then after this soon they had sight of land, and when they were there, a husbandman of that country came and told him there was a great giant which had slain, murdered, and devoured much people of the country, and had been sustained seven year with the children of the commons of that land, insomuch that all the children be all slain and destroyed.

"And now late," saith this countryman, "he hath taken the Duchess of Brittany as she rode with her train, and hath led her to this lodging which is in a mountain, for to keep her to her life's end ; and many people followed her, more than five hundred, but all they might not rescue her, but they left her shrieking and crying lamentably, wherefore I suppose that he hath slain her. Now as thou art a rightful king have pity on this lady, and revenge us all as thou art a noble conqueror."

"Alas ! " said King Arthur, "this is a great mischief, I had rather than the best realm that I have that I had been a furlong way tofore him, for to have rescued that lady. Canst thou bring me where this giant haunteth ?"

"Yea, sir," said the good man, "lo, yonder where as thou seest those two great fires, there thou shalt find him, and more treasure than I suppose is in all France."

When the king had understood this piteous case he returned into his tent.

Then he called unto him Sir Kay and Sir Bedivere, and commanded them secretly to make ready horse and harness for himself and them twain, for after evensong he would ride on pilgrimage with them two only unto Saint Michael's Mount. And then anon he made him ready and armed him at all points, and took his horse and his shield. And so they three departed thence, and rode forth

G

as fast as ever they might till that they came unto the foot
of that mount. And there they alighted, and the king
commanded them to tarry there, for he would himself go up
into that mount. And so he ascended up into that hill
till he came to a great fire, and there he found a careful
widow wringing her hands and making great sorrow, sitting
by a grave new made.

King Arthur saluted her, and demanded of her wherefore she made such lamentation : to whom she answered
and said, "Sir knight, speak soft, for yonder is a demon :
if he hear thee speak he will come and destroy thee; I
hold thee unhappy ; what dost thou here in this mountain?
for if ye were such fifty as ye be, ye were not able to make
resistance against this devil : here lieth a duchess dead, the
which was the fairest of all the world, wife to Sir Howell,
Duke of Brittany ; he hath murdered her."

"Dame," said the king, "I come from the noble
conqueror King Arthur, for to treat with that tyrant for
his liege people."

"Fie upon such treaties," said the widow, "he setteth
not by the king, nor by no man else. Beware, approach
him not too nigh, for he hath vanquished fifteen kings,
and hath made him a coat full of precious stones, embroidered with their beards, which they sent him to have
his love for salvation of their people at this last Christmas.
And if thou wilt, speak with him at yonder great fire at
supper."

"Well," said Arthur, "I will accomplish my message for
all your fearful words."

And he went forth by the crest of that hill, and saw
where the giant sat at supper gnawing on a limb of a
man, baking his broad limbs by the fire, and three fair
damsels turning three spits, whereon were broached twelve
young children like young birds.

When King Arthur beheld that piteous sight he had
great compassion on them so that his heart bled for
sorrow, and hailed him saying in this wise,—

"He that all the world wieldeth, give thee short life and
shameful death. Why hast thou murdered these young
innocent children, and murdered this duchess? Therefore arise and dress thee, thou glutton ; for this day shalt
thou die of my hand."

"THEREFORE ARISE AND DRESS THEE, THOU GLUTTON;
FOR THIS DAY THOU SHALT DIE OF MY HAND."

Then the glutton anon started up and took a great club in his hand, and smote at the king that his coronal fell to the ground. And the king hit the giant again, and carved his body till his blood fell down in two streams. Then the giant threw away his club, and caught the king in his arms that he crushed his ribs. Then the three maidens kneeled down and called to Christ for help and comfort of Arthur. And then Arthur weltered and wrestled with the giant, that he was other while under and another time above. And so weltering and wallowing they rolled down the hill till they came to the sea mark, and ever as they so weltered Arthur smote him with his dagger, and it fortuned they came to the place where as the two knights were that kept Arthur's horse. Then when they saw the king fast in the giant's arms they came and loosed him.

And then the king commanded Sir Kay to smite off the giant's head, and to set it upon a truncheon of a spear, and bear it to Sir Howell, and tell him that his enemy was slain. "After this," said the king, " let his head be bound to a barbican that all the people may see and behold it ; and go ye two up to the mountain and fetch me my shield, my sword, and the club of iron. And as for the treasure take ye it, for ye shall find there goods out of number. So I have the kirtle and the club, I desire no more. This was the fiercest giant that ever I met with, save one in the mount of Arabe which I overcame, but this was greater and fiercer."

Then the knights fetched the club and the kirtle, and some of the treasure they took to themselves, and returned again to the host. And anon this was known through all the country, wherefore the people came and thanked the king. And he said again, "Give the thanks to God, and part the goods among you." And after that, King Arthur said and commanded his cousin Howell that he should ordain for a church to be builded on the same hill, in the worship of Saint Michael.

THE FAIRIES' FROLIC

Scene from a Fairy Play

Human Characters :—Mopso, Joculo, and Frisio.

Enter Fairies, singing and dancing.

Fairy Song.

> By the moon we sport and play,
> With the night begins our day ;
> As we dance the dew doth fall—
> Trip it, little urchins all,
> Lightly as the little bee,
> Two by two, and three by three ;
> And about go we, and about go we.

Jo. What mawmets [1] are these ?
Fris. O they be the fairies that haunt these woods.
Mop. O we shall be pinched most cruelly !
1st Fai. Will you have any music, sir ?
2d Fai. Will you have any fine music ?
3d Fai. Most dainty music ?
Mop. We must set a face on it now ; there is no flying.
No, sir, we very much thank you.
1st Fai. O but you shall, sir.
Fris. No, I pray you, save your labour.
2d Fai. O, sir ! it shall not cost you a penny.
Jo. Where be your fiddles ?
3d Fai. You shall have most dainty instruments, sir ?
Mop. I pray you, what might I call you ?
1st Fai. My name is Penny.
Mop. I am sorry I cannot purse you.
Fris. I pray you, sir, what might I call you ?
2d Fai. My name is Cricket.

[1] Dolls, puppets.

Fris. I would I were a chimney for your sake.

Jo. I pray you, you pretty little fellow, what's your name?

3d Fai. My name is little little Puck.

Jo. Little little Puck? O you are a dangerous fairie!
I care not whose hand I were in, so I were out of yours.

   1st Fai. I do come about the cops,
        Leaping upon flowers' tops;
        Then I get upon a fly,
        She carries me about the sky,
        And trip and go.

   2d Fai. When a dew-drop falleth down,
        And doth light upon my crown,
        Then I shake my head and skip,
        And about I trip.

   3d Fai. When I see a girl asleep,
        Underneath her curls I peep,
        There to sport, and there I play,
        When she wakes, I run away.

   Jo. I thought where I should have you.

   1st Fai. Will 't please you dance, sir?

   Jo. Indeed, sir, I cannot handle my legs.

   2d Fai. O you must needs dance and sing,
        Which if you refuse to do,
        We will pinch you black and blue;
        And about we go.

FAIRIES *sing.*

Round about, round about, in a fine ring a,
Thus we dance, thus we dance, and thus we sing a;
Trip and go, to and fro, over this green a,
All about, in and out, for our brave queen a.

Round about, round about, in a fine ring a,
Thus we dance, thus we dance, and thus we sing a;
Trip and go, to and fro, over this green a,
All about, in and out, for our brave queen a.

We have danced round about, in a fine ring a,
We have danced lustily, and thus we sing a;
All about, in and out, over this green a,
To and fro, trip and go, to our brave queen a.

JACK AND THE BEAN-STALK

HERE once lived a poor widow, in a cottage which stood in a country village, a long distance from London, for many years.

The widow had only a child named Jack, whom she gratified in everything; the end of her foolish kindness was, that Jack paid little attention to any-hing she said; and he was heedless and naughty. His follies were not owing to bad nature, but to his mother never having chided him. As she was not rich, and he would not work, she was obliged to support herself and him by selling everything she had. At last nothing remained, only a cow.

The widow, with tears in her eyes, could not help scolding Jack. "Oh! you wicked boy," said she, "by your naughty course of life you have now brought us both to fall! Heedless, heedless boy! I have not money enough to buy a bit of bread for another day: nothing remains but my poor cow, and that must be sold, or we must starve!"

Jack was in a degree of tenderness for a few minutes, but soon over; and then becoming very hungry for want of food he teased his poor mother to let him sell the cow; which at last she sadly allowed him to do.

As he went on his journey he met a butcher, who asked why he was driving the cow from home? Jack replied he was going to sell it. The butcher had some wonderful beans, of different colours, in his bag, which caught Jack's fancy. This the butcher saw, who, knowing Jack's easy temper, made up his mind to take advantage of it, and offered all the beans for the cow. The foolish boy thought it a great offer. The bargain was momently struck, and the cow exchanged for a few paltry beans. When Jack hastened home with the beans and told his mother, and showed them to her, she kicked the beans away in a great passion. They flew in all directions, and fell as far as the garden.

Early in the morning Jack arose from his bed, and seeing something strange from the window, he hastened downstairs into the garden, where he soon found that some of the beans had taken root, and sprung up wonderfully: the stalks grew of an immense thickness, and had so entwined, that they formed a ladder like a chain in view.

Looking upwards, he could not descry the top, it seemed to be lost in the clouds. He tried it, found it firm, and not to be shaken. A new idea immediately struck him: he would climb the bean-stalk, and see whither it would lead. Full of this plan, which made him forget even his hunger, Jack hastened to tell it to his mother.

He at once set out, and after climbing for some hours, reached the top of the bean-stalk, tired and almost exhausted. Looking round, he was surprised to find himself in a strange country; it seemed to be quite a barren desert; not a tree, shrub, house, or living creature was to be seen.

Jack sat himself pensively upon a block of stone, and thought of his mother; his hunger attacked him, and now he felt sorrowful for his disobedience in climbing the bean-stalk against her will; and made up his mind that he must now die for want of food.

However, he walked on, hoping to see a house where he might beg something to eat. Suddenly he saw a beautiful young woman at some distance. She was dressed in an elegant manner, and had a small white wand in her hand, on the top of which was a peacock of pure gold. She came near and said: " I will tell to you a story your mother dare not. But before I begin, I require a solemn promise on your part to do what I command. I am a fairy, and unless you perform exactly what I direct you to do, you will take from me the power to assist you; and there is little doubt but that you will die in the attempt." Jack was rather frightened at this caution, but promised to follow her directions.

"Your father was a rich man, with a greatly generous nature. It was his practice never to refuse help to the

poor people about him ; but, on the contrary, to seek out
the helpless and distressed. Not many miles from your
father's house lived a huge giant, who was the dread of
the country around for cruelty and wickedness. This
creature was moreover of a very envious spirit, and dis-
liked to hear others talked of for their goodness and
humanity, and he vowed to do him a mischief, so that he
might no longer hear his good actions made the subject of
everyone's talk. Your father was too good a man to fear
evil from others ; so it was not long before the cruel
giant found a chance to put his wicked threats into
practice ; for hearing that your parents were about passing
a few days with a friend at some distance from home, he
caused your father to be waylaid and murdered, and your
mother to be seized on their way homeward.

"At the time this happened, you were but a few months
old. Your poor mother, almost dead with affright and
horror, was borne away by the cruel giant's servants, to a
dungeon under his house, in which she and her poor babe
were both long kept prisoners. Distracted at the absence
of your parents, the servants went in search of them ; but
no tidings of either could be got. Meantime he caused
a will to be found making over all your father's property to
him as your guardian, and as such he took open possession.

"After your mother had been some months in prison,
the giant offered to restore her to liberty, on condition
that she would solemnly swear that she would never tell
the story of her wrongs to any one. To put it out of her
power to do him any harm, should she break her oath, the
giant had her put on shipboard, and taken to a distant
country ; where she was left with no more money for her
support than what she got by selling a few jewels she had
hidden in her dress.

"I was appointed your father's guardian at his birth ;
but fairies have laws to which they are subject as well as
mortals. A short time before the giant killed your father,
I transgressed ; my punishment was the loss of my power
for a certain time, which, alas, entirely prevented my
helping your father, even when I most wished to do so.
The day on which you met the butcher, as you went to
sell your mother's cow, my power was restored. It was I

who secretly prompted you to take the beans in exchange for the cow. By my power the bean-stalk grew to so great a height, and formed a ladder. The giant lives in this country; you are the person who must punish him for all his wickedness. You will meet with dangers and difficulties, but you must persevere in avenging the death of your father, or you will not prosper in any of your doings.

"As to the giant's goods, everything he has is yours, though you are deprived of it; you may take, therefore, what part of it you can. You must, however, be careful, for such is his love for gold, that the first loss he discovers will make him outrageous and very watchful for the future. But you must still pursue him; for it is only by cunning that you can ever hope to get the better of him, and become possessed of your rightful property, and the means of justice overtaking him for his barbarous murder. One thing I desire is, do not let your mother know you are aware of your father's history till you see me again.

"Go along the direct road; you will soon see the house where your cruel enemy lives. While you do as I order you, I will protect and guard you; but remember, if you disobey my commands, a dreadful punishment awaits you."

As soon as she had made an end she disappeared, leaving Jack to follow his journey. He walked on till after sunset, when, to his great joy, he espied a large mansion. This pleasant sight revived his drooping spirits; he redoubled his speed, and reached it shortly. A well-looking woman stood at the door: he spoke to her, begging she would give him a morsel of bread and a night's lodging. She expressed the greatest surprise at seeing him; and said it was quite uncommon to see any strange creature near their house, for it was mostly known that her husband was a very cruel and powerful giant, and one that would eat human flesh, if he could possibly get it.

This account terrified Jack greatly, but still, not forgetting the fairy's protection, he hoped to elude the giant, and therefore he begged the woman to take him in for one night only, and hide him where she thought proper

The good woman at last suffered herself to be persuaded for she had a kind heart, and at last led him into the house.

First they passed an elegant hall, finely furnished ; they then went through several spacious rooms, all in the same style of grandeur, but they seemed to be quite forsaken and desolate. A long gallery came next ; it was very dark, just large enough to show that, instead of a wall each side, there was a grating of iron, which parted off a dismal dungeon, from whence issued the groans of several poor victims whom the cruel giant kept shut up in readiness for his very large appetite. Poor Jack was in a dreadful fright at witnessing such a horrible scene, which caused him to fear that he would never see his mother, but be captured lastly for the giant's meat ; but still he recollected the fairy, and a gleam of hope forced itself into his heart.

The good woman then took Jack to a large kitchen, where a great fire was kept ; she bade him sit down, and gave him plenty to eat and drink. When he had done his meal and enjoyed himself, he was disturbed by a hard knocking at the gate, so loud as to cause the house to shake. Jack was hidden in the oven, and the giant's wife ran to let in her husband.

Jack heard him accost her in a voice like thunder, saying : "Wife ! wife ! I smell fresh meat !" "Oh ! my dear," replied she, "it is nothing but the people in the dungeon." The giant seemed to believe her, and at last seated himself by the fireside, whilst the wife prepared supper.

By degrees Jack managed to look at the monster through a small crevice. He was much surprised to see what an amazing quantity he devoured, and supposed he would never have done eating and drinking. After his supper was ended, a very curious hen was brought and placed on the table before him. Jack's curiosity was great to see what would happen. He saw that it stood quiet before him, and every time the giant said : "Lay !" the hen laid an egg of solid gold. The giant amused himself a long time with his hen ; meanwhile his wife went to bed. At length he fell asleep, and snored like the roaring of a cannon. Jack, finding him still asleep at daybreak, crept

Jack and the Bean-stalk 109

softly from his hiding-place, seized the hen, and ran off with her as fast as his legs could possibly carry him.

Jack easily found his way to the bean-stalk, and came down better and quicker than he expected. His mother was overjoyed to see him. "Now, mother," said Jack, "I have brought you home that which will make you rich." The hen laid as many golden eggs as they desired ; they sold them, and soon had as much riches as they wanted.

For a few months Jack and his mother lived very happy, but he longed to pay the giant another visit. Early one morning he again climbed the bean-stalk, and reached the giant's mansion late in the evening : the woman was at the door as before. Jack told her a pitiful tale, and prayed for a night's shelter. She told him that she had admitted a poor hungry boy once before, and the little ingrate had stolen one of the giant's treasures, and ever since that she had been cruelly used. She however led him to the kitchen, gave him a supper, and put him in a lumber closet. Soon after the giant came in, took his supper, and ordered his wife to bring down his bags of gold and silver. Jack peeped out of his hiding-place, and observed the giant counting over his treasures, and after which he carefully put them in bags again, fell asleep, and snored as before. Jack crept quietly from his hiding-place, and approached the giant, when a little dog under the chair barked furiously. Much to his surprise, the giant slept on soundly, and the dog ceased. Jack seized the bags, reached the door in safety, and soon arrived at the bottom of the bean-stalk. When he reached his mother's cottage, he found it quite deserted. Full of astonishment he ran into the village, and an old woman directed him to a house, where he found his mother apparently dying. On being told of our hero's safe return, his mother revived and soon recovered. Jack then presented two bags of gold and silver to her.

His mother saw that something preyed upon his mind heavily, and tried to find out the cause ; but Jack knew too well what the consequence would be should he discover the cause of his melancholy to her. He did his utmost therefore to conquer the great desire which now forced itself upon him in spite of himself for another journey up the bean-stalk, but in vain.

On the longest day Jack arose as soon as it was light, climbed the bean-stalk, and reached the top with some little trouble. He found the road, journey, etc., the same as before. He arrived at the giant's house in the evening, and found his wife standing as usual at the door. Jack now appeared a different character, and had disguised himself so completely that she did not appear to remember him. However, when he begged admittance, he found it very difficult to persuade her. At last he prevailed, was allowed to go in, and was hidden in the copper.

When the giant returned, he said, as usual: "Wife! wife! I smell fresh meat!" But Jack felt quite composed, as he had said so before, and had soon been satisfied. However, the giant started up suddenly, and notwithstanding all his wife could say, he searched all round the room. Whilst this was going forward, Jack was much terrified, and ready to die with fear, wishing himself at home a thousand times; but when the giant approached the copper, and put his hand upon the lid, Jack thought his death was certain. Fortunately the giant ended his search there, without moving the lid, and seated himself quietly by the fireside.

When the giant's supper was over, he commanded his wife to fetch down his harp. Jack peeped under the copper-lid, and soon saw the most beautiful one that could be imagined. It was put by the giant on the table, who said: "Play," and it instantly played of its own accord. The music was uncommonly fine. Jack was delighted, and felt more anxious to get the harp into his possession than either of the former treasures.

The giant's soul was not attuned to harmony, and the music soon lulled him into a sound sleep. Now, therefore, was the time to carry off the harp, as the giant appeared to be in a more profound sleep than usual. Jack soon made up his mind, got out of the copper, and seized the harp; which, however, being enchanted by a fairy, called out loudly: "Master, master!"

The giant awoke, stood up, and tried to pursue Jack; but he had drank so much that he could not stand. Jack ran as quick as he could. In a little time the giant was well enough to walk slowly, or rather to reel after him.   Had he been sober, he must have overtaken Jack instantly ; but as he then was, Jack contrived to be first at the top of the bean-stalk.   The giant called to him all the way along the road in a voice like thunder, and was sometimes very near to him.

The moment Jack got down the bean-stalk, he called out for a hatchet : one was brought him directly.   Just at that instant the giant began to descend, but Jack with his hatchet cut the bean-stalk close off at the root, and the giant fell headlong into the garden.   The fall instantly killed him.

Jack heartily begged his mother's pardon for all the sorrow and affliction he had caused her, promising most faithfully to be dutiful and obedient to her in future. He proved as good as his word, and became a pattern of affectionate behaviour for the rest of her life ; and, let us hope, he never lost his mother-wit.

QUEEN MAB'S GOOD GRACE

IF ye will with Mab find grace,
  Set each platter in his place;
Rake the fire up, and get
Water in, ere sun be set,
Wash your pails and cleanse your dairies,
Sluts are loathsome to the fairies;
Sweep your house; who doth not so,
Mab will pinch her by the toe.

OLD FORTUNATUS

F AR from here in the famous isle of Cyprus there is a stately city called Famagosta. There, a long time ago, lived one Theodorus, descended of noble parents, who left him with a great estate. But being brought up to nothing but idleness, he soon wasted the greater half of his riches to the great grief of his relations, who, thinking to make him leave these courses, determined to match him to a rich merchant's daughter in the city of Nicovia, named Graciana.

Now for a time, Theodorus was content to lead a quiet life, and Graciana brought her husband a fine little son, who was named Fortunatus. So one would think nothing could have kept Theodorus from being the most happy person in the world. But this was not long the case; for when he had enjoyed these things for some time, he grew tired of them, and began to keep company with young noblemen of the Court, and in a few years spent all his fortune. He was now very sorry for what he had done, but it was too late; and there was nothing he could do, but to work at some trade to support his wife and child. For all this Graciana never found fault with him, but still loved her husband the same as before, saying,—

"Dear Theodorus, to be sure I do not know how to work at any trade; but if I cannot help you in earning money, I will help you to save it."

So Theodorus set to work; and though the Lady Graciana had always been used only to ring her bell for everything that she wanted, she now scoured the kettles and washed the clothes with her own hands.

They went on in this manner till Fortunatus was sixteen years of age. When that time came, one day, as they were all sitting at dinner, Theodorus fixed his eyes on his son, and sighed deeply.

"What is the matter with you, father?" said Fortunatus.

"Ah! my child," said Theodorus, "I have reason enough to be sorry, when I think of the noble fortune which I have spent, and that my folly will force you to labour for your living."

"Father," replied Fortunatus, "do not grieve about it. I have often thought that it was time I should do something for myself; and though I have not been brought up to any trade, yet I hope I can contrive to support myself somehow."

When Fortunatus had done his dinner, he took his hat and walked to the sea-side, thinking of what he could do, so as to be no longer a burden to his parents. Just as he reached the sea-shore, the Earl of Flanders, who had been to Jerusalem, was embarking on board his ship with all his servants, to set sail for Flanders. Fortunatus now thought he would offer himself to be the Earl's page. When the Earl saw that he was a smart-looking lad, and heard the quick replies which he made to his questions, he took him into his service; so at once they all went on board. On their way the ship stopped a short time at the port of Venice, where Fortunatus saw many strange things, which made him wish still more to travel, and taught him much that he did not know before.

Soon after they came to Flanders; and they had not been long on shore, before the Earl, his master, was married to the daughter of the Duke of Cleves. The wedding was kept with all sorts of public feasting, and games on horseback called tilts, which lasted many days; and, among the rest, the Earl's lady gave two jewels as prizes to be played for, each of them the value of a hundred crowns. One of them was won by Fortunatus, and the other by Timothy, a servant of the Duke of Burgundy; who afterwards ran another tilt with Fortunatus, so that the winner was to have both the jewels. So they tilted, and, at the fourth course, Fortunatus hoisted Timothy a full spear's length from his horse, and thus won both the jewels; which pleased the Earl and Countess so much that they praised Fortunatus, and thought better of him than ever. At this time, also, Fortunatus had many rich presents given him by the lords and ladies of the Court. But the high favour shown him made his fellow-servants jealous; and one, named Robert, who had always pretended a great friendship for Fortunatus, made him believe that for all his seeming kindness, the Earl in secret envied him his great skill in tilting. Robert said, too, that he had heard the Earl give private orders to one of his servants to find some way of killing him next day, while they should all be out hunting.

Fortunatus thanked the wicked Robert for what he thought a great kindness; and the next day, at daybreak, he took the swiftest horse in the Earl's stables, and left the country. When the Earl heard that Fortunatus had gone away in a hurry, he was much surprised, and asked all his servants what they knew about the matter; but they all denied knowing anything of it, or why he had left them. The Earl then said: "Fortunatus was a lad for whom I had a great esteem; I am sure some of you must have given him an affront; if I discover it, I shall not fail to punish the guilty person." In the meantime Fortunatus, when he found himself out of the Earl's country, stopped at an inn to refresh himself, and began to reckon how much he had about him. He took out all his fine clothes and jewels, and could not help putting them on. He then looked at himself in the glass, and thought that, to be sure, he was quite a fine smart fellow. Next he took out his purse, and counted the money that had been given him by the lords and ladies of the Earl's court. He found that in all he had five hundred crowns; so he bought a horse, and took care to send back the one that he had taken from the Earl's stable.

He then set off for Calais, crossed the Channel, landed safely at Dover, and went on to London, where he soon made his way into genteel company, and had once the honour to dance with the daughter of a duke at the lord mayor's ball. This sort of life, as anybody may well think, soon made away with his little stock of money. When Fortunatus found that he had not a penny left, he began to think of going back again to France; and soon after went on board a ship bound to Picardy. He landed in that country; but finding no employment he set off for Brittany, when he lost his way in crossing a wood, and was forced to stay in it all night. The next morning he was little better off, for he could find no path. So he walked about from one part of the wood to another, till at last, on the evening of the second day, he saw a spring, at which he drank very heartily; but still he had nothing to eat, and was ready to die with hunger. When night came on, he heard the growling of wild beasts, so he climbed up a high tree for safety; and he had hardly seated himself in it, before a lion walked fiercely up to the spring to drink. This made him very much afraid. When the lion had gone away, a bear came to drink also; and, as the moon shone very bright, the beast looked up, and saw Fortunatus, and straightway began to climb up the tree to get at him.

Fortunatus drew his sword, and sat quiet till the bear was come within arm's length; and then he ran him through the body. This drove the bear so very savage, that he made a great spring to get at him; the bough broke, and down he fell, and lay sprawling and howling on the ground. Fortunatus now looked around on all sides; and as he saw no more wild beasts near, he thought this would be a good time to get rid of the bear at once; so down he came, and killed him at a single blow. Being almost starved for want of food, the poor youth stooped down, and was going to suck the blood of the bear; but looking round once more, to see if any wild beast were coming, he on a sudden beheld a beautiful lady standing by his side, with a bandage over her eyes, leaning upon a wheel, and looking as if she were going to speak, which she soon did, in these words: " Know, young man, that my name is Fortune; I have the power to bestow wisdom, strength, riches, health, beauty, and long life: one of these I am willing to grant you—choose for yourself which it shall be."

Fortunatus was not a moment before he answered: " Good lady, I wish to have riches in such plenty that I may never again know what it is to be so hungry as I now find myself." The lady then gave him a purse, and told him that in all the countries where he might happen to be, he need only put his hand into the purse as often as he pleased, and he would be sure to find in it ten pieces of gold; that the purse should never fail of yielding the same sum as long as it was kept by him and his children; but that when he and his children should be dead, then the purse would lose its power.

The Lady then gave him a purse

. Fortunatus now did not know what to do with himself for joy, and began to thank the lady very much ; but she told him that he had better think of making his way out of the wood. She then directed him which path to take, and bade him farewell. He walked by the light of the moon, as fast as his weakness and fatigue would let him, till he came near an inn. But before he went into it, he thought it would be best to see whether the Lady Fortune had been as good as her word; so he put his hand into his purse, and to his great joy he counted ten pieces of gold. Having nothing to fear, Fortunatus walked boldly up to the inn, and called for the best supper they could get ready in a minute; "For," said he, "I must wait till to-morrow before I am very nice. I am so hungry now, that almost anything will do." Fortunatus very soon ate quite enough, and then called for every sort of wine in the house, and drank his fill. After supper, he began to think what sort of life he should lead; "For," said he to himself, "I shall now have money enough for everything I can desire." He slept that night in the very best bed in the house ; and the next day he ordered the finest victuals of all kinds. When he rang his bell, all the waiters tried who should run fastest, to ask him what he pleased to want; and the landlord himself, hearing what a noble guest was come to his house, took care to be standing at the door to bow to him when he should be passing out.

Fortunatus asked the landlord whether any fine horses could be got near at hand; also, if he knew of some smart-looking, clever men-servants who wanted places. By chance the landlord was able to provide him with both. As he had now got everything he wanted, he set out on the finest horse that was ever seen, with two servants, for the nearest town. There he bought some grand suits of clothes, put his two servants into liveries laced with gold, and then went on to Paris. Here he took the best house that was to be had, and lived in great pomp. He invited the nobility, and gave grand balls to all the most beautiful ladies of the Court. He went to all public places of amusement, and the first lords in the country invited him to their houses. He had lived in this manner for about a year, when he began to think of going to Famagosta to visit his parents, whom he had left very poor.

"But," thought Fortunatus, "as I am young and have not seen much of the world, I should like to meet with some person of more knowledge than I have, who would make my journey both useful and pleasing to me." Soon after this he met with an old gentleman, called Loch-Fitty, who was a native of Scotland, and had left a wife and ten children a great many years ago, in hopes to better his fortune ; but now, owing to many accidents, was poorer than ever, and had not money enough to take him back to his family.

When Loch-Fitty found how much Fortunatus wished to obtain knowledge, he told him many of the strange adventures he had met with, and gave him an account of all the countries he had been in, as well as of the customs, dress, and manners of the people. Fortunatus thought to himself, "This is the very man I stand in need of ;" so at once he made him a good offer, which the old gentleman agreed to, but made the bargain that he might first go and visit his family. Fortunatus told him that he should. "And," said he, "as I am a little tired of being always in the midst of such noisy pleasures as we find at Paris, I will, with your leave, go with you to Scotland, and see your wife and children." They set out the very next day, and came safe to the house of Loch-Fitty ; and in all the journey, Fortunatus did not once wish to change his kind companion for all the pleasures and grandeur he had left behind. Loch-Fitty kissed his wife and children, five of whom were daughters, and the most beautiful creatures that were ever beheld. When they were seated, his wife said to him : "Ah ! dear Lord Loch-Fitty, how happy I am to see you once again ! Now I hope we shall enjoy each other's company for the rest of our lives. What though we are poor ! We will be content if you will but promise not to think of leaving us again to get riches, only because we have a noble title."

Fortunatus heard this with great surprise. "What !" said he, "are you a lord ? Then you shall be a rich lord too. And that you may not think I lay you under any burden in the fortune I shall give you, I will put it in your power to make me your debtor instead. Give me your youngest daughter, Cassandra, for a wife, and accompany us as far as Famagosta, and take all your family with you, that you may have pleasant company on your way back, when you have rested in that place from your fatigue."

Lord Loch-Fitty shed some tears of joy to think he should at last see his family again raised to all the honours which it had once enjoyed. He gladly agreed to the marriage of Fortunatus with his daughter Cassandra, and then told him the reasons that had forced him to drop his title and live poor at Paris. When Lord Loch-Fitty had ended his story, they agreed that the very next morning the Lady Cassandra should be asked to accept the hand of Fortunatus; and that, if she should consent, they would set sail in a few days for Famagosta. The next morning the offer was made to her, as had been agreed on; and Fortunatus had the pleasure of hearing from the lips of the beautiful Cassandra, that the very first time she cast her eyes on him she thought him the most handsome gentleman in the world.

Everything was soon ready for them to set out on the journey. Fortunatus, Lord Loch-Fitty, his lady, and their ten children, then set sail in a large ship: they had a good voyage, and landed safe at the port of Famagosta. There, however, Fortunatus found, with great grief and self-reproach, that his father and mother were both dead. However, as he was an easy-tempered gentleman, and had his betrothed Cassandra and her whole family to reconcile him to his grief, it did not last very long; the wedding took place almost immediately; so they lived all together in Famagosta, and in very great style. By the end of the first year, the Lady Cassandra had a little son, who was christened Ampedo; and the next year another, who was christened Andolucia. For twelve years Fortunatus lived a very happy life with his wife and children, and his wife's kindred; and as each of her sisters had a fortune given her from the purse of Fortunatus, they soon married very well. But by this time he began to long to travel again; and he thought, as he was now so much older and wiser than when he was at Paris, he might go by himself, for Lord Loch-Fitty was at this time too old to bear fatigue. After he had, with great trouble, got the consent of the Lady Cassandra, and made her a promise to stay away only two years, he made all things ready for his journey; and taking his lady into one of his private rooms, he showed her three chests of gold. He told her to keep one of these for herself, and take charge of the other two for their sons, in case any evil should happen to him. He then led her back to the room where the whole family were sitting, embraced them all tenderly one by one, and set sail with a fair wind for Alexandria.

When Fortunatus came to this place, he was told it was the custom to make a handsome present to the sultan ; so he sent him a piece of plate that cost five thousand pounds. The sultan was so much pleased with this, that he ordered a hundred casks of spices to be given to Fortunatus in return. Fortunatus sent these straight to the Lady Cassandra, with the most tender letters, by the same ship that brought him, which was then going back to Famagosta. Having stated that he wished to travel through his country by land, he obtained from the sultan such passports and letters as he might stand in need of, to the other princes in those parts. He then bought a camel, hired proper servants, and set off on his travels. He went through Turkey, Persia, and from thence to Carthage ; he next went into the country of Prester John, who rides upon a white elephant, and has kings to wait on him. Fortunatus made him some rich presents, and went on to Calcutta ; and, in coming back, he took Jerusalem in the way, and so came again to Alexandria, where he had the good fortune to find the same ship that had brought him, and to learn from the captain that his wife and family were all in perfect health. The first thing he did was to pay a visit to his old friend the sultan, to whom he again make a handsome present, and was invited to dine at his palace. After dinner, the sultan said : " It must be vastly amusing, Fortunatus, to hear an account of all the places you have seen ; pray favour me with a history of your travels." Fortunatus did as he was desired, and pleased the sultan very much by telling him the many odd adventures he had met with ; and, above all, the manner of his first becoming known to the Lord Loch-Fitty, and the desire of that lord to maintain the honours of his family. When he had ended, the sultan said he was greatly pleased with what he had heard, but that he possessed a more curious thing than any Fortunatus had told him of. He then led him into a room almost filled with jewels, opened a large closet,

Old Fortunatus 123

and took out a cap, which he said was of greater value than all the rest. Fortunatus thought the sultan was joking, and told him he had seen many a better cap than that. " Ah ! " said the sultan, " that is because you do not know its value. Whoever puts this cap on his head, and wishes to be in any part of the world, will find himself there in a moment."

"Indeed ! " said Fortunatus ; " and pray, is the man living who made it ? "

" I know nothing about that," said the sultan.

"One would hardly believe it," said Fortunatus. " Pray, sir, is it very heavy ? "

"Not at all," replied the sultan ; " you may feel it."

Fortunatus took up the cap, put it on his head, and could not help wishing himself on board the ship that was going back to Famagosta. In less than a moment he was carried on board of her, just as she was ready to sail ; and there being a brisk gale, they were out of sight in half an hour, before the sultan had even time to repent of his folly for letting Fortunatus try the cap on his head. The ship came safe to Famagosta, after a happy passage, and Fortunatus found his wife and children well ; but Lord Loch-Fitty and his lady had died of old age, and were buried in the same grave.

Fortunatus now began to take great pleasure in teaching his two boys all sorts of useful learning, and also such manly sports as wrestling and tilting. Now and then he thought about the curious cap which had brought him home, and then would wish he could just take a peep at what was passing in other countries ; which wish was always fulfilled : but he never stayed there more than an hour or two, so that the Lady Cassandra did not miss him, and was no longer made uneasy by his love of travelling.

At last, Fortunatus began to grow old, and the Lady Cassandra fell sick and died. The loss of her caused him so much grief, that soon after he fell sick too. As he thought he had not long to live, he called his two sons to his bedside, and told them the secrets of the purse and the cap, which he begged they would not, on any account, make known to others. " Follow my example," said he : " I have had the purse these forty years, and no living person knew from what source I obtained my riches." He

then told them to make use of the purse between them
and to live together in friendship; and embracing them,
died soon after.   Fortunatus was buried with great pomp
by the side of Lady Cassandra, in his own chapel, and
was for a long time mourned by the people of Famagosta.

DICK WHITTINGTON AND HIS CAT

I N the reign of the famous King Edward III. there was a little boy called Dick Whittington, whose father and mother died when he was very young, so that he remembered nothing at all about them, and was left a ragged little fellow, running about a country village. As poor Dick was not old enough to work, he was very badly off; he got but little for his dinner, and sometimes nothing at all for his breakfast; for the people who lived in the village were very poor indeed, and could not spare him much more than the parings of potatoes, and now and then a hard crust of bread.

For all this Dick Whittington was a very sharp boy, and was always listening to what everybody talked about. On Sunday he was sure to get near the farmers, as they sat talking on the tombstones in the churchyard, before the parson was come; and once a week you might see little Dick leaning against the sign-post of the village alehouse, where people stopped to drink as they came from the next market town; and when the barber's shop door was open, Dick listened to all the news that his customers told one another.

In this manner Dick heard a great many very strange things about the great city called London; for the foolish country people at that time thought that folks in London were all fine gentlemen and ladies; and that there was singing and music there all day long; and that the streets were all paved with gold.

One day a large waggon and eight horses, all with bells at their heads, drove through the village while Dick was standing by the sign-post. He thought that this waggon must be going to the fine town of London; so he took courage, and asked the waggoner to let him walk with him by

125

the side of the waggon.   As soon as the waggoner heard that
poor Dick had no father or mother, and saw by his ragged
clothes that he could not be worse off than he was, he told
him he might go if he would, so they set off together.

I could never find out how little Dick contrived to get
meat and drink on the road; nor how he could walk so
far, for it was a long way; nor what he did at night for a
place to lie down to sleep in.   Perhaps some good-natured
people in the towns that he passed through, when they saw
he was a poor little ragged boy, gave him something to
eat; and perhaps the waggoner let him get into the waggon
at night, and take a nap upon one of the boxes or large
parcels in the waggon.

Dick, however, got safe to London, and was in such a
hurry to see the fine streets paved all over with gold, that
I am afraid he did not even stay to thank the kind
waggoner; but ran off as fast as his legs would carry him,
through many of the streets, thinking every moment to
come to those that were paved with gold; for Dick had
seen a guinea three times in his own little village, and
remembered what a deal of money it brought in change;
so he thought he had nothing to do but to take up some
little bits of the pavement, and should then have as much
money as he could wish for.

Poor Dick ran till he was tired, and had quite forgot his
friend the waggoner; but at last, finding it grow dark, and
that every way he turned he saw nothing but dirt instead of
gold, he sat down in a dark corner and cried himself to sleep.

Little Dick was all night in the streets; and next
morning, being very hungry, he got up and walked about,
and asked everybody he met to give him a halfpenny to
keep him from starving; but nobody stayed to answer
him, and only two or three gave him a halfpenny; so that
the poor boy was soon quite weak and faint for the want
of victuals.

At last a good-natured looking gentleman saw how
hungry he looked.   "Why don't you go to work, my lad?"
said he to Dick.   "That I would, but I do not know how
to get any," answered Dick.   "If you are willing, come
along with me," said the gentleman, and took him to a
hay-field, where Dick worked briskly, and lived merrily till
the hay was made.

After this he found himself as badly off as before; and
being almost starved again, he laid himself down at the
door of Mr. Fitzwarren, a rich merchant. Here he was
soon seen by the cook-maid, who was an ill-tempered
creature, and happened just then to be very busy dressing
dinner for her master and mistress; so she called out to
poor Dick: "What business have you there, you lazy
rogue? there is nothing else but beggars; if you do not
take yourself away, we will see how you will like a sousing
of some dish-water; I have some here hot enough to make
you jump."

Just at that time Mr. Fitzwarren himself came home to
dinner; and when he saw a dirty ragged boy lying at the
door, he said to him: "Why do you lie there, my boy?
You seem old enough to work; I am afraid you are
inclined to be lazy."

"No, indeed, sir," said Dick to him, "that is not the
case, for I would work with all my heart, but I do not
know anybody, and I believe I am very sick for the want
of food." "Poor fellow, get up; let me see what ails you."

Dick now tried to rise, but was obliged to lie down
again, being too weak to stand, for he had not eaten any
food for three days, and was no longer able to run about
and beg a halfpenny of people in the street. So the kind
merchant ordered him to be taken into the house, and
have a good dinner given him, and be kept to do what
dirty work he was able for the cook.

Little Dick would have lived very happy in this good
family if it had not been for the ill-natured cook, who was
finding fault and scolding him from morning to night, and
besides, she was so fond of basting, that when she had no
meat to baste, she would baste poor Dick's head and
shoulders with a broom, or anything else that happened to
fall in her way. At last her ill-usage of him was told to
Alice, Mr. Fitzwarren's daughter, who told the cook she
should be turned away if she did not treat him kinder.

The ill-humour of the cook was now a little amended;
but besides this Dick had another hardship to get over.
His bed stood in a garret, where there were so many holes
in the floor and the walls that every night he was tormented
with rats and mice. A gentleman having given Dick a
penny for cleaning his shoes, he thought he would buy a

cat with it. The next day he saw a girl with a cat, and asked her if she would let him have it for a penny. The girl said she would, and at the same time told him the cat was an excellent mouser.

Dick hid his cat in the garret, and always took care to carry a part of his dinner to her; and in a short time he had no more trouble with the rats and mice, but slept quite sound every night.

Soon after this, his master had a ship ready to sail; and as he thought it right that all his servants should have some chance for good fortune as well as himself, he called them all into the parlour and asked them what they would send out.

They all had something that they were willing to venture except poor Dick, who had neither money nor goods, and therefore could send nothing.

For this reason he did not come into the parlour with the rest; but Miss Alice guessed what was the matter, and ordered him to be called in. She then said she would lay down some money for him, from her own purse; but the father told her this would not do, for it must be something of his own.

When poor Dick heard this, he said he had nothing but a cat which he bought for a penny some time since of a little girl.

"Fetch your cat then, my good boy," said Mr. Fitzwarren, "and let her go."

Dick went upstairs and brought down poor puss, with tears in his eyes, and gave her to the captain; for he said he should now be kept awake again all night by the rats and mice.

All the company laughed at Dick's odd venture; and Miss Alice, who felt pity for the poor boy, gave him some money to buy another cat.

This, and many other marks of kindness shown him by Miss Alice, made the ill-tempered cook jealous of poor Dick, and she began to use him more cruelly than ever, and always made game of him for sending his cat to sea. She asked him if he thought his cat would sell for as much money as would buy a stick to beat him.

At last poor Dick could not bear this usage any longer, and he thought he would run away from his place; so he packed up his few things, and started very early in the morning, on All-Hallow's Day, which is the first of November. He walked as far as Holloway; and there sat down on a stone, which to this day is called Whittington's stone, and began to think to himself which road he should take as he went onwards.

While he was thinking what he should do, the Bells of Bow Church, which at that time had only six, began to ring, and he fancied their sound seemed to say to him,—

> "Turn again, Whittington,
> Lord Mayor of London."

"Lord Mayor of London!" said he to himself. "Why, to be sure, I would put up with almost anything now, to be Lord Mayor of London, and ride in a fine coach, when I grow to be a man! Well, I will go back, and think nothing of the cuffing and scolding of the old cook, if I am to be Lord Mayor of London at last."

Dick went back, and was lucky enough to get into the house, and set about his work, before the old cook came downstairs.

The ship, with the cat on board, was a long time at sea; and was at last driven by the winds on a part of the coast of Barbary, where the only people were the Moors, that the English had never known before.

The people then came in great numbers to see the sailors, who were of different colour to themselves, and treated them very civilly; and, when they became better acquainted, were very eager to buy the fine things that the ship was loaded with.

When the captain saw this, he sent patterns of the best things he had to the king of the country; who was so much pleased with them, that he sent for the captain to the palace. Here they were placed, as it is the custom of the country, on rich carpets marked with gold and silver flowers. The king and queen were seated at the upper end of the room; and a number of dishes were brought in for dinner. They had not sat long, when a vast number of rats and mice rushed in, helping themselves from almost every dish. The captain wondered at this, and asked if these vermin were not very unpleasant.

"Oh, yes," said they, "very destructive; and the king

I

would give half his treasure to be freed of them, for they not only destroy his dinner, as you see, but they assault him in his chamber, and even in bed, so that he is obliged to be watched while he is sleeping for fear of them."

The captain jumped for joy; he remembered poor Whittington and his cat, and told the king he had a creature on board the ship that would despatch all these vermin immediately. The king's heart heaved so high at the joy which this news gave him that his turban dropped off his head. "Bring this creature to me," says he; "vermin are dreadful in a court, and if she will perform what you say, I will load your ship with gold and jewels, in exchange for her." The captain, who knew his business, took this opportunity to set forth the merits of Miss Puss. He told his majesty that it would be inconvenient to part with her, as, when she was gone, the rats and mice might destroy the goods in the ship—but to oblige his majesty he would fetch her. "Run, run!" said the queen; "I am impatient to see the dear creature."

Away went the captain to the ship, while another dinner was got ready. He put puss under his arm, and arrived at the place soon enough to see the table full of rats.

When the cat saw them, she did not wait for bidding, but jumped out of the captain's arms, and in a few minutes laid almost all the rats and mice dead at her feet. The rest of them in their fright scampered away to their holes.

The king and queen were quite charmed to get so easily rid of such plagues, and desired that the creature who had done them so great a kindness might be brought to them for inspection. Upon which the captain called: "Pussy, pussy, pussy!" and she came to him. He then presented her to the queen, who started back, and was afraid to touch a creature who had made such a havoc among the rats and mice. However, when the captain stroked the cat and called: "Pussy, pussy," the queen also touched her and cried: "Putty, putty," for she had not learned English. He then put her down on the queen's lap, where she, purring, played with her majesty's hand, and then sung herself to sleep.

The king, having seen the exploits of Mrs. Puss, and being informed that her kittens would stock the whole

country, bargained with the captain for the whole ship's
cargo, and then gave him ten times as much for the cat
as all the rest amounted to.

The captain then took leave of the royal party, and set
sail with a fair wind for England, and after a happy voyage
arrived safe in London.

One morning Mr. Fitzwarren had just come to his
counting-house and seated himself at the desk, when somebody came tap, tap, at the door. "Who's there! ' says
Mr. Fitzwarren. "A friend," answered the other ; "I come
to bring you good news of your ship *Unicorn*." The
merchant, bustling up instantly, opened the door, and
who should be seen waiting but the captain and factor,
with a cabinet of jewels, and a bill of lading, for which the
merchant lifted up his eyes and thanked heaven for sending him such a prosperous voyage.

They then told the story of the cat, and showed the
rich present that the king and queen had sent for her to
poor Dick.   As soon as the merchant heard this, he called
out to his servants,—

> " Go fetch him—we will tell him of the same ;
> Pray call him Mr. Whittington by name."

Mr. Fitzwarren now showed himself to be a good man ;
for when some of his servants said so great a treasure was
too much for Dick, he answered : "God forbid I should
deprive him of the value of a single penny."

He then sent for Dick, who at that time was scouring
pots for the cook, and was quite dirty.

Mr. Fitzwarren ordered a chair to be set for him, and
so he began to think they were making game of him, at
the same time begging them not to play tricks with a poor
simple boy, but to let him go down again, if they pleased,
to his work.

"Indeed, Mr. Whittington," said the merchant, "we are
all quite in earnest with you, and I most heartily rejoice
in the news these gentlemen have brought you ; for the
captain has sold your cat to the King of Barbary, and
brought you in return for her more riches than I possess in
the whole world ; and I wish you may long enjoy them ! "

Mr. Fitzwarren then told the men to open the great
treasure they had brought with them ; and said : "Mr.

Whittington has nothing to do but to put it in some place of safety."

Poor Dick hardly knew how to behave himself for joy. He begged his master to take what part of it he pleased, since he owed it all to his kindness. "No, no," answered Mr. Fitzwarren, "this is all your own; and I have no doubt but you will use it well."

Dick next asked his mistress, and then Miss Alice, to accept a part of his good fortune; but they would not, and at the same time told him they felt great joy at his good success. But this poor fellow was too kind-hearted to keep it all to himself; so he made a present to the captain, the mate, and the rest of Mr. Fitzwarren's servants; and even to the ill-natured old cook.

After this Mr. Fitzwarren advised him to send for a proper tradesman and get himself dressed like a gentleman; and told him he was welcome to live in his house till he could provide himself with a better.

When Whittington's face was washed, his hair curled, his hat cocked, and he was dressed in a nice suit of clothes, he was as handsome and genteel as any young man who visited at Mr. Fitzwarren's; so that Miss Alice, who had once been so kind to him, and thought of him with pity, now looked upon him as fit to be her sweetheart; and the more so, no doubt, because Whittington was now always thinking what he could do to oblige her, and making her the prettiest presents that could be.

Mr. Fitzwarren soon saw their love for each other, and proposed to join them in marriage; and to this they both readily agreed. A day for the wedding was soon fixed; and they were attended to church by the Lord Mayor, the court of aldermen, the sheriffs, and a great number of the richest merchants in London, whom they afterwards treated with a very rich feast.

History tells us that Mr. Whittington and his lady lived in great splendour, and were very happy. They had several children. He was Sheriff of London, also Mayor, and received the honour of knighthood by Henry V.

The figure of Sir Richard Whittington with his cat in his arms, carved in stone, was to be seen till the year 1780 over the archway of the old prison of Newgate, that stood across Newgate Street.

THE KING OF THE VIPERS

NEAR Norman Cross was a large lake or "mere," about whose borders tall reeds were growing, and beyond this, at a somewhat greater distance, was a wild sequestered spot surrounded with woods and thick groves, the deserted seat of some ancient family. A place more solitary and wild could scarcely be imagined; the garden and walks were overgrown with weeds and briers, and the woods were tangled and unpruned. About this domain I would wander till overtaken by fatigue, and there I would sit down with my back against some beech, elm or stately alder tree, and, taking out my book, would pass hours in a state of unmixed enjoyment, my eyes now fixed on the wondrous pages, now glancing at the sylvan scene around; and sometimes I would drop the book and listen to the voice of the rooks and wild pigeons, or to the croaking of multitudes of frogs from the neighbouring swamps and fens.

In going to and fro from this place I frequently passed a tall, elderly individual, dressed in rather a quaint fashion, with a skin cap on his head and stout gaiters on his legs; on his shoulders hung a moderate sized leathern sack; he seemed fond of loitering near sunny banks, and of groping amidst furze and low scrubby bramble bushes, of which there were plenty in the neighbourhood of Norman Cross. Once I saw him standing in the middle of a dusty road, looking intently at a large mark which seemed to have been drawn across it, as if by a walking-stick.

"He must have been a large one," the old man muttered half to himself, "or he would not have left such a trail; I wonder if he is near; he seems to have moved this way."

He then went behind some bushes which grew on the right side of the road, and appeared to be in quest of something, moving behind the bushes with his head downwards, and occasionally striking their roots with his foot. At length he exclaimed, "Here he is !" and I saw him dart amongst the bushes. There was a kind of scuffling noise, the rustling of branches, and the crackling of dry sticks. "I have him," said the man at last; "I have got him !" and presently he made his appearance about twenty yards down the road, holding a large viper in his hand. "What do you think of that, my boy?" said he, as I went up to him; "what do you think of catching such a thing with the naked hand?" "What do I think?" said I. "Why, that I could do as much myself." "You do, do you?" said the man; and opening his bag he thrust the reptile into it, which was far from empty.

As I was returning, towards the evening, I overtook the old man, who was wending in the same direction. "Good evening to you, sir," said I, taking off my cap. "Good evening," said the old man; and then looking at me, "How's this?" said he, "you aren't, sure, the child I met in the morning? Why, you were then all froth and conceit, and now you take off your cap to me." "I beg your pardon," said I, "if I was frothy and conceited: it ill becomes a child like me to be so." "That's true, dear," said the old man; "well, as you have begged my pardon, I truly forgive you." "Thank you," said I; "have you caught many more of those things?" "Only four or five," said the old man; "they are getting scarce, though this used to be a great neighbourhood for them. I hunt them mostly for the fat they contain, which is good for various sore troubles, especially for the rheumatism." "And do you get your living by hunting these creatures?" I demanded. "Not altogether," said the old man. "I am what they call a herbalist, one who knows the virtue of particular herbs; I gather them at the proper season to make medicines for the sick, but I do not live in this neighbourhood in particular, I travel about; I have not been here for many years."

.   .   .   .

From this time the old man and myself formed an acquaintance; I often accompanied him in his wanderings about the neighbourhood, and on two or three occasions assisted him in catching the reptiles which he hunted. He was fond of telling me anecdotes connected with his adventures with reptiles. "But," said he one day, sighing, "I must shortly give up this business, I am no longer the man I was, I am become timid, and when a person is timid in viper-hunting he had better leave off, as it is clear his virtue is forsaking him. I got a fright some years ago, which I am sure I shall never get the better of; my hand

has been shaky more or less ever since." "What frightened you?" I asked. "I had better not tell you," said the old man, "or you may be frightened too, lose your virtue, and be no longer good for the business." "I don't care," said I; "I don't intend to follow the business: I daresay I shall be an officer, like my father." "Well," said the old man, "I once saw the king of the vipers, and since then—" "The king of the vipers!" said I, interrupting him, "have the vipers a king?" "As sure as we have," said the old man, "as sure as we have King George to rule over us, have these reptiles a king to rule over them." "And where did you see him?" said I. "I will tell you," said the old man, "though I don't like talking about the matter. About seven years ago I happened to be far down yonder to the west, on the other side of England. It was a very sultry day, about three o'clock in the afternoon, when I found myself on some heathy land near the sea, on the ridge of a hill, the side of which, nearly as far down as the sea, was heath; but on the top there was ground which had been planted, and from which the harvest had been gathered—oats or barley, I know not which—but I remember that the ground was covered with stubble. Well, from the heat of the day and from having walked about for hours, I felt very tired; so I laid myself down, my head just on the ridge of the hill, towards the field, and my body over the side down amongst the heath. My bag, which was nearly filled with creatures, lay at a little distance from my faee; the creatures were struggling in it, I remember, and I thought to myself, how much more comfortably off I was than they; I was taking my ease on the nice open hill, cooled by the breezes, whilst they were in the nasty close bag, coiling about one another, and breaking their very hearts. Little by little I closed my eyes, and fell into the sweetest snooze; and there I lay over the hill's side, I don't know how long. At last it seemed to me that I heard a noise in my sleep, something like a thing moving, very faint, however, far away; then it died, and then it came again upon my ear as I slept, and now it appeared almost as if I heard crackle, crackle; then it died again, or I became yet more dead asleep than before, I know not which, but I certainly lay some time without hearing it. All of a sudden I became awake, and there was I, on the ridge of the hill, with my cheek on the ground towards the stubble, with a noise in my ear like that of something moving towards me, among the stubble of the field; well, I lay a moment or two, listening to the noise, and then I became frightened, for I did not like the noise at all, it sounded so odd; so I rolled myself over, and looked towards the stubble. Mercy upon us! there was a huge snake, or rather a dreadful viper, for it was all yellow and gold, moving towards me, bearing its head about a foot and a half above the ground, the dry stubble crackling beneath it. It might be about five yards off

when I first saw it, making straight towards me, child, as
if it would devour me.   I lay quite still, for I was stupefied
with horror, whilst the creature came still nearer; and
now it was nearly upon me, when it suddenly drew back a
little, and then—what do you think?—it lifted its head
and chest high in the air, and high over my face as I
looked up, flickering at me with its tongue as if it would
fly at my face.   Child, what I felt at that moment I can
scarcely say, but it was a sufficient punishment for all the
sins I ever committed : and there we two were, I looking
up at the viper, and the viper looking down upon me,
flickering at me with its tongue.   It was only the kindness
of God that saved me : all at once there was a loud noise,
the report of a gun, for a fowler was shooting at some
birds, a little way off in the stubble.   Whereupon the viper
sunk its head and immediately made off over the ridge of
the hill, down in the direction of the sea.   As it passed by
me, however—and it passed close by me—it hesitated a
moment, as if it was doubtful whether it should not seize
me ; it did not, however, but made off down the hill.   It
has often struck me that he was angry with me, and came
upon me unawares for presuming to meddle with his people,
as I have always been in the habit of doing."

'But," said I, "how do you know that it was the king
of the vipers?"

"How do I know?" said the old man, "who else
should it be?   There was as much difference between
it and other reptiles as between King George and other
people.

THE KING OF THE CATS

ONCE upon a time there were two brothers who lived in a lonely house in a very lonely part of Scotland; an old woman used to do the cooking, and there was no one else, unless we count her cat and their own dogs, within miles of them.

One autumn afternoon the elder of the two, whom we will call Elshender, said he would not go out, so the younger one, Fergus, went alone to follow the path where they had been shooting the day before, far across the mountains. He meant to return home before the early sunset; however, he did not do so, and Elshender became very uneasy as he watched and waited in vain till long after their usual supper-time. At last Fergus returned, wet and exhausted, nor did he explain why he was so late.

But after supper when the two brothers were seated before the fire, on which the peat crackled cheerfully, the dogs lying at their feet, and the old woman's black cat sitting gravely with half-shut eyes on the hearth between them, Fergus recovered himself and began to tell his adventures.

"You must be wondering," said he, "what made me so late? I have had a very, very strange adventure to-day; I hardly know what to say about it. I went, as I told you I should, along our yesterday's track; a mountain fog came on just as I was about to turn homewards, and I completely lost my way. I wandered about for a long time not knowing where I was, till at last I saw a light, and made for it, hoping to get help. As I came near it, it disappeared, and I found myself close to an old oak tree. I climbed into the branches the better to look for the light, and, behold! there it was right beneath me, inside the hollow trunk of the tree. I seemed to be looking

138

down into a church, where a funeral was taking place. I
heard singing, and saw a coffin surrounded by torches, all
carried by— But I know you won't believe me,
Elshender, if I tell you!"

His brother eagerly begged him to go on, and threw a
dry peat on the fire to encourage him. The dogs were
sleeping quietly, but the cat was sitting up and seemed to
be listening just as carefully and cannily as Elshender
himself. Both brothers indeed turned their eyes on the
cat as Fergus took up his story.

"Yes," he continued, "it is as true as I sit here. The
coffin and the torches were both carried by cats, and upon
the coffin were marked a crown and a sceptre!"

He got no further, for the black cat started up shrieking:
"My stars! old Peter's dead, and I'm the King o' the
Cats!"—then rushed up the chimney and was seen no
more.

CHICKEN-LICKEN

S Chicken-licken went one day to the wood, an acorn fell upon her poor bald pate, and she thought the sky had fallen. So she said she would go and tell the King the sky had fallen. So Chicken-licken turned back, and met Hen-len. "Well, Hen-len, where are you going?" And Hen-len said, "I'm going to the wood for some meat." And Chicken-licken said, "Oh! Hen-len, don't go, for I was going, and the sky fell upon my poor bald pate, and I'm going to tell the King." So Hen-len turned back with Chicken-licken, and met Cock-lock. "Oh! Cock-lock, where are you going?" And Cock-lock said, "I'm going to the wood for some meat." Then Hen-len said, "Oh! Cock-lock, don't go, for I was going, and I met Chicken-licken, and Chicken-licken had been at the wood, and the sky had fallen on her poor bald pate, and we are going to tell the King."

So Cock-lock turned back, and met Duck-luck. "Well, Duck-luck, where are you going?" And Duck-luck said, "I'm going to the wood for some meat." Then Cock-lock said, "Oh! Duck-luck, don't go, for I was going, and I met Hen-len, and Hen-len met Chicken-licken, and Chicken-licken had been at the wood, and the sky had fallen on her poor bald pate, and we are going to tell the King."

So Duck-luck turned back, and met Drake-lake. "Well, Drake-lake, where are you going?" And Drake-lake said, "I'm going to the wood for some meat." Then Duck-luck said, "Oh! Drake-lake, don't go, for I was going, and I met Cock-lock, and Cock-lock met Hen-len, and Hen-len met Chicken-licken, and Chicken-licken had been at the wood, and the sky had fallen on her poor bald pate, and we are going to tell the King."

So Drake-lake turned back, and met Goose-loose.

"Well, Goose-loose, where are you going?" And Goose-loose said, "I'm going to the wood for some meat." Then Drake-lake said, "Oh! Goose-loose, don't go, for I was going, and I met Duck-luck, and Duck-luck met Cock-lock, and Cock-lock met Hen-len, and Hen-len met Chicken-licken, and Chicken-licken had been at the wood, and the sky had fallen on her poor bald pate, and we are going to tell the King."

So Goose-loose turned back, and met Gander-lander. "Well, Gander-lander, where are you going?" And Gander-lander said, "I'm going to the wood for some meat." Then Goose-loose said, "Oh! Gander-lander, don't go, for I was going, and I met Drake-lake, and Drake-lake met Duck-luck, and Duck-luck met Cock-lock, and Cock-lock met Hen-len, and Hen-len met Chicken-licken, and Chicken-licken had been at the wood, and the sky had fallen on her poor bald pate, and we are going to tell the King."

So Gander-lander turned back, and met Turkey-lurkey. "Well, Turkey-lurkey, where are you going?" And Turkey-lurkey said, "I'm going to the wood for some meat." Then Gander-lander said, "Oh! Turkey-lurkey, don't go, for I was going, and I met Goose-loose, and Goose-loose met Drake-lake, and Drake-lake met Duck-luck, and Duck-luck met Cock-lock, and Cock-lock met Hen-len, and Hen-len met Chicken-licken, and Chicken-licken had been at the wood, and the sky had fallen on her poor bald pate, and we are going to tell the King."

So Turkey-lurkey turned back, and walked with Gander-lander, Goose-loose, Drake-lake, Duck-luck, Cock-lock, Hen-len, and Chicken-licken. And as they were going along, they met Fox-lox. And Fox-lox said, "Where are you going, my pretty maids?" And they said, "Chicken-licken went to the wood, and the sky fell upon her poor bald pate, and we are going to tell the King." And Fox-lox said, "Come along with me, and I will show you the way." But Fox-lox took them into the fox's hole, and he and his young ones soon ate up poor Chicken-licken, Hen-len, Cock-lock, Duck-luck, Drake-lake, Goose-loose, Gander-lander, and Turkey-lurkey, and they never saw the King to tell him that the sky had fallen.

QUEEN MAB'S BED

UPON six plump dandelions, high-
   Reared, lies her elvish majesty,
Whose woolly bubbles seemed to drown
Her Mabship in obedient down ;
And next to these, two blankets o'er-
Cast of the finest gossamer ;
And then a rug of carded wool,
Which, sponge-like, drinking in the dull
Light of the moon, seemed to comply,[1]
Cloud-like, the dainty deity.
Thus soft she lies ; and over-head
A spinner's[2] circle is bespread
With cobweb curtains, from the roof
So neatly sunk, as that no proof
Of any tackling can declare
What gives it hanging in the air.
And now sleeps Mab : out goes the light ;
I wish both her and thee good-night.

[1] Enfold·   [2] Spider's.

PART II
MOTHER JACK'S FAIRY-BOOK

PART II

MOTHER JACK'S FAIRY-BOOK

It had once been an old Cookery Book with brown covers, into which Mother Jack used to paste recipes for Twelfth Cakes and custards, and those which tell the three ways of jugging a hare, or the way to make a Cornish pie. But when she grew old she gave up cooking and took to nursing, and then she filled up the pages at the end of her book with old Nursery Rhymes, and odds and ends of stories, and some of Æsop's Fables. But afterwards some of the leaves were torn out to make jam-covers, and these are all that remain.

LEAF TWENTY

THE "FARY" NURSLING

A COTTAGER, who lived with his wife at Nether Wilton, was one night visited by two of the little people,—a "fary" and his spouse. They brought a child with them, which they wished to put out to nurse. The goodman and his wife agreed to take care of the child for a certain period, until such time as it had to be taken away. The "fary" gave the man a box of ointment with which to anoint the child's eyes ; but he had not on any account to touch himself with it, or some misfortune would befall him.

For a long time he and his wife were very careful to avoid the "fary" ointment, but one day when his wife was out curiosity overcame him, and he anointed his eyes without feeling any bad effect. But after a while, when walking through Long Horsley Fair, he met the male "fary" and accosted him. The "fary" started back in amazement at the recognition ; and then, instantly guessing the truth, he blew on the eyes of the cottager, and instantly blinded him.

But the "fary" was never more seen after the day of the Fair.

K   145

LEAF TWENTY-THREE

A CONJURATION FOR A FAIRY

TAKE one pint of sweet oil, and put it into a vial glass, but first wash it with rose-water, and marigold-flower-water, whose flowers be gathered towards the East. Wash it till the oil come white ; then put it into the glass, and then put thereto the buds of hollyhock, the flowers of marigold, the flowers or tops of wild thyme, the buds of young hazel, and the thyme must be gathered near the side of a hill where fairies used to be, and the grass of a fairy throne there. All these put into the oil in the glass, and set it to dissolve three days in the sun, and then keep it for thy use.

LEAF TWENTY-FOUR

THE LITTLE PORTUNES

THERE is a queer kind of smallish creatures in some parts of England, which the country people call the Portunes. They live the life of plain farmers ; but the country folk say, when they sit up late in winter nights, and the doors are shut, they warm themselves at the fire, and take little frogs out of their bosom, roast them on the coals, and eat them. They have the faces of old men, with wrinkled cheeks, and they are of a very small stature, not being quite half-an-inch high. They wear little patched coats, and if anything is to be carried into the house, or any laborious work to be done, they lend a hand, and finish it sooner than any man could. It is their nature to have the power to serve, but not to injure. They have, however, one little mode of annoying. When in the uncertain shades of night the English are riding any where alone, the Portune sometimes invisibly joins the horseman ; and when he has accompanied him a good while, he at last takes the reins, and leads the horse into a neighbouring slough. Then, when the rider is fixed and floundering in it, the Portune goes off with a loud laugh, crying " Ho, ho, ho ! " like Robin Goodfellow, who must be come of their kindred.

LEAF TWENTY-FIVE

FAIRY FOOD

Two lads were ploughing in a field, in the middle of which was an old thorn-tree, a trysting-place of the Fairy-folk. One of them described a circle round the thorn, within which the plough should not go. They were surprised, on ending the furrow, to behold a green table placed there, heaped up with excellent bread and cheese, and even wine. The lad who had drawn the circle sat down without hesitation, ate and drank heartily, saying, "Fair fa' the hands whilk gie." His companion whipped on the horses, refusing to partake of the Fairy-food. The other, who had eaten of it, was lucky all the rest of his life.

A FAIRY BANQUET

There was once a young shepherd of Nithsdale, who, one summer night, heard most delicious music, and advancing to the spot whence the sound appeared to come, he suddenly found himself the spectator of a Fairy banquet. A green table with feet of gold was laid across a small rivulet, and supplied with the finest of bread and the richest of wines. The music proceeded from instruments formed of reeds and stalks of corn. He was invited to join in the dance, and presented with a cup of wine. He was allowed to depart in safety, and ever after possessed the gift of second sight. He said he saw there several of his old acquaintances, who were become Fairy-folk.

LEAF TWENTY-SIX

THE TRUE HISTORY OF JACK SPRAT, HIS WIFE AND HIS CAT

I

WHEN Jack Sprat was young,
   He dressed very smart,
He courted Joan Cole,
   And he gained her heart;
In his fine leather doublet,
   And old greasy hat,
O what a smart fellow
   Was little Jack Sprat.

II

Jack Sprat was the bridegroom,
   Joan Cole was the bride,
Jack said, from the church
   His Joan home should ride;
But no coach could take her,
   The lane was so narrow,
Said Jack, then I'll take her
   Home in a wheel-barrow.

III

As Jack Sprat was wheeling
   His wife by the ditch,
The barrow turned over,
   And in she did pitch.
Says Jack, "You'll be drowned!"
   But Joan did reply,—
" I don't think I shall,
   For the ditch is quite dry."

149

IV

Jack brought home his Joan,
  And she sat on a chair,
When in came his cat,
  That had got but one ear.
Says Joan, " I'm come home, puss,
  Pray how do you do ? "
The cat wagg'd her tail,
  And said nothing but " Mew ! "

V

Then Joan went to market,
  To buy her some fowls,
She bought a jackdaw
  And a couple of owls ;
The owls they were white,
  The jackdaw was black,
" They'll lay brindled eggs,"
  Says little Joan Sprat.

VI

Joan Sprat went to brewing
  A barrel of ale,
She put in some hops
  That it might not turn stale,
But as for the malt,
  She forgot to put that,
" This is sober liquor,"
  Says little Jack Sprat.

VII

Jack Sprat could eat no fat,
  His wife could eat no lean,
And so between them both,
  They lick'd the platter clean ;
Jack eat all the lean,
  Joan eat all the fat,
The bone they pick'd it clean,
  Then gave it to the cat.

VIII

Jack Sprat went to market,
  And bought him a mare,
She was lame of three legs,
  And as blind as a bat,
Her ribs they were bare,
  For the mare had no fat,
"She looks like a racer,"
  Says little Jack Sprat.

IX

Now I have told you the story
  Of little Jack Sprat,
Of little Joan Cole,
  And the one-ear'd cat.
Now Jack has got rich,
  And has plenty of pelf,
If you'd know any more,
  You may tell it yourself.

LEAF TWENTY-SEVEN

THE PIXY'S CLOTHES

THERE was once an old dame, who lived by her spinning wheel; and who often of a morning found the flax she had left overnight all spun and done with. One evening, coming suddenly into the room, she spied by her wheel a ragged little creature, who jumped out of the door. Well, she thought she would try still further to win the services of her pixy friend, and so she bought some smart new clothes, as big as those made for a doll. These pretty things she placed by the side of her wheel. The Pixy returned, and put them on; when, clapping her tiny hands, she was heard to exclaim—

Pixy spin,—Pixy gay,
Pixy now will run away;

and off she went. But the ungrateful little creature never spun for the poor old woman after.

THE PIXY GARDEN

AN old woman who lived near Tavistock had in her garden a splendid bed of tulips. To these the Pixies of the neighbourhood loved to resort, and often at midnight might they be heard singing their babes to rest among them. By their Pixy power they made the tulips more beautiful and more lasting than any other tulips, and they caused them to emit a fragrance equal to that of the rose. The old woman was so fond of her tulips that she would never let one of them be plucked, and thus the Pixies were never deprived of their floral bowers.

But at length the old woman died; the tulips were taken up, and the place converted into a parsley-bed. Again, however, the power of the Pixies was shown; the parsley withered, and nothing would grow even in the other beds of the garden. On the other hand, they tended diligently the grave of the old woman, around which they were heard lamenting and singing dirges. They suffered not a weed to grow on it ; they kept it always green, and evermore in spring-time spangled with wild flowers.

LEAF TWENTY-EIGHT

THE BOGGART

In an old farm-house in Yorkshire, where lived an honest farmer named George Gilbertson, a Boggart had taken up his abode. He caused a good deal of trouble, and he kept tormenting the children, day and night, in various ways. Sometimes their bread and butter would be snatched away, or their porringers of bread and milk be capsized by an invisible hand; for the Boggart never let himself be seen; at other times, the curtains of their beds would be shaken backwards and forwards, or a heavy weight would press on and nearly suffocate them. Their mother had often, on hearing their cries, to fly to their aid.

There was a kind of closet, formed by a wooden partition on the kitchen-stairs, and a large knot having been driven out of one of the deal-boards of which it was made, there remained a round hole. Into this one day the farmer's youngest boy stuck the shoe-horn with which he was amusing himself, when immediately it was thrown out again, and struck the boy on the head. Of course it was the Boggart did this, and it soon became their sport, which they called *larking with Boggart*, to put the shoe-horn into the hole and have it shot back at them.

But the gamesome Boggart at length proved such a torment that the farmer and his wife resolved to quit the house and let him have it all to himself. This settled, the flitting day came, and the farmer and his family were following the last loads of furniture, when a neighbour named John Marshall came up.

"Well, Georgey," said he, "and so you're leaving t'ould hoose at last?"

"Heigh, Johnny, my lad, I'm forced to it; for that bad Boggart torments us so, we can neither rest night nor day for't. It seems to have such a malice against t'poor

154

bairns, it almost kills my poor dame here at thoughts on't, and so, ye see, we're forced to flitt loike."

He scarce had uttered the words when a voice from a deep upright churn cried out. "Aye, aye, Georgey, we're flitting, ye see!"

"Ods, alive!" cried the farmer, "if I'd known thou would flit too, I'd not have stirred a peg!"

And with that, he turned about to his wife, and told her they might as well stay in the old house, as be bothered by the Boggart in a new one. So stay they did.

LEAF THIRTY

COME, follow, follow me,
You, fairy elves that be:
Which circle on the green,
Come follow Mab, your queen
Hand in hand let's dance around,
For this place is fairy ground.

When mortals are at rest,
And snoring in their nest;
Unheard, and unespy'd,
Through key-holes we do glide;
Over tables, stools, and shelves,
We trip it with our fairy elves.

And, if the house be foul
With platter, dish or bowl,
Upstairs we nimbly creep,
And find the sluts asleep:
There we pinch them as they lie,
None escapes and none dare cry.

But if the house be swept,
And from uncleanness kept,
We praise the household maid,
And duly she is paid:
For we use before we go,
To drop a tester [1] in her shoe.

Upon a mushroom's head
Our tablecloth we spread;
A grain of rye, or wheat,
Is manchet,[2] which we eat;
Pearly drops of dew we drink
In acorn cups filled to the brink.

[1] A silver sixpence.   [2] Fine white bread.

The brains of nightingales,
With unctuous fat of snails,
Between two cockles stew'd,
Is meat that's easily chew'd;
Tails of worms, and marrow of mice,
Do make a dish that's wondrous nice.

H C.

Grasshopper, gnat, and fly,
Serve for our minstrelsy;
Grace said, we dance awhile,
And so the time beguile:
And if the moon doth hide her head,
The glow-worm lights us home to bed.

On tops of dewy grass,
So nimbly do we pass,
The young and tender stalk
Ne'er bends when we do walk :
Yet in the morning may be seen
Where we the night before have been.

LEAF THIRTY-ONE

MR. AND MRS. VINEGAR

MR. and Mrs. Vinegar lived in a vinegar-bottle. Now one day, when Mr. Vinegar was from home, Mrs. Vinegar, who was a very good housewife, was busily sweeping her house, when an unlucky thump of the broom brought the whole house clitter-clatter, clitter-clatter about her ears. In floods of tears she rushed forth to meet her husband. On seeing him she exclaimed,—

"Oh, Mr. Vinegar, Mr. Vinegar, we are ruined, we are ruined! I have knocked the house down, and it is all to pieces!"

Mr. Vinegar then said, "My dear, let us see what can be done. Here is the door; I will take it on my back, and we will go forth to seek our fortune."

They walked all that day, and at nightfall entered a thick forest. They were both very tired, and Mr. Vinegar said,—

"My love, I will climb up into a tree, drag up the door, and you shall follow."

This he did, and they both stretched their weary limbs upon the door, and fell fast asleep. In the middle of the night Mr. Vinegar was disturbed by the sound of voices beneath, and to his great dismay perceived that a party of thieves were met to divide their booty.

"Here, Jack," said one, "here's five pounds for you; here, Bill, here's ten pounds for you; here, Bob, here's three pounds for you."

Mr. Vinegar could listen no longer; his terror was so intense that he trembled most violently, and shook down the door on their heads. Away scampered the thieves, but Mr. Vinegar dared not quit his retreat till broad daylight.

He then scrambled out of the tree, and went to lift up the door. What did he behold but a number of golden guineas!

"Come down, Mrs. Vinegar," he cried, "come down, I

say; our fortune's made, our fortune's made! come down, I say."

Mrs. Vinegar got down as fast as she could, and saw the money with equal delight.

"Now, my dear," said she, "I'll tell you what you shall do. There is a fair at the town hard by; you shall take these forty guineas and buy a cow. I can make butter and cheese, which you shall sell at market, and we shall then be able to live very comfortably."

Mr. Vinegar joyfully agrees, takes the money, and goes off to the fair. When he arrived, he walked up and down, and at length saw a beautiful red cow.

Oh! thought Mr. Vinegar, if I had but that cow I should be the happiest man alive. So he offers the forty guineas for the cow, and the owner declaring that, as he was a friend, he'd oblige him, the bargain was made. Proud of his purchase, he drove the cow backwards and forwards to show it. By-and-bye he saw a man playing the bagpipes—tweedledum, tweedledee; the children followed him about, and he appeared to be pocketing money on all sides. Well, thought Mr. Vinegar, if I had but that beautiful instrument I should be the happiest man alive—my fortune would be made.

So he went up to the man.

"Friend," says he, "what a beautiful instrument that is, and what a deal of money you must make."

"Why, yes," said the man, "I make a great deal of money, to be sure, and it is a wonderful instrument."

"Oh!" cried Mr. Vinegar, "how I should like to possess it!"

"Well," said the man, "as you are a friend, I don't much mind parting with it; you shall have it for that red cow."

"Done," said the delighted Mr. Vinegar; so the beautiful red cow was given for the bagpipes.

He walked up and down with his purchase, but in vain he attempted to play a tune, and instead of pocketing pence, the boys followed him hooting, laughing, and pelting.

Poor Mr. Vinegar, his fingers grew very cold, and, heartily ashamed and mortified, he was leaving the town, when he met a man with a fine thick pair of gloves.

"Oh, my fingers are so very cold," said Mr. Vinegar to himself; "if I had but those beautiful gloves I should be the happiest man alive."

He went up to the man, and said to him,—

"Friend, you seem to have a capital pair of gloves there."

"Yes, truly," cried the man; "and my hands are as warm as possible this cold November day."

"Well," said Mr. Vinegar, "I should like to have them."

"What will you give?" said the man; "as you are a friend, I don't much mind letting you have them for those bagpipes."

"Done," cried Mr. Vinegar. He put on the gloves, and felt perfectly happy as he trudged homewards.

At last he grew very tired, when he saw a man coming towards him with a good stout stick in his hand. "Oh," said Mr. Vinegar, "if I had but that stick I should then be the happiest man alive !"

He accosted the man—

"Friend, what a rare good stick you have got."

"Yes," said the man, "I have used it for many a long mile, and a good friend it has been; but if you have a fancy for it, as you are a friend, I don't mind giving it to you for that pair of gloves."

Mr. Vinegar's hands were so warm, and his legs so tired, that he gladly exchanged.

As he drew near to the wood where he had left his wife, he heard a parrot on a tree calling out his name,—

"Mr. Vinegar, you foolish man, you blockhead, you simpleton ! you went to the fair, and laid out all your money in buying a cow; not content with that you changed it for bagpipes, on which you could not play, and which were not worth one-tenth of the money. Then you had no sooner got the bagpipes than you changed them for the gloves, which were not worth one-quarter of the money; and when you had got the gloves, you changed them for a miserable walking stick, and now for your forty guineas, cow, bagpipes, and gloves, you have nothing to show but a stick, which you might have cut in any hedge."

On this the bird laughed, and laughed again, and Mr.

L

Vinegar, falling into a violent rage, threw the stick at its head. The stick lodged in the tree, and he returned to

his wife without money, cow, bagpipes, gloves, or stick, and she instantly gave him such a sound cudgelling that she almost broke every bone in his sour skin.

LEAF THIRTY-TWO

THE FAIRY FAIR

THE Fairy Fair, as I am told, used to be held on the side of a hill, named Black-down, between the parishes of Pittminster and Chestonford, not many miles from Taunton. Those countryfolk that have had occasion to travel that way have frequently seen the fairies crowded there, appearing like men and women, of a stature generally near the smaller size of men. Their habits used to be of red, blue, or green, according to the old way of country garb, with high-crowned hats. One time, about fifty years since, a farmer living at Comb St. Nicholas, a parish lying on one side of that hill, near Chard, was riding towards his home that way, and saw, just before him, on the side of the hill, a great company of people, that seemed to him like country folks assembled as at a fair. There were all sorts of commodities, as at our ordinary fairs; and pewterers, shoe-makers, pedlars with all kinds of trinkets, fruit and drinking-booths. He could not remember anything he had ever seen at a fair but what he saw there. All he bought was a pewter pot, and when he got home, there was only a puff-ball in its place.

CINDERELLA, OR THE LITTLE GLASS SLIPPER

THERE lived once a gentleman who married for his second wife the proudest woman ever seen. She had two daughters of the same spirit, who were indeed like her in all things. On his side, her husband had a young daughter, who was of great goodness and sweetness of temper; in this she was like her mother, who was the best woman in the world.

No sooner was the wedding over than the step-mother began to show her ill-humour; she could not bear her young step-daughter's gentle ways, because they made those of her own daughters appear a thousand times more odious and disagreeable. So she employed her in the meanest work of the house; she it was who must wash the dishes and rub the tables and chairs, and it was her place to clean madam's chamber and that of the misses, her daughters. She herself slept up in a sorry garret, upon a wretched straw bed, while her sisters' rooms had shining floors and curtained beds, and looking-glasses so long and broad that they could see themselves from head to foot in them.

The poor girl bore everything with patience, not daring to complain to her father. When she had finished her work she used to sit down in the chimney corner among the cinders; so that in the house she went by the name of Cinderwench. The youngest of the two sisters, however, being rather more civil than the eldest, called her Cinderella. But Cinderella, ragged as she was, looked a hundred times more charming than her sisters, decked out in all their splendour.

It happened that the king's son gave a ball, to which he

invited all the persons of fashion for miles around; our
two misses were among the number, for they made a great
figure in the country. They were delighted with this in-
vitation, and were wonderfully busy choosing such dresses
as might become them. This was a new trouble for
Cinderella, for it was she who ironed her sisters' linen,
and plaited their ruffles. There was little then talked of
but what dresses should be worn at the ball. "I," said
the eldest, "will wear my crimson velvet gown. "I," said
the youngest, "will wear a dress all flowered with gold and
a brooch of diamonds in my hair." Yet they sent for
Cinderella to ask her advice, for she had excellent taste.
She helped them as much as she could, and even offered
to dress their hair, which was exactly what they wanted.

While she was busy over this, her sisters said to her,
"Cinderella, should not you be glad to go to the ball?"
"Ah," said she, "you must mock me; it is not for such as
I am to go thither." "You are in the right of it," replied
they, "it would make the folk laugh to see a Cinderwench
at a ball." Any other than Cinderella would have dressed
their hair awry, but she was good and did nothing but her
best.

At last the happy moment arrived: they all set off, and
Cinderella looked after them till they passed from her
sight, when she sat down and began to cry.

Her godmother came in, and seeing her in tears, asked
what ailed her. "I want—oh, I want—" sobbed poor
Cinderella, without being able to say another word.

Her godmother, who indeed was a fairy, said to her,
"You want to go to the ball, isn't it so?" "Oh, yes!"
said Cinderella, sighing. "Well, then," said her godmother, "be but a good girl, and I will contrive that you
shall go."

Then taking her kindly by the hand, she said, "Run
now into the garden, and bring me a pumpion." Cinderella flew at her bidding, and brought back the finest she
could get. Her godmother scooped out the inside, leaving nothing but the rind; this done, she struck it with
her wand, and the pumpion was instantly changed into a
fine coach, gilded all over with gold. She then went to
look into the mouse-trap, where she found six mice, all
alive; she told Cinderella to raise the door of the mouse-

trap, and as each mouse came out, at one tap of her wand
they changed into splendid horses; so that now Cinderella
had a coach and six horses of a fine dappled mouse-colour.
"Here, my child, are your coach and horses," said the
godmother; "but what shall we do for a coachman? run
and see if there be not a rat in the trap." Cinderella
brought the trap, and in it were three huge rats. The
fairy made choice of the biggest of the three, and having
touched him, he was turned into a fat jolly coachman, who
mounted the hammer-cloth in a trice.

She next said to Cinderella—"Go again into the garden,
and you will find six lizards behind the watering-pot;
bring them hither." She had no sooner done so, than
her godmother turned them into smart footmen, who at
once skipped up behind the coach.

Then said the fairy, "Now, then, here is something
that will take you to the ball; are you pleased with it?"
"Oh, yes," cried she, "but must I go in these dirty
clothes?"

Her godmother only touched her with her wand, and
her clothes were turned into cloth of gold and silver, all
beset with jewels. This done, she gave her a pair of glass
slippers, the prettiest in the world.

Being thus decked out, she got into her coach; but
her godmother bade her, above all things, not to stay past
midnight, telling her that if she stayed a single moment
longer, all her fine things would return to what they had
been before.

She promised her godmother she would not fail to leave
the ball before midnight, and then away she drove.

The king's son, being told that a great princess had
come, ran out to receive her; he gave her his hand as she
stepped from her coach, and led her among all the
company.

Cinderella no sooner appeared than every one was
silent; both the dancing and the music stopped and then
all the guests might be heard whispering, "Ah, how handsome she is." All the ladies were busied in gazing at her
clothes and head-dress, that they might have some made
after the same pattern. The king's son took her to dance
with him: she danced so gracefully that they all more and
more admired her.

Cinderella

A fine supper was served up, whereof the young prince ate not a morsel, so intently was he busied in gazing on her. She sat down by her sisters, giving them part of the fruit which the prince had presented her with; which very much surprised them. While Cinderella was thus talking with her sisters, she heard the clock strike eleven and three-quarters, whereupon she immediately made a curtsey to the company and then hastened away. Being got home, she thanked her godmother, and said she could not but wish she might go next day to the ball, because the king's son had desired her.

While she was telling her godmother all that had passed, her two sisters knocked at the door, and Cinderella opened. "How long you have stayed!" cried she, pretending to yawn. "If you had been at the ball," said one of them, "let me tell you, sleepiness would not have fallen on you. There came thither the very handsomest princess ever seen with eyes; she showed us a thousand kindnesses, and gave us oranges and citrons." Cinderella asked the name of the princess, but they told her they did not know it, and that the king's son was uneasy, and would give all the world to know who she was.

At this, Cinderella, smiling, replied, "She must be very beautiful: could I not see her? Ah! dear Miss Charlotte, do lend me your yellow suit of clothes that you wear every day?"—"Oh, indeed!" cried Miss Charlotte, "lend my clothes to such a dirty Cinderwench as thou art!"

The next day the two sisters went to the ball and so did Cinderella, dressed still more magnificently than she had been on the first night.

The king's son was always by her, and said the kindest things to her imaginable. She was so far from feeling wearied by this, that she forgot the charge her godmother had given her; so she at last counted the clock striking twelve when she took it to be no more than eleven: she then fled as nimble as a deer. The prince followed, but could not overtake her; she dropped one of her glass slippers, which the prince carefully took up. She got home all out of breath, without coach or footmen, and in her old clothes, having nothing left of all her finery but one of the little slippers. The guards of the gate were asked if they had seen a princess go out, but they said they had seen nobody except a young girl very meanly dressed.

When the two sisters returned, Cinderella asked them if they had been as much amused as the night before, and if the beautiful princess had been there? They told her, yes, but that she hurried away at twelve o'clock, so fast that she dropped one of her glass slippers, which the king's son had taken up; and that he was surely in love with the person to whom the slipper belonged.

What they said was perfectly true, for the king's son caused it to be given out that he would marry her whose foot this slipper would exactly fit. So they began by trying it on the princesses, then on the duchesses, and all the court, but in vain; they then brought it to the two sisters, who both tried all they could to force their feet into the slipper, but without success.

Cinderella, who was looking at them all the while, could not help smiling, and said, "Let me see what I can do with the slipper," which made her sisters laugh heartily. "Very likely," said they, "that it will fit your clumsy foot!" The gentleman who was sent to try the slipper saw that she was very handsome, and said he had been ordered to try it on everyone that pleased. Then, putting the slipper to her foot, he found that it went on very easily, and fitted her as though it had been made of wax.

The astonishment of the two sisters was great, but still greater when Cinderella drew out of her pocket the other slipper, and put it on! At that very moment in came her godmother, and with one touch of her wand, made Cinderella appear more magnificent than ever.

The sisters knew her again at once, and throwing themselves at her feet, begged pardon for the ill-treatment they had made her undergo. Cinderella forgave them with all her heart, and begged they would always love her.

She was then led to the palace where the young prince received her with great joy, and in a few days they were married. Cinderella, who was as good as she was beautiful, took her sisters to live in the palace, and shortly afterwards matched them to two great lords of the court, and they all lived happily ever afterwards.

LEAF THIRTY-FIVE

THE FAIRY THIEVES

ONCE upon a time there was an old farmer who was sorely
bothered by the unsettling of his barn. However straight
he laid his sheaves over-night on the threshing-floor for the
morning's flail, when morning came, all was topsy-turvy,
higgledy-piggledy, though the
door remained
locked. Re-
solved to find out
who played him
these pranks, he
couched himself
one night deeply
among the
sheaves, and
watched for the
enemy. At
length midnight
arrived, the barn
was lit up as if
by moonbeams
of wonderful
brightness, and
through the key-
hole came thou-
sands of elves,
the tiniest that
could be im-
agined. They immediately began their gambols among
the straw, which was soon in wild disorder. He wondered,
but interfered not ; and at last the fairy thieves began to
busy themselves in a new way, for each elf set about con-
veying the crop away, a straw at a time with astonishing

activity, through the keyhole, which resembled the door
of a bee-hive, on a sunny day in June. The goodman
was already in a rage at seeing his corn vanish in this
fashion, when one of the fairies said to another in the
tiniest voice that ever was heard,—

"*I weat, you weat?*"

He could contain himself then no longer. He leaped
out crying,—

> "*The foul fiend 'weat' ye.*
> *Let me get at ye!*"

With that, they all flew away, so frightened that they
never disturbed him or his barn any more.

LEAF THIRTY-SIX

THE FAIRY FISH

THE dolphin is a monster of the sea, and it hath no voice, but it singeth like a man, and toward a tempest it playeth upon the water. Some say when they be taken that they weep. The dolphin hath no ears for to hear nor no nose for to smell, yet it smelleth very well and sharp. And it sleepeth upon the water very heartily, that they be heard snore afar off, and they live a hundred and forty years, and they gladly hear playing on instruments, as lutes, harps, tabors and pipes. They have many young, and among them all be two old ones, that if it fortuned one of the young to die, then these old ones will bury them deep in the ground of the sea, because other fishes should not eat this dead dolphin; so well they love their young. There was once a king that had taken a dolphin, which he caused to be bound with chains fast at a haven where the ships come in at, and there was always the most piteous weeping and lamenting that the king could not bear it for pity, but let him go again.

H·C.

LEAF THIRTY-SEVEN

ECHEOLA

ECHEOLA is a mussel in which fish is a precious stone. For by night they float to the water-side and there they receive the heavenly dew, wherethrough there groweth in them a costly margaret, or Orient pearl. There they float a great many together, and he that knoweth the water best goeth before and leadeth the other ; and when he is taken, all the others scatter abroad and get them away.

LEAF THIRTY-EIGHT

SERRA

SERRA is a fish with great teeth, and on his back he hath sharp fins like the comb of a cock and jagged like a saw, wherewith this monstrous fish cutteth a ship through, and when he seeth a ship coming, then he setteth up his fins and thinketh to sail with the ship as fast as it, but when he seeth that he cannot continue, then he letteth his fins fall again and destroyeth the ship with the people, and then eateth the dead bodies.

Note.—Scylla is a monster in the sea between Italy and Sicily; it is a great enemy unto man. It is faced and handed like a gentlewoman, but it hath a wide mouth and fearful teeth, and it is tailed like a dolphin. It heareth gladly singing. It is in the water so strong that it cannot be overcome, but on the land it is but weak.

LEAF THIRTY-NINE

THE MERMAID

SYREN, the mermaid, is a deadly beast that bringeth a man gladly to death. From the middle up she is like a woman, with a dreadful face and long, slimy hair, and

great body, and is like the eagle in the lower part, having feet and talons to tear asunder such as she getteth. Her tail is scaled like a fish, and she singeth a manner of sweet song, and therewith deceiveth many a good mariner, for when they hear it they fall asleep commonly, and then she cometh, and draweth them out of the ship, and teareth them a- sunder; but the wise mariners stop their ears when they see her, for when she playeth on the water, they all be in fear, and then they cast out an empty barrel to let her play with it till they be past her. This is specified of them that have seen it. There be also in some places in Arabia serpents named sirens, that run faster than a horse and have wings to fly.

H. C.

174

THE SLEEPING BEAUTY

 HERE was formerly, in a distant country, a king and a queen, the most beautiful and happy in the world; having nothing to cloud their delight, but the want of children to share in their happiness. This was their whole concern: physicians, waters, vows and offerings were tried, but all to no purpose. At last, however, after long waiting, a daughter was born. At the christening the princess had seven fairies for her godmothers, who were all they could find in the whole kingdom, that every one might give her a gift.

The christening being over, a grand feast was prepared to entertain and thank the fairies: before each of them was placed a magnificent cover, with a spoon, a knife, and a fork, of pure gold and exquisite workmanship, set with divers precious stones; but as they were all sitting down at the table, they saw come into the hall a very old fairy, whom they had not invited, because it was near fifty years since she had been out of a certain tower, and was thought to have been either dead or enchanted.

The king ordered her a cover, but could not furnish her with such a case of gold as the others had, because he had only seven made for the seven fairies. The old fairy, thinking she was slighted by not being treated in the same manner as the rest, murmured out some threats between her teeth.

One of the young fairies who sat by her, overheard how she grumbled, and judging that she might give the little princess some unlucky gift, she went, as soon as she rose from the table, and hid herself behind the hangings, that she might speak last, and repair, as much as she possibly could, the evil which the old fairy might intend.

In the meantime all the fairies began to give their gifts to the princess in the following manner :—

The youngest gave her a gift that she should be the most beautiful person in the world.

The second, that she should have wit like an angel.

The third, that she should have a wonderful grace in everything that she did.

The fourth, that she should sing like a nightingale.

The fifth, that she should dance like a flower in the wind.

And the sixth, that she would play on all kinds of musical instruments to the utmost degree of perfection.

The old fairy's turn coming next, she advanced forward, and, with a shaking head, that seemed to shew more spite than age, she said,—That the princess, when she was fifteen years old, would have her hand pierced with a spindle, and die of the wound.

This terrible gift made the whole company tremble, and every one of them fell a-crying.

At this very instant the young fairy came out from behind the curtains and spoke these words aloud: " Assure yourselves, O King and Queen, that your daughter shall not die of this disaster. It is true, I have not the power to undo what my elder has done. The princess shall indeed pierce her hand with a spindle ; but, instead of dying, she shall only fall into a profound sleep, which shall last a hundred years, at the end of which time a king's son shall come, and awake her from it."

The king, to avoid this misfortune told by the old malicious fairy, caused at once his royal command to be issued forth, whereby every person was forbidden, upon pain of death, to spin with a distaff or spindle ; nay, even so much as to have a spindle in any of their houses.

About fifteen or sixteen years after, the king and queen being gone to one of their houses of pleasure, the young princess happened one day to divert herself by wandering up and down the palace, when, going up from one apartment to another, she at length came into a little room at the top of the tower, where an old woman, all alone, was spinning with her spindle.

Now either she had not heard of the king's command issued forth against spindles, or else it was the wicked fairy who had taken this disguise.

"What are you doing here, Goody?" said the princess. "I am spinning, my pretty child," said the old woman. "Ha!" said the princess, "that is very amusing: how do you do it? give it to me that I may see if I can do so too." The old woman gave it her. She had no sooner taken it into her hand than, whether being very hasty at it, and somewhat awkward, or that the decree of the spiteful fairy had caused it, is not to be certainly known ; but, however, sure it is that the spindle immediately ran into her hand, and she directly fell down upon the ground in a swoon. Thereupon the old woman cried out for help, and people came in from every quarter in great numbers : some threw water upon the princess's face, unlaced her, struck her on the palms of her hands, and rubbed her temples with Hungary water ; but all they could do did not bring her to herself.

The good fairy who had saved her life, by condemning her to sleep one hundred years, was in the kingdom of Matakin, twelve thousand leagues off, when this accident befell the princess ; but she was instantly informed of it by a little dwarf, who had boots of seven leagues, that is, boots with which he could tread over seven leagues of ground at one stride. The fairy left the kingdom immediately, and arrived at the palace about an hour after, in a fairy chariot drawn by dragons.

The king handed her out of the chariot and she approved of everything he had done ; but as she had a very great foresight, she thought that when the princess should awake, she might not know what to do with herself, being all alone in the old palace ; therefore she touched with her wand everything in the palace, except the king and the queen— governesses, maids of honour, ladies of the bed-chamber, gentlemen, officers, stewards, cooks, under-cooks, scullions, guards, with their beef-eaters, pages, and footmen ; she likewise touched all the horses that were in the stables, as well pads as others, the great dog in the outer court, and the little spaniel that lay by her on the bed.

Immediately on her touching them they all fell asleep, that they might not wake before their mistress, and that they might be ready to wait upon her when she wanted them. The very spits at the fire, as full as they could be of partridges and pheasants, and everything in the place, whether alive or not, fell asleep also.

M

All this was done in a moment, for fairies are not long in doing their business.

And now the king and queen, having kissed their child without waking her, went very sorrowfully forth from the palace, and issued a command that no one should come near it. This, however, was not needed ; for in less than a quarter of an hour, there got up all round the park such a vast number of trees, great and small bushes, and brambles, twined one within the other, that neither man nor beast could pass through, so that nothing could be seen but the very tops of the towers, and not that even, unless it were a good way off. Nobody doubted but that here was an extraordinary example of the fairies' art, that the princess, while she remained sleeping, might have nothing to fear from any curious people.

When a hundred years were gone and past, the son of a king then reigning, who was of another family from that of the sleeping princess, being out a-hunting on that side of the country, asked what these towers were which he saw in the midst of a great thick wood. Every one answered according as they had heard ; some said it was an old ruinous castle haunted by spirits ; others, that all the sorcerers and witches kept their sabbath or weekly meeting in that place.

The most common opinion was, that an ogre lived there, and that he carried thither all the little children he could catch, that he might eat them up at his leisure, without anybody being able to follow him, as having himself only power to pass through the wood.

The prince was at a stand, not knowing what to believe, when an aged man spoke to him thus,—

"May it please your highness, it is about fifty years since I heard from my father, who heard my grandfather say, that there was then in that castle a princess, the most beautiful that was ever seen ; that she must sleep there for a hundred years, and would be wakened by a king's son, whom she was a-waiting."

The young prince was all on fire at these words, believing without considering the matter, that he could put an end to this rare adventure ; and pushed on by love and ambition, resolved at that moment to attempt it.

Scarce had he advanced towards the wood, when all the

great trees, the bushes, the brambles, gave way of their own accord, and let him pass through. He went up to the castle, which he saw at the end of a large avenue, and entered into it; what not a little surprised him was, he saw none of his people could follow him, because the trees closed again, as soon as he passed through them.

However, he did not cease from valiantly pursuing his way. He came into a spacious outward court, where everything he saw might have frozen up the most hardy person with horror. There reigned all over a most frightful silence, the image of death everywhere showing itself, and there was nothing to be seen but stretched out bodies of men and animals, seeming to be dead. He, however, very well knew by the rosy faces and red noses of the beef-eaters that they were only asleep; and their goblets, wherein still remained some few drops of wine, plainly showed that they had fallen asleep while drinking.

He then, crossing a court paved with marble, went upstairs, and came into the guard-chamber, where the guards were standing in their ranks, with their halberds on their shoulders, and snoring as loud as they could. After that he went through several rooms full of gentlemen and ladies all asleep, some sitting and some standing.

At last he came into a chamber all gilt with gold; here he saw, upon a bed, the curtains of which were all open, the fairest sight that ever he beheld—a princess who appeared to be about fifteen or sixteen years of age, and whose resplendent beauty had in it something divine. He approached with trembling and admiration, and fell down before her on his knees. And now the enchantment was at an end; the princess awaked, and looking at him kindly, said, " Is it you, my prince? I have waited for you a long time?"

The prince, charmed with these words, and much more with the manner in which they were spoken, answered that he loved her better than the whole world. Then they talked for four hours together and yet said not half of what they had got to say.

In the meantime all the palace awaked, every one thinking on his particular business. The chief lady of honour, being ready to die of hunger, grew very impatient, and told the princess aloud, that supper was served up. The prince then gave her his hand ; though her attire was very magnificent, his royal highness did not forget to tell her that she was dressed like his great-grandmother ; but however, she looked not the less beautiful and charming for all that. They went into the great hall of looking-glasses, where they held the wedding supper, and were served by the officers of the princess ; the violins and hautboys played all old tunes, but very excellent, though it was now about a hundred years since they had any practice. After supper the lord almoner married them in the chapel of the castle, and they lived happily ever afterwards.

LEAF FORTY-ONE

THE FAIRY BANQUET

THERE is a town a few miles distant from the Eastern Sea, near which are those celebrated waters commonly called Gipse. . . . A tinsmith of this town went once to see a friend who lived in the next town, and it was late at night when he was riding back, not very sober; when lo! from the adjoining barrow, which I have often seen, and which is not much over a quarter of a mile from the town, he heard the voices of people singing, and, as it were joyfully feasting.

He wondered who they could be that were breaking in that place, by their merriment, the silence of the dead night, and he wished to examine into the matter more closely. Seeing a door open in the side of the barrow, he went up to it, and looked in; and there he beheld a large and luminous house, full of people, women as well as men, who were reclining as at a solemn banquet. One of the fairy servants, seeing him standing at the door, offered him a cup of wine. He took it, but would not drink; and pouring out the contents he kept the cup, and made haste away with it.

A great tumult arose at the banquet on account of his taking away the cup, and all the guests pursued him; but he escaped by the fleetness of the pony he rode, and got into the town with his booty. Finally, this vessel of some unknown metal, of rare colour and extraordinary form, was presented to Henry the Elder, king of the English, as a valuable gift. It was then given to the queen's brother David, king of the Scots, and was kept for several years in the treasury of Scotland; and a few years ago (as I have heard), it was given by William, king of the Scots, to Henry the Second.

LEAF FORTY-TWO

TWO CHARMS

I. *A charm at bedtime*

BRING the holy crust of bread,
Lay it underneath the head ;
'Tis a certain charm to keep
Hags away while children sleep !

II. *A charm at getting-up-time*

In the morning when ye rise,
Wash your hands and cleanse your eyes,
Next, be sure ye have a care
To disperse the water far :
For as far as that doth light,
So far keeps the evil sprite.

LEAF FORTY-THREE

LITTLE RED RIDING-HOOD

ONCE upon a time there was a little village-girl, the prettiest ever seen : her mother doted upon her, and so did her grandmother. She, good woman, made for her a little red hood which suited her so well, that everyone called her Little Red Riding-Hood.

One day her mother, who had just made some cakes, said to her : " My dear, you shall go and see how your grandmother is, for I have heard she is ailing ; take her this cake and this little pot of butter."

Litte Red Riding-Hood started off at once for her grandmother's cottage, which was in another village.

While passing through a wood she met a wolf, who would have liked well to have eaten her ; but he dared not, because of some wood-cutters who were hard by in the forest. So he asked her where she was going.

The poor child, who did not know it was dangerous to listen to a wolf, answered, " I am going to see my grandmother, to take her a cake and a little pot of butter that my mother sends her."—" Does she live a great way off ? " said the wolf.—" Oh, yes ! " said Little Red Riding-Hood, "she lives beyond the mill you see right down there, in the first house in the village."—" Well," said the wolf, " I shall go and see her too. I shall take this road, and do you take that one, and let us see who will get there first ! "

The wolf set off at a gallop along the shortest road ; but the little girl took the longest way and amused herself by gathering nuts, running after butterflies, and plucking daisies and buttercups.

The wolf soon reached her grandmother's cottage ; he knocks at the door, rap, rap. " Who's there ? " " 'Tis your grand-daughter Little Red Riding-Hood," said the wolf in a shrill voice, " and I have brought you a cake and a little pot of butter that my mother sends you." The good old grandmother, who was ill in bed, called out, "Pull the bobbin and the latch will go up!" The wolf pulled the bobbin, and the door opened. He leaped on the old woman and gobbled her up in a minute; for he had had no dinner for three days past.

Then he shut the door and rolled himself up in the grandmother's bed, to wait for Little Red Riding-Hood.

In a while she came knocking at the door, rap, rap. "Who's there?" Little Red Riding-Hood, who heard the

gruff voice of the wolf, was frightened at first, but thinking that her grandmother had a cold, she answered, "'Tis your grand daughter, Little Red Riding-Hood, and I have brought you a cake and a little pot of butter that my mother sends you." Then the wolf called to her in as soft a voice as he could, "Pull the bobbin and the latch will go up." Little Red Riding-Hood pulled, the bobbin and the door opened.

When the wolf saw her come in he covered himself up with the clothes, and said, "Put the cake and the little pot of butter on the chest, and come and lie down beside me." Little Red Riding-Hood took off her cloak and went over to the bed; she was full of surprise to see how strange her grandmother looked in her night-cap. She said to her then, "Oh, grandmamma, grandmamma, what great arms you have got!"

"All the better to hug you with, my dear!"

"Oh, grandmamma, grandmamma, what great legs you have got!"

"All the better to run with, my dear!"

"Oh, grandmamma, grandmamma, what great ears you have got!"

"All the better to hear with, my dear!"

"Oh, grandmamma, grandmamma, what great eyes you have got!"

"All the better to see with, my dear!"

"Oh, grandmamma, grandmamma, what great *teeth* you have got!"

"All the better to gobble you up!"

So saying, the wicked wolf leaped on Little Red Riding-Hood and gobbled her up.

LEAF FORTY-SIX

THE PARTING OF THE FAIRIES

On a Sabbath morning, all the inmates of a little hamlet had gone to church, except a herd-boy, and a little girl, his sister, who were lounging beside one of the cottages, when just as the shadow of the garden-dial had fallen on the line of noon, they saw a long cavalcade ascending out of the ravine, through the wooded hollow. It wound among the knolls and bushes, and turning round the nothern gable of the cottage, beside which the sole spectators of the scene were stationed, began to ascend the eminence towards the south. The horses were shaggy diminutive things, speckled dun and grey; the riders stunted, misgrown, ugly creatures, attired in antique jerkins of plaid, long grey cloaks, and little red caps, from under which their wild uncombed locks shot out over their cheeks and foreheads. The boy and his sister stood gazing in utter dismay and astonishment, as rider after rider, each more uncouth and dwarfish than the other which had preceded it, passed the cottage and disappeared among the brushwood, which at that period covered the hill, until at length the entire rout, except the last rider, who lingered a few yards behind the others, had gone by.

"What are you, little mannie? and where are ye going?" inquired the boy, his curiosity getting the better of his fears.

"Not of the race of Adam," said the creature, turning for a moment in its saddle, "the people of peace shall never more be seen in Scotland.'

LEAF FORTY-NINE

THE WEE WEE MAN

As I was walking all alone,
    Between the water and the green ;
There I spied a wee wee man,
    The least wee man that ever was seen.

H.C.

His legs were scarce an effet's length,
    But thick his arm as any tree ;
Between his brows there was a span,
    Between his shoulders there were three.

187

He took up a boulder stone,
   And flung it far as I could see;
Though I had been a miller's man,
   I could not lift it to my knee.

"O, wee wee man, but thou art strang!
   O tell me where thy haunt may be?"
"My dwelling's down by yon bonny bower,
   O will you mount and ride with me?"

On we leapt, and off we rode,
   Till we came to far-away;
We lighted down to bait our horse,
   And out there came a bonny may.

Four-and-twenty at her back,
   And they were all dressed out in green;
And though King Harry had been there,
   The worst o' them might be his queen.

On we leapt, and off we rode,
   Till we came to yon bonny hall:
The roof was o' the beaten gold,
   Of gleaming crystal was the wall.

When we came to the door of gold,
   The pipes within did whistle and play;
But ere the tune of it was told,
   My wee wee man was clean away.

LEAF FIFTY

THE FAREWELL TO THE FAIRIES

Farewell, you elves and Fairies !
  Good housewives now may say ;
For now foul sluts in dairies,
  Do fare as well as they.
And though they sweep their hearths no less
  Than maids were wont to do,
Yet who of late for cleanliness
  Finds sixpence in her shoe ?

At morning and at evening both
  You merry were and glad ;
So little care of sleep and sloth,
  These pretty ladies had.
When Tom came home from labour,
  Or Ciss to milking rose,
Then merrily went their tabour
  And nimbly went their toes.

A tell-tale in their company
  They never could endure ;
And whoso kept not secretly
  Their mirth was punish'd sure.
But now, alas ! they all are dead,
  Or else they take their ease,
Or far in fairyland are fled,
  Or gone beyond the seas.

PART III
LATER FAIRY TALES AND RHYMES

MELILOT

I

THE THREE NEIGHBOURS OF MELILOT

IT had been raining for ten months, and everybody felt as if it had been raining for ten years. In the driest part of the country, in the driest corners of the driest houses, there was damp. Whoever came near a fire began to steam; whoever left the fire began to moisten as the damp entered the clothes. There was a breath of wet on everything in-doors, and Melilot was wet through when she came to the door of a broken-roofed cottage that stood in a marsh between two lakes.

Melilot was a pretty girl of twelve, who had lived in a cottage up the mountains, as the only child of hard-working parents, who taught her all that was good, and whose one worldly good she was ; for they had nothing to eat but what they could force to grow out of a stony patch of ground upon the mountain-side. They had loved Melilot, and they loved each other. To feed their little one they had deprived themselves, till when the rain running down the mountain-side had washed away their little garden crops, first the mother died—for she it was who had denied herself the most—and then the father also died in a long passion of weeping. The nearest neighbours occupied the cottage in the valley on the marsh between the lakes. In hunger and grief, therefore, Melilot went down to them to ask for human help.

From Melilot's home it was a long way up to the peak of the mountains, and a long way down to the marshy valley in which lay the two lakes with a narrow spit of earth between them, and a black rocky mountain overhanging them upon the other side. A gloomy defile, between high rocks, led out of the valley on the one side, and on the other side it opened upon a waste of bog, over which the thick mist brooded, and the rain now fell with never-ending plash.

The runlets on the mountain formed a waterfall that, dashing over a smooth wall of rock, broke into foam on the ragged floor of a great rocky basin near Melilot's cottage door. Then after a short rush, seething and foaming down a slope rugged with granite boulders, the great cataract fell with a mighty roar over another precipice upon the stream that, swollen by the rains almost into a river, carried its flood into one of the lakes. It was partly by this waterfall that the path down into the valley ran.

Melilot knew that her father, when alive, had avoided the people in the lake cottage, and had forbidden her, although they were the only neighbours, to go near their dwelling. But her father now was dead, and her mother was dead, and there was need of human help if she would bury them. Her father, too, had told her that when she was left helpless she would have to go out and serve others for her daily bread. To what others than these could the child look ? So by the stony side of the stream, and by the edge of the lake, her only path in the marsh, Melilot came down shivering and weeping through the pitiless rain, and knocked at the door of the lake cottage.

"Who's that ? " asked a hoarse voice inside.

"That's Melilot from up above us," said a hoarser voice.

" Come in then, little Melilot," another voice said, that was the hoarsest of the three.

The child flinched before opening the door, but she did open it, and set one foot over the threshold ; then she stopped. There was nothing in the cottage but a muddy puddle on the floor, into which rain ran from the broken roof. Three men sat together in the puddle, squatted like frogs. They had broad noses and spotted faces, and the brightest of bright eyes, which were all turned to look at Melilot when she came in.

" We are glad to see you, Melilot," said the one who sat in the middle, holding out a hand that had all its fingers webbed together. He was the one who had the hoarsest voice. "My friend on the right is Dock, Dodder sits on my left, and I am Squill. Come in and shut the door behind you."

Melilot had to choose between the dreary, empty world outside, and trust in these three creatures—who were more horrible to look at than I care to tell. She hesitated only for an instant, then went in and shut the door behind her.

"A long time ago your father came to us, and he went out and shut the door upon us. You are wiser than your father, little girl."

"My father, oh, my dear father!" began Melilot, and fell to weeping bitterly.

"Her father is dead," said Dock, who was the least hoarse.

"And her mother too," said Dodder, who was hoarser.

"And she wants us to help her to bury them," croaked Squill.

"She is fainting with hunger," said Dock.

"She is dying of hunger and grief," said Dodder.

"And we have nothing to offer her but tadpoles, which she cannot eat," said Squill.

"Dear neighbours, I am nothing," said the child. "I do not know that I am hungry. But if you would come with me and help me."

"She asks us to her house," said Dock.

"We may go," said Dodder, "if we are invited."

"Little Melilot," said Squill then, in his hoarsest tone of all, "we will all follow you to the mountain hut." Then the three ugly creatures splashed out of their pool, and moved, web-footed too, about their cottage with ungainly hopping. Melilot all the while only thanked them, frankly looking up into their bright eyes, that were eager, very eager, but not cruel.

II

THE MOUNTAIN HUT

MELILOT, with her three wonderful neighbours, Dock, Dodder and Squill, hopping arm in arm behind her, and getting a good hold on the stones with their web feet, began to climb the mountain. Rain still poured out of the sky ; runlets flooded their path, and the great cataract roared by their side.   The faint and hungry child had climbed but half the way to her desolate home when she swooned, and was caught in the arms of Squill.

" Sprinkle water," said Dock.

" No need of that," said Dodder.

" It will not be right for us to carry her," said Squill.

Either because there was more than a sprinkling of water, or because of her own stout young heart, Melilot recovered and climbed on.   They reached the hut, and when there, the three neighbours at once bestirred themselves.   Because of the flood outside, they dug the graves under the roof, one on each side of the hearth, for Melilot's dead father and mother, and so buried them. Then the child made her friends sit down to rest ; one in her father's chair, one in her mother's, and one on her own little stool.   She raked the embers of the fire and put on fresh wood until a blaze leapt up that was strong enough to warm them before she would turn aside.   Then standing in a corner by the morsel of window that looked out towards the waterfall, she gave way to her sobbing.   But again—brave little heart—conquering herself, she came forward to where the monsters were sitting, with their legs crossed, basking in the firelight, and said, " I am sorry, dear, kind neighbours, that I have no supper to offer you."

" Nay, but you have," said Dock.

The child followed the glance of his eyes, and saw that on her father's grave there stood a loaf of bread, and on her mother's grave a cup of milk.

"They are for you, from the good angels." She said, " Oh, I am thankful ! "   Then Melilot broke the bread into three pieces, and gave a piece to each, and held the milk for them when they would drink.

" She is famished herself," said Dodder.

" We must eat all of it up," said Squill.

So they ate all of it up ; and while they ate, there was no thought in the child's heart but of pleasure that she had this bread to give.

When they had eaten all, there was another loaf upon the father's grave, and on the mother's grave another and a larger cup of milk.

" See there ! " Dock said.

"Whose supper is that?" asked Dodder.

"It must be for the pious little daughter Melilot, and no one else," said Squill.

The three neighbours refused to take another crumb; they had eaten so much tadpole, they said, for their dinners. Melilot, therefore, supped, but left much bread and milk, secretly thinking that her friends would require breakfast, if they should consent to stay with her throughout the night. It was long since the sun set, reddening the mists of the plain, and now the mountain path beside the torrent was all dark and very perilous. The monsters eagerly watched their little hostess with their brilliant eyes, and assented, as it seemed, with exultation, to her wish that they would sleep in the hut. There were but two beds under its roof—Melilot's own little straw pallet, and that on which her parents were to sleep no more, on which she was no more to kneel beside them in the humble morning prayer. With sacred thoughts of hospitality the child gave up to the use of those who had smoothed for her dear parents a new bed, the bed that was no longer theirs; and the three monsters, after looking at her gratefully, lay down on it together and went to sleep on it, with their arms twisted about each other's necks. The child looked down upon them, clinging together in their sleep as in their talk, and saw a weariness of pain defined in many a kindly-turned line of their half frog-like faces. If one stirred in sleep, it was to nestle closer to the other two. "How strange," she said to herself, "that I should at first have thought them ugly!" Then she knelt in prayer by her little nest of straw, and did not forget them in her prayers. There was a blessing on them in her heart as she lay down to sleep.

But when Melilot lay down with her face towards the hearth, the dying embers shone with a red light on the two solemn graves. She turned her face to the wall, and the rush of the torrent on the other side was louder than the passion of her weeping. But the noise of the waterfall first soothed her, and then, fixing her attention, drew her from her bed towards the little window, from which she was able to look out into the black night through which it roared. A night not altogether black, for there was a short lull in the rain, though the wind howled round

the mountain, and through a chance break in the scurrying
night-clouds the full moon now and then flashed, lighting
the lakes in the valley far below, and causing the torrent
outside the window to gleam through the night shadows
of the great rocks among which it fell.   Could it be the
song of busy Fairies that came thence to the child's ear?

> " Up to the moon and cut down that ray !
> In and out the foam-wreaths plaiting ;
> Spin the froth and weave the spray !
> Melilot is watching !   Melilot is waiting !
> Pick the moonbeam into shreds,
> Twist it, twist it into threads !
> Threads of the moonlight, yarn of the bubble,
> Weave into muslin, double and double !
> Fold all and carry it, tarry ye not,
> To the chamber of gentle and true Melilot."

Almost at the same moment the door of the hut opened
and Melilot, turning round, saw two beautiful youths enter,
bright as the moonlight, who laid a white bale at her feet,
and said that it came from the Fairy Muslin Works.
Having done that, they flew out in the shape of fire-flies,
and Melilot herself closed the door after them.   It was
her first act to shut the door, because she was bred to be
a careful little housewife, and she thought the night-air
would not be good for the sleepers.

Then the child looked again at the three monsters
cuddled together on her father's and mother's bed.   "The
Fairies have done this for me," she considered to herself,
"that I might not have to send away kind helpers without
a gift.   White muslin is not quite the dress that will suit
lodging such as theirs, but it is all I have !   If I could
make them, by the time they wake, three dresses, they
would see, at any rate, that I was glad to work for them
as they had worked for me."

So Melilot began measuring her neighbours with the
string of her poor little apron ; and when she had
measured them all, shrank, with her scissors and thread
and the bale of fairy muslin, into the farthest corner of
her hut, and set to work by the light of a pine-stick,
shaded from the eyes of her guests with a screen made of
her own ragged old frock.

While the child stitched, the Fairies sang, and it was a
marvel to her that her needle never wanted threading.

Melilot and Sir Crucifer

Keeping time with her fingers to the fairy song, she worked with a speed that almost surpassed her desire, and altogether surpassed understanding. One needleful of thread made the three coats, and the thread, when the coats were made, was as long as it had been when they were begun.

Very soon after dawn the white dresses were made, and all the muslin had been used in making them, except what was left in the small litter of fragments round the stool upon which Melilot had been at work. Three coats of white muslin, daintily folded, were laid by the bed of the three guests, and each was folded with that corner uppermost on which there had been written in thread its owner's name. Dock was worked in the corner of one; Dodder in the corner of another; and in the corner of the third coat, Squill.

Then Melilot lay down for an hour's sleep, and, weary with grief as with toil, slept heavily. Dock, Dodder, and Squill were awake before her, and the first thing that each of them did upon waking was to look upon his new coat. The next thing that each of them did was to put on his new coat; and after this the next thing they all did was to change into three beautiful Fairy youths — Dock with yellow hair, Dodder with brown, and Squill with black. Thus they stood hand in hand by the little girl's bed.

"She has freed us, the dear child!" said Dock.

"She," said Dodder, "she, our darling, and our brothers of the waterfall."

"She has saved nothing for herself," said Squill. "Did not the child once wish to wear muslin in place of these poor rags? I kiss them, brothers, for her sake." But Squill's kiss on the girl's ragged frock made it a treasure for an empire.

"And I kiss the walls that sheltered us," said Dodder. But Dodder's kiss upon the walls changed them into a close network of fragrant blossoms.

"And I kiss the lips that bade us hither," Dock said; and at his kiss the child smiled, and her eyes opened upon the three Fairies in the muslin dresses she had made.

"Ah, Fairies," she said, "those are the dresses I made for my three dear neighbours. Do not take back your gift, although the muslin is indeed yours, and the thread too, I know, and—and the work too, for surely it was you who made the needle run. I have done nothing, and am but a poor little child ; only I thought you meant to give me something to be grateful with."

"We did not give you your good heart, dear little Melilot," the Fairies said ; and now their speaking was in softest unison. " That has done more for us than all our love and service will repay. We were your neighbours, but we are your servants now."

"No, no, no," said the child. " I was afraid to ask to be your servant, because I thought last night you were too poor to feed me, as I am too poor and weak to feed myself. The angels themselves gave me bread yesterday, and I have some yet. But all is changed about me. Why do the walls flower, and why is my dress covered with glittering stones? Ah, yes, I am at home," she said, for her eyes fell on the two graves.

Then, as she rose to her knees, with quivering lips, the three Fairies went out into the sun, and stood at the door to see how all the rains were gone, and the bright morning beams played in the spray of the cataract.

" Do you see anything between us and the sun ? " Dock asked of the other two.

" A speck," said Dodder.

" Frogbit herself," said Squill.

III

SIR CRUCIFER

PRESENTLY Melilot bade the three Fairies come in to share her breakfast. She had saved bread from last night, and while she took it from its place among the blossoms that last night were mud, again the loaf of bread stood on her father's, and the cup of milk upon her mother's grave. "The angels of my father and mother feed me still," she said ; " I must abide under the shelter of their wings."

The Fairies came at her bidding to eat with her ; but Squill, excusing himself, went to the stool about which were the chips and shreds of Fairy muslin. There, joining each to each with a stroke of his finger, he was shaping them into a little net, when Melilot, who had been sent out to feel the sunshine, came in, saying that there was a chill wind; and though it was foolishness to think so, it did really seem to have come with a black raven that was sitting on the roof.

"You had better strike through the roof, Frogbit," Squill cried, looking up. The bird croaked as if in defiance, and at once began to beat a way in through the flowers. As it did so, the leaves of the bower withered, and the blossoms all began to stink.

But Squill leapt up, and holding the net he had made under the hole Frogbit was making, caught her as she fell through, and held her captured in the folds of Fairy muslin that seemed to stand like iron against the beating of her wings.

"Poor bird!" said Melilot.

"Our enemy, who came on a bad errand, is our prisoner," said Dock.

"Cleverly done," said Dodder. "Very cleverly done, brother Squill."

But Melilot, who loved man, beast, and bird, bent over the fluttering raven, and was not hindered from taking it, net and all, to her bosom, though it struck at her fiercely with its great bill that, strong as it was, could not tear through the muslin net.

"Poor bird!" said the child; "how can a raven be your enemy?"

"Theirs and yours!" the raven herself shrieked. "Theirs and yours!"

"And mine, bird! I would do you no hurt. See, I kiss you." When Melilot stooped to kiss through the thin muslin the raven's head, the bird struggled to escape from the kiss with an agony of terror.

"Nay," said the gentle child, "no evil can come of a true kiss."

Good came of it; for at the touch of her kiss, the wicked Fairy Frogbit dropped out of the form of a raven into a black, shapeless lump of earth.

"What have I done?" the child cried, weeping.

Then the three Fairies threw the lump of earth into the waterfall, and told her all that she had done. They told her how of old they had lived with their brother Fairies of

the Torrent till the wicked Frogbit came and turned the
land below into a marshy wilderness, in which she ruled
over her own evil race.   One day she and her people had
contrived to seize Titania herself, as she flew over the
marsh on the way to her subjects of the mountain.   They
could not change her beauty, or stain her bright nature,
but they held her prisoner for a time among their stagnant
pools, till she was rescued in a moonlight attack by the
Fairies of the waterfall, who left three prisoners, Dock,
Dodder, and Squill, in the hands of the enemy.   Those
prisoners Frogbit had shut up in loathsome frog-like bodies,
and set in the cottage between the lakes, while she brought
down never-ending rain over the whole district, to make
their prison more gloomy.   The Fairies of the bright
running and leaping water were condemned to sit in
stagnant puddle, and eat tadpoles, having their own bright
natures shut up in forms so detestable, that Frogbit hoped
to make their case more wretched by a mockery of hope.

"Live there," she said, "till a mortal child can look at you
without being afraid : till there is a little girl in the world
bold enough to seek you out, and trust you with all that she
holds most sacred ; to shut herself up with you, and believe
in you entirely ; to give up to you her own supper, and of
her own free thought make white muslin dresses to your
filthy shapes."

She spoke mockingly of white muslin, because she knew
of the old Fairy trade that had been carried on for ages on
the mountains.   There the Fairies weave after their own
fashion into muslin the white sheets of foam ; and when
the three prisoners had heard their doom they were not in
despair.   For although Frogbit, who had never been up
the mountain, knew nothing of the one little hut there was
upon it, yet all the Fairies knew it, and they knew well the
little Melilot.

"Then I have really been a friend to you," the child
said.

"Ay," they replied, "and to Frogbit a friend.   An
innocent kiss is the charm that breaks all evil spells, and
you have with a kiss broken the spell that raised in her a
clod of earth into a creature of mischief.   We of the
torrent will direct the waters that they wash that clod of
earth from which evil is banned to a place where it may

yield lilies and violets, of which good Fairies shall be born."

The three Fairies returning to their own race, were still Melilot's neighbours and friends, and the child grew up to womanhood, the favourite of all the Fairies of the waterfall. Her bower blossomed, and the ground about it was made into a delicious garden. Her dress of precious stones was thrown into a corner, and she was arrayed by the Fairies in their shining muslin that would take no soil. But still she found, morning and night, the only bread she ate upon her father's grave, and upon her mother's grave the milk that nourished her.

Whether the bad Fairies over whom Frogbit had ruled left the marsh, Melilot did not know, but the marsh dried and became a great plain, which men tilled, and upon which at last men fought.

Sobbing and panting, Melilot ran down the hillside when she saw men cased in iron galloping to and fro, and falling wounded to lie bleeding and uncared for on the quaking ground. Every fear was mastered by her sacred pity, and her Fairy muslin was unstained, though she knelt on the red mud of the battle-field and laid the wounded soldier's head upon her lap. None, even in the direst madness of the strife, could strike upon the frail white girl, who saw only the suffering about her, and thought only of wounds that she might bind. Had any struck, her muslin was an armour firmer than all steel; and there was no rent in her dress, as she tore from it strip after strip, to bind rents in the flesh of men who lay in their death-agonies about her.

In the tumult of flight, the defeated host parted before her, and sped on, still leaving her untrampled and un-touched. But once, reaching a white arm into the crowd, she caught from it a wounded soldier as he fell, and with the other hand seized the shaft of the spear that a fierce youth, hot in pursuit, thrust on his falling enemy. She fainted as she did so; and the youth, letting his spear drop, knelt beside her, and looked down into her face. His tears presently were falling on her lifeless cheek. The flight and the pursuit rushed by, and he was still kneeling beside her, when the moon rose, and three youths, dressed in white, stood near.

"Are you her brothers?" he asked. "Who is this, with a dress that has passed unstained through blood and mire, and with a face so holy?"

"Take her up in your arms," they said, "and we will show you where to carry her."

The young soldier lifted her with reverence, and took her up the mountain to the bower by the waterfall. The scent of the flowers, when they came into its garden, gave fresh life to her. The soldier gently laid her down upon a bank of wild thyme, and looked up for the three youths, but they were gone. He went into the bower, and saw therein scanty furniture, a dress of jewels worth an empire thrown into a corner, and two graves, on one of which stood bread, and on the other milk. He brought the food out to the girl, and, at her bidding, broke bread with her.

Now Dock, Dodder, and Squill were match-makers. They had made up their minds that Melilot should be to Sir Crucifer—that was the soldier's name—as near in trust and in love as her mother had been to her father. So they put the cottage between the two lakes into repair, and made him a home out of the place in which they had been imprisoned. There he dreamt, all the night through, sacred dreams of her by whose side he spent all his days.

Much the girl heard, as she sat with the soldier by the waterfall, of the high struggle for all that makes man good and glorious, that bred the strife out of which she had drawn him for a little time. Much the soldier learnt as he sat with the girl, from a companion whose thoughts purified his zeal, and made his aspirations happier and more unbounded. One day there were words said that made the girl a woman; and when she awoke on the next morning, her father's grave was overgrown with laurel bushes, and her mother's grave was lost under a wealth of flowering myrtle.

But there was no food provided.

When Sir Crucifer came to her that sunny morning, "I have a sign," she said. "It is time that I also take my part in the struggle of which you have told me. Let us go down together to the plains."

She gathered for him a branch of laurel, and she plucked a sprig of myrtle for herself. These never faded; they remained green as the daughter's memory of those two dear ones from whose graves they came. But in all their long after-lives of love and labour, neither of them remembered the worth of an empire in stone that they left unguarded in a corner of the hut.

The spray was radiant, and the foam was white as her bright Fairy muslin, as it floated over the strength of the waterfall, when Melilot and her soldier, hand in hand, went down the mountain. They passed out of her bower, she in the full flood of the sunshine, with an arm raised upward and a calm face turned towards him, as he, walking in her shadow, pointed to the plains below.

THE DEFEAT OF TIME;

A TALE OF THE FAIRIES

ITANIA and her moonlight elves were assembled under the canopy of a huge oak, that served to shelter them from the moon's radiance, which, being now at her full moon, shot forth intolerable rays,—intolerable I mean to the subtile texture of their little shadowy bodies,— but dispensing an agreeable coolness to us grosser mortals. An air of discomfort sate upon the queen and upon her courtiers. Their tiny friskings and gambols were forgot; and even Robin Goodfellow, for the first time in his little airy life, looked grave. For the queen had had melancholy forebodings of late, founded upon an ancient prophecy laid up in the records of Fairyland, that the date of fairy existence should be *then* extinct when men should cease to believe in them. And she knew how that the race of the Nymphs, which were her predecessors, and had been the guardians of the sacred floods, and of the silver fountains, and of the consecrated hills and woods, had utterly disappeared before the chilling touch of man's incredulity; and she sighed bitterly at the approaching fate of herself and of her subjects, which was dependent upon so fickle a lease as the capricious and ever-mutable faith of man. When, as if to realise her fears, a melancholy shape came gliding in, and *that* was— Time, who with his intolerable scythe mows down kings and kingdoms; at whose dread approach the fays huddled together as a flock of timorous sheep; and the most courageous among them crept into acorn-cups, not enduring the sight of that ancientest of monarchs. Titania's first impulse was to wish the presence of her false lord, King Oberon,—who was far away, in the pursuit of a strange beauty, a fay of Indian Land,—that with his good lance and sword, like a faithful knight and husband, he

might defend her against Time.   But she soon checked
that thought as vain; for what could the prowess of the
mighty Oberon himself, albeit the stoutest champion in
Fairyland, have availed against so huge a giant, whose
bald top touched the skies?   So, in the mildest tone, she
besought the spectre, that in his mercy he would overlook
and pass by her small subjects, as too diminutive and
powerless to add any worthy trophy to his renown.   And
she besought him to employ his resistless strength against
the ambitious children of men, and to lay waste their
aspiring works; to tumble down their towers and turrets,
and the Babels of their pride,—fit objects of his devouring
scythe,—but to spare her and her harmless race, who had
no existence beyond a dream; frail objects of a creed that
lived but in the faith of the believer.   And with her little
arms, as well as she could, she grasped the stern knees of
Time; and, waxing speechless with fear, she beckoned to
her chief attendants and maids of honour to come forth
from their hiding-places, and to plead the plea of the
fairies.   And one of those small, delicate creatures came
forth at her bidding, clad all in white like a chorister, and
in a low melodious tone, not louder than the hum of a
pretty bee—when it seems to be demurring whether it
shall settle upon this sweet flower or that before it settles,
—set forth her humble petition.   "We fairies," she said,
"are the most inoffensive race that live, and least deserving
to perish.   It is we that have the care of all sweet melodies
that no discords may offend the sun, who is the great soul
of music.   We rouse the lark at morn; and the pretty
Echoes, which respond to all the twittering choir, are of
our making.   Wherefore, great King of Years, as ever you
have loved the music which is raining from a morning
cloud sent from the messenger of day, the lark, as he
mounts to heaven's gate, beyond the ken of mortals; or if
ever you have listened with a charmed ear to the nightbird,
that—

> " ' In the flowery spring,
> Amidst the leaves set, makes the thickets ring
> Of our sour sorrows, sweeten'd with her song—'

spare our tender tribes, and we will muffle up the sheep-
bell for thee, that thy pleasure take no interruption whenever thou shalt listen unto Philomel."

o

And Time answered, that "he had heard that song toc long; and he was even wearied with that ancient strain that recorded the wrong of Tereus. But, if she would know in what music Time delighted, it was, when sleep and darkness lay upon crowded cities, to hark to the midnight chime which is tolling from a hundred clocks, like the last knell over the soul of a dead world; or to the crash of the fall of some age-worn edifice, which is as the voice of himself when he disparteth kingdoms."

A second female fay took up the plea, and said, "We be the handmaids of the Spring, and tend upon the birth of all sweet buds: and the pastoral cowslips are our friends; and the pansies and the violets, like nuns; and the quaking harebell is in our wardship; and the hyacinth, once a fair youth, and dear to Phœbus."

Then Time made answer, in his wrath striking the harmless ground with his hurtful scythe, that, "they must not think that he was one that cared for flowers, except to see them wither, and to take her beauty from the rose."

And a third fairy took up the plea, and said, "We are kindly things: and it is we that sit at evening, and shake rich odours from sweet bowers upon discoursing lovers, that seem to each other to be their own sighs; and we keep off the bat and the owl from their privacy, and the ill-boding whistler; and we flit in sweet dreams across the brains of infancy, and conjure up a smile upon its soft lips to beguile the careful mother, while its little soul is fled for a brief minute or two to sport with our youngest fairies."

Then Saturn (which is Time) made answer, that "they should not think that he delighted in tender babes, that had devoured his own, till foolish Rhea cheated him with a stone, which he swallowed, thinking it to be the infant Jupiter." And thereat, in token, he disclosed to view his enormous tooth, in which appeared monstrous dents left by that unnatural meal; and his great throat, that seemed capable of devouring up the earth and all its inhabitants at one meal. "And for lovers," he continued, "my delight is, with a hurrying hand to snatch them away from their love-meetings by stealth at nights; and, in absence, to stand like a motionless statue, or their leaden planet of mishap (whence I had my name), till I make their minutes seem ages."

Next stood up a male fairy, clad all in green, like a forester or one of Robin Hood's mates, and, doffing his tiny cap, said, "We are small foresters, that live in woods, training the young boughs in graceful intricacies, with blue snatches of the sky between : we frame all shady roofs and arches rude ; and sometimes, when we are plying our tender hatchets, men say that the tapping woodpecker is nigh. And it is we that scoop the hollow cell of the squirrel, and carve quaint letters upon the rinds of trees, which in sylvan solitudes sweetly recall to the mind of the heat-oppressed swain, ere he lies down to slumber, the name of his fair one, dainty Aminta, gentle Rosalind, or chastest Laura, as it may happen."

Saturn, nothing moved with this courteous address, bade him begone, or "if he would be a woodman, to go forth and fell oak for the fairies' coffins which would forthwith be wanting. For himself he took no delight in haunting the woods, till their golden plumage (the yellow leaves) were beginning to fall, and leave the brown-black limbs bare, like Nature in her skeleton dress."

Then stood up one of those gentle fairies that are good to man, and blushed red as any rose while he told a modest story of one of his own good deeds. "It chanced upon a time," he said, "that while we were looking for cowslips in the meads, while yet the dew was hanging on the buds like beads, we found a babe left in its swathing-clothes,—a little sorrowful, deserted thing, begot of love, but begetting no love in others ; guiltless of shame, but doomed to shame for its parents' offence in bringing it by indirect courses into the world. It was pity to see the abandoned little orphan left to the world's care by an unnatural mother. How the cold dew kept wetting its childish coats ! and its little hair, how it was bedabbled, that was like gossamer ! Its pouting mouth, unknowing how to speak, lay half opened like a rose-lipped shell ; and its cheek was softer than any peach, upon which the tears, for very roundness, could not long dwell, but fell off, in clearness like pearls,—some on the grass, and some on his little hand ; and some haply wandered to the little dimpled well under his mouth, which Love himself seemed to have planned out, but less for tears than for smilings. Pity, it was, too, to see how the burning sun had scorched its helpless limbs; for it lay without shade or shelter, or mother's breast, for foul weather or fair. So, having compassion on its sad plight, my fellows and I turned ourselves into grasshoppers, and swarmed about the babe, making such shrill cries as that pretty little chirping creature makes in its mirth, till with our noise we attracted the attention of a passing rustic, a tender-hearted hind, who, wondering at our small but loud concert, strayed aside curiously, and found the babe, where it lay in the remote grass, and taking it up, lapped it in his russet coat, and bore it to his cottage, where his wife kindly nurtured it till it grew up a goodly personage. How this babe prospered afterwards, let proud London tell. This was that famous Sir Thomas Gresham, who was the chiefest of her merchants, the richest, the wisest. Witness his many goodly vessels on the Thames, freighted with costly merchandise, jewels from Ind, and pearls for courtly dames, and silks of Samarcand. And witness, more than all, that stately Bourse (or Exchange) which he caused to be built, a mart for merchants from east and west, whose graceful summit still bears, in token of the fairies' favours, his chosen crest, the grasshopper. And, like the grasshopper, may it please you, great king, to suffer us also to live, partakers of the green earth!"

The fairy had scarce ended his plea, when a shrill cry, not unlike the grasshopper's was heard. Poor Puck—or Robin Goodfellow, as he is sometimes called—had recovered a little from his first fright, and, in one of his mad freaks, had perched upon the beard of old Time, which was flowing, ample, and majestic; and was amusing himself with plucking at a hair, which was indeed so massy that it seemed to him that he was removing some huge beam of timber, rather than a hair: which Time, by some ill chance perceiving, snatched up the impish mischief with his great hand, and asked what it was.

"Alas!" quoth Puck, "a little random elf am I, born in one of Nature's sports; a very weed, created for the simple, sweet enjoyment of myself, but for no other purpose, worth, or need, that ever I could learn. 'Tis I that bob the angler's idle cork, till the patient man is ready to breathe a curse. I steal the morsel from the gossip's fork, or stop the sneezing chanter in mid psalm; and when an infant has been born with hard or homely features, mothers say I changed the child at nurse : but to fulfil any graver purpose I have not wit enough, and hardly the will. I am a pinch of lively dust to frisk upon the wind: a tear would make a puddle of me ; and so I tickle myself with the lightest straw, and shun all griefs that might make me stagnant. This is my small philosophy."

Then Time, dropping him on the ground, as a thing too inconsiderable for his vengeance, grasped fast his mighty scythe : and now, not Puck alone, but the whole state of fairies, had gone to inevitable wreck and destruction, had not a timely apparition interposed, at whose boldness Time was astounded ; for he came not with the habit of the forces of a deity, who alone might cope with Time, but as a simple mortal, clad as you might see a forester that hunts after wild conies by the cold moonshine ; or a stalker of stray deer, stealthy and bold.   But by the golden lustre in his eye, and the passionate wanness in his cheek, and by the fair and ample space of his forehead, which seemed a palace framed for the habitation of all glorious thoughts, he knew that this was his great rival, who had power given him to rescue whatsoever victims Time should clutch, and to cause them to live for ever in his immortal verse.   And, muttering the name of Shakspere, Time spread his roc-like wings, and fled the controlling presence ; and the liberated court of the fairies, with Titania at their head, flocked around the gentle ghost, giving him thanks, nodding to him, and doing him courtesies, who had crowned them henceforth with a permanent existence, to live in the minds of men, while verse shall have power to charm, or midsummer moons shall brighten.

   .   .   .   .   .   .

What particular endearments passed between the fairies and their poet, passes my pencil to delineate ; but, if you are curious to be informed, I must refer you, gentle reader, to the " Plea of the Midsummer Fairies," [1] a most agree-

---

[1] Four verses from Tom Hood's poem follow, which show to what kind of tune he set the music of his Midsummer Fairies :—

'Twas in that mellow season of the year,
When the hot Sun singes the yellow leaves

able poem lately put forth by my friend Thomas Hood;
of the first half of which the above is nothing but a
meagre and harsh prose abstract. Farewell!

The words of Mercury are harsh after the songs of Apollo.

Till they be gold,——and with a broader sphere
The Moon looks down on Ceres and her sheaves;
When more abundantly the spider weaves,
And the cold wind breathes from a chillier clime;
That forth I fared, on one of those still eves,
Touch'd with the dewy sadness of the time,
To think how the bright months had spent their prime.

And lo! upon my fix'd delighted ken
Appear'd the loyal Fays.——Some by degrees
Crept from the primrose buds that open'd then,
And some from bell-shap'd blossoms like the bees,
Some from the dewy meads, and rushy leas,
Flew up like chafers when the rustics pass;
Some from the rivers, others from tall trees
Dropp'd, like shed blossoms, silent to the grass,
Spirits and elfins small, of every class.

Peri and Pixy, and quaint Puck the Antic,
Brought Robin Goodfellow, that merry Swain;
And stealthy Mab, queen of old realms romantic,
Came too, from distance, in her tiny wain,
Fresh dripping from a cloud——some bloomy rain,
Then circling the bright Moon, had wash'd her car,
And still bedew'd it with a various stain:
Lastly came Ariel, shooting from a star,
Who bears all fairy embassies afar.

Anon I saw one of those elfin things,
Clad all in white like any chorister,
Come fluttering forth on his melodious wings,
That made soft music at each little stir,
But something louder than a bee's demur
Before he lights upon a bunch of broom,
And thus 'gan he with Saturn to confer,——
And O his voice was sweet, touch'd with the gloom
Of that sad theme that argued of his doom!

ELAN THE ARMOURER

HERE no ship is sailing, and no bird is flying, far away from all land, the great waves mingle their foam with the low, scudding clouds. Sea and air break in storm against each other. The lightning leaps over the rolling hills of water ; over the falling hill-tops the wind hisses and the thunder - crash descends ; but the hills fall to rise as mountains, and the mountains rise to be dashed through the sky in powder by the fierce stroke of the gale. The roar of the beaten water, and the hiss of the foam swept by the hurricane into the upper sky, are as a whisper to the thunder-peals that crack as if the globe itself were being rent in twain.

There is a red gleam tossing between heaven and earth. It cannot be a·ship's light, for no ship could live in such a gale. The lightning flashes into it ; the thunder rattles over it. The water beats it up into the battling clouds, and leaves it to fall back into the depths ; but the hills of the sea do not cover it. Out of the lowest abyss it mounts again, and grows as a fire. It is a floating forge-fire, and a mighty anvil rides beside it, upon which a giant beats. The giant's calm face and his yellow hair, dragged by the wind, are ruddy in the blaze of his own furnace. The flame of the forge flickers on his naked arm as, when it is raised, the hammer-head plunges among the thunder-clouds before it falls upon the armour he is shaping. That is Elan who rides the Waters, terrible in strength.

Of his strength the sea-nymphs are enamoured. In calm weather they play about his forge, and delight more in the ring of his hammer through the vault of heaven than in softest music of the sirens.

From afar over the waves, the sound of the hammer could be heard on the shores of the kingdom of Cock-paidle, when there was a clear sea and no speck on the

horizon. Sometimes at night, watchmen upon some coast
cliff of Cockpaidle saw, like the gleam of a distant lighthouse, the moving forge-fire of Elan of the Waters twinkle
between sky and ocean.   Then the watchmen lighted their
own signal fires upon the hill-top, and height after height
was tipped with flame as the quick signal passed.   Armed
knights and cross-bow men then crowded the Cockpaidle
war-galleys.   The rowers strained their arms, obedient to
the whip that urged them ; for they were in no haste of
their own to come within reach of the giant's hammer.
Every King Pipit, down to Pipit the Twenty-ninth-and-a-
third, who ruled at the time of which this story tells (there
had been ninety-one kings of the name, but many had
their tenths and their thirds reckoned as fractions, so that
Pipit the Eleventh had been held to mean, not the
Eleventh King Pipit, but Pipit the Eleventh of a king)—
every Pipit had laboured to make Elan his prisoner.   For
there was an ancient prophecy, boding destruction to the
race of Pipits when the chained Fairy Euroe should come
to Cockpaidle with a sword of Elan's sharpening and
armour shapen at his ever-blazing forge.

Pipit the Twenty-ninth-and-a-third, King of Cockpaidle,
was the most bewildering of sovereigns.   Traitors among
his subjects dared to ask each other, very secretly, whether
his real face must not be something shameful ; for he
never went abroad without a mask.   He had indeed a
closet full of masks, all differing from each other, and
cunningly devised to imitate a real face of some sort.
Without one of these over his face—if he had a face—
Pipit was never seen, even by the friend—if he had a
friend—of his bosom.   He was nothing in the world but
the King of Cockpaidle.   You may say, it was something
to be that.   Perhaps he himself thought so, when he stocked
his cupboard, but he soon found it the least of a something to be nothing in the world but that.   A man who in
one day might eat his breakfast with his cat's face on, ride
out in his ape's face, dine in his dog's face, receive friends
from behind a cock's face, and go to bed in the face of a
lynx, bewildered everybody.   The face he chose was
always at odds with the mind in which he wore it.   His
words were always at odds with his thoughts, in order that
he might be too dark for any man to see into ; he was as

careful to avoid a true word as most men are to keep their
mouths clean from a false one. Therefore, as people who
speak truth are apt to believe they hear the truth from
others, King Pipit over-reached so many neighbours during
the first few years of his reign, that he was supposed to
have a wonderfully clever head.

King Pipit, in his mask as a vulture, sat on a very high
throne in the middle of his Court.

"Ambassador from the Estates of Brill, begone !" he
said ; whereupon a gentleman, in a gold coat and amber-
satin stockings, advanced to the steps of his throne and
knelt before him. It was etiquette in Pipit's Court, and
held to be useful discipline for all who waited on it, that
when "come" was meant the word was "go," and so
"begone" was of course Pipit for "come before me."

"Be silent," said Pipit. Thereupon the ambassador
from Brill began to speak, and spoke officially, saying,—

"Sire, I am not ignorant that you wish not ill to Euroe.
Therefore I come not to tell you that her raft is not
wrecked upon a shoal not far from the Brill coast, and
were it not that we do not hear from afar, day and night,
not a sound of the hammer of Elan the Armourer, our
ships would not have rescued her, and not have brought
her as a guest to your great capital."

"Tell my Admiral I shall not want him for ten years,"
King Pipit cried to his attendants. Thereupon the
Admiral was summoned by a breathless messenger to
come, without a moment's loss of time, into the sublimest
presence.

"Draw up my war-galleys on all my coasts. Let them
lie high and dry upon the shore," said Pipit, while the
Admiral was coming. Messengers were sent at once to
all the coasts, ordering the war-galleys to be got ready for
instant service.

"When anybody sees my Admiral, let him be told,"
said Pipit, "that as there is no more work for him upon
the seas, I shall be glad if he will look in and play
beggar-my-neighbour with me in my private cabinet. I
shall sit here all day to hear petitions." Thereupon he
retired immediately, and the Court broke up. A great
concourse of petitioners that waited at the gate was at the
same time kicked back into holes and corners of the city.

Stripped of her ornaments and chained down to a raft, the Fairy Euroe, in form of a fair woman, had been tossed for many years on the wide waters. So wide were the waters upon which she was tossed, that never once had her path crossed that of the strong giant Elan. At last—though it may not have been clear to any one but Pipit, from the guarded language of the Brill ambassador—her raft had really struck upon a bank of sand, hardly within sight of the shores of Brill. Then the planks parted from under her, and from the chains that bound her to them. She stood in her fetters knee-deep in the shallow waves, imperishable as a Fairy, but much suffering.

So she stood, on a warm and breezy summer's day, when there was no sound to be heard but the far, far distant clang of Elan's hammer. A flock, as it were, of white pigeons crossing the horizon, spread over the sea. They were King Pipit's war-galleys, with the sails spread, and a watchman upon every one of their crows' nests and high swan-like prows. The ships, when Euroe had been descried, drew together in a long line between her and the point from which the sound of the Sea Armourer's hammer seemed to come. Towards that point every knight pointed his lance, every bowman his arrow. A gilded boat, with a silk canopy, put off from the chief galley, and the Admiral himself was rowed to the fair Euroe, whose limbs were veiled only by the trickling ringlets of her hair.

"Madam," the Admiral said, "seeing you wrecked, I stay to rescue you, although our fleet is bound upon a distant expedition. Suffer me to throw over you this robe of honour." As he said this, his men threw over her shoulders a white sheet of penance, painted over with all manner of horrid shapes. "I very deeply regret," he said, "that we cannot strike your chains off without hurting you. Believe, however, that I have a master who will gild them." Poor Euroe! Her power as a Fairy was bound by those chains, and she was carried off a helpless prisoner, while all the fleets of Cockpaidle covering her capture were manned with knights and bowmen ready to fight Elan the Armourer, should he attempt a rescue.

When Euroe stood in the Court of Pipit, the false King made so low and courteous an obeisance to her that she was immediately seized and conveyed to his secret

ELAN the Armourer

dungeons. These dungeons were built under and near the royal bed-chamber. A pipe carried from each cell every sound of complaint, every groan, every restless shuffle of a foot or clank of a chain, to a reservoir in the air-pillow of the royal bed. When King Pipit went to bed, his pillow was stuffed with those sounds, that soothed him into easy slumber with assurance that his enemies were safe. Pipit the Twenty-ninth-and-a-third, like his royal predecessors, knew every captive by the sound of his or of her footstep, by the rub of the chain, or the tone of the cry of suffering, or nightly prayer. He made sure that he had all his groans before he slept in peace, counting them as a good monk might count his beads. Whenever he missed the stir of any one prisoner, he sent one of the jailers, who served as his grooms of the bedchamber to see that all was safe, and to fetch out a groan in some way for his full and perfect satisfaction. Obstinately silent prisoners were scourged when Pipit went to bed. If then they persisted in defrauding his pillow of a portion of its stuffing, at least there was contributed the sound made by the falling of the lash upon their skin. Into a dark cave beneath the royal chamber Euroe was dragged, and the low song she murmured was the last sound in the tyrant's ear before he slept.

But in the darkness of the night there was a cry, "Elan! Elan!" Elan the Armourer had come to Cockpaidle, and was walking on the land. He had discerned from afar the galleys of King Pipit, and the planks of Euroe's broken raft had floated round his anvil. The armour was forged, and the sharp sword was tempered. Therefore, shouldering his mighty hammer, and with the Fairy sword and armour upon his left arm, Elan marched over the waves to the shore of Cockpaidle, and strode over cliffs and hills, rivers and woods, to Pipit's capital. He struck no blow, but steadily walked forward with his hammer on his shoulder, and he walked so carefully that there was not a field-mouse crushed under his tread.

But when he came to Pipit's palace he stood still, and raising the great hammer high into the night, struck one blow on the corner-stone. Then all the outer walls fell forward with a mighty crash, and the stones that fell upon the giant hurt him no more than if they had been falling

dust.   When the walls fell the prisons were laid open,
and the false King felt the night air blowing in upon him
as he was awakened.   The shock of the ruin woke him,
and the glad shout of the captives who had made his
pillow tremble.   Pipit sat up in his bed, shivering with
fear, and looking straight before him through the ape-faced
mask in which it had pleased him to go to bed, dimly saw
Elan the Armourer, who filled the night with his great
presence.   The giant had already rubbed to dust with his
strong hand the chains of Euroe, and now a light suddenly
poured from the cave below.   The Fairy had regained her
power as she buckled on the breastplate he had made for
her, crowned her head with the helmet, and grasped the
keen sword in her right hand.   From the Fairy in the
fulness of her power the light poured.

In all the houses servant-maids jumped out of bed,
accusing the false house-clocks ; mistresses jumped out of
bed, accusing the overslept maids ; masters jumped out of
bed and clamoured for their breakfasts, wondering how
they could have slept till it was blazing noon.   But maids,
mistresses, and masters were soon running to the palace,
crowding the great square and all the streets that led into
it, looking up, with their hands over their eyes, at the
blinding beauty of Euroe.   She had risen as an airy spirit
through the solid stone roof of her cave into the chamber
of the miserable naked Pipit, and stood fully armed over
the bed in which he knelt.   He clasped his trembling
hands before her in entreaty, and turned up to her glorious
face his ape-mask.   The terrors of the dungeons were laid
bare to every eye ; and in the full light of Euroe's brightness Elan the Armourer stood like a massive tower.

Then Euroe, before all the people, stretched towards
King Pipit her unarmed hand, and plucking from his face
the mask he wore, laid bare what was beneath that had so
long been hidden.   A great shudder ran through the
crowd, and Pipit spread his hands over the unmasked
horror.

" Live the great Fairy ! " cried the people.

" Live Euroe ! " Elan cried, with a voice that was heard
to the remotest village on the borders of Cockpaidle.
" Live Euroe ! Queen Euroe ! " replied in a glad shout
every voice of man upon the land ; and upon the cry of

the throng about the palace there seemed to roll back as
thunder from all corners of the sky, "Live Queen Euroe."

Then a low murmur arising grew among the crowd, and
confused voices joined in words that altogether meant,
"We have been Pipit's; Pipit now is ours!" The
miserable king grasped at the robe of Euroe, the robe
of shame in which he had clothed her, but upon which
the foul painted shapes were changed to happy visions,
glowing, as it seemed, with colour from the rainbow.
There was no hold for Pipit on that robe. It was to his
strained fingers as if he caught at air.

Then Elan took up in his hand the quivering and
quaking Pipit, as a man might grasp a sparrow, and
lifting him out of his nest, laid him upon the ground
among his people. There, while he still covered his
foul face with both his hands, he knelt and prayed that
none would trust the dangerous Euroe; knelt and
promised, knelt and swore, that he would constitute his
people, if they only trusted him again, partners with
him in power, and devote his whole life to their welfare.
"Ah! ah!" they answered; "but we know that to be
Pipit for Grind us in slavery and make us wretched."
"Believe me! believe me!" Pipit mourned. But the
people, looking at the dungeons under dungeons exposed
by the falling of the palace walls, pronounced this
sentence on him and his race :—

"Henceforth the Pipits follow their true calling. Let
them be slaves to the turnkeys who are servants of the
keepers in the common jails!"

With his hands bound to his side, so that his unmasked
face should be open to sight, causing all by whom he
passed to turn away their eyes in sudden loathing, Pipit
was led to his jail-work; and as the crowd that opened to
make way for him closed behind him into one dense mass,
again there rolled up to heaven the great shout, and there
rolled back as a low thunder from all corners of the sky,
"Live Euroe! Queen Euroe!"

The high throne of the Pipits was uprooted from its
place, and borne by a great concourse of men, women, and
children, out into the free air. There it was set up in the
sight of all the people.

For two thousand years and more the bright Fairy

Euroe reigned over Cockpaidle in truth, justice, and mercy, and the place of the giant Elan was at her feet, sunning himself always in the light of her pure beauty. All who knew her loved her, but it was Elan who had been born to love her most of all.   All who served her were true to her, but of her world of friends old Elan was the trustiest.

THE PIED PIPER OF HAMELIN

A CHILD'S STORY

I

HAMELIN Town's in Brunswick,
  By famous Hanover city;
The River Weser, deep and wide,
  Washes its wall on the southern side;
  A pleasanter spot you never spied;
But, when begins my ditty,
  Almost five hundred years ago,
  To see townsfolk suffer so
From vermin, was a pity.

II

  Rats!
They fought the dogs, and killed the cats,
  And bit the babies in the cradles,
  And ate the cheeses out of the vats,
    And lick'd the soup from the cook's own ladles,
  Split open the kegs of salted sprats,
  Made nests inside men's Sunday hats,
  And even spoiled the women's chats,
    By drowning their speaking
    With shrieking and squeaking
  In fifty different sharps and flats.

III

  At last the people in a body
    To the Town Hall came flocking:
  "'Tis clear," cried they, "our Mayor's a noddy;
    And as for our Corporation—shocking
  To think we buy gowns lined with ermine
  For dolts that can't or won't determine
  What's best to rid us of our vermin!

P   225

You hope, because you're old and obese,
To find in the furry civic robe ease?
Rouse up, Sirs! Give your brains a racking
To find the remedy we're lacking,
Or, sure as fate, we'll send you packing!"
At this the Mayor and Corporation
Quaked with a mighty consternation.

IV

An hour they sate in council,
   At length the Mayor broke silence:
"For a guilder I'd my ermine gown sell,
   I wish I were a mile hence!
It's easy to bid one rack one's brain—
I'm sure my poor head aches again
I've scratched it so, and all in vain.
Oh, for a trap, a trap, a trap!"
Just as he said this, what should hap
At the chamber door but a gentle tap?
"Bless us," cried the Mayor, "what's that?"
(With the Corporation as he sat,
Looking little though wondrous fat;
Nor brighter was his eye, nor moister
Than a too-long-opened oyster,
Save when at noon his paunch grew mutinous
For a plate of turtle green and glutinous)
"Only a scraping of shoes at the mat?
Anything like the sound of a rat
Makes my heart go pit-a-pat!

V

"Come in!"—the Mayor cried, looking bigger:
And in did come the strangest figure!
His queer long coat from heel to head
Was half of yellow and half of red;
And he himself was tall and thin,
With sharp blue eyes, each like a pin,
And light loose hair, yet swarthy skin,
No tuft on cheek nor beard on chin,
But lips where smiles went out and in
There was no guessing his kith and kin
And nobody could enough admire

The tall man and his quaint attire:
Quoth one: "It's as my great-grandsire,
Starting up at the Trump of Doom's tone,
Had walked this way from his painted tombstone!"

VI

He advanced to the council-table:
And, "Please your honours," said he, "I'm able,
By means of a secret charm, to draw
All creatures living beneath the sun,
That creep, or swim, or fly, or run,
After me so as you never saw!
And I chiefly use my charm
On creatures that do people harm,
The mole, and toad, and newt, and viper;
And people call me the Pied Piper."
(And here they noticed round his neck
A scarf of red and yellow stripe,
To match with his coat of the self same check;
And at the scarf's end hung a pipe;
And his fingers, they noticed, were ever straying
As if impatient to be playing
Upon this pipe, as low it dangled
Over his vesture so old-fangled.)
"Yet," said he, "poor piper as I am,
In Tartary I freed the Cham,
Last June, from his huge swarms of gnats;
I eased in Asia the Nizam
Of a monstrous brood of vampire-bats:
And, as for what your brain bewilders,
If I can rid your town of rats
Will you give me a thousand guilders?"
"One? fifty thousand!"—was the exclamation
Of the astonished Mayor and Corporation.

VII

Into the street the Piper stept,
    Smiling first a little smile,
As if he knew what magic slept
    In his quiet pipe the while;
Then, like a musical adept,
To blow the pipe his lips he wrinkled,

And green and blue his sharp eyes twinkled
Like a candle flame where salt is sprinkled ;
And ere three shrill notes the pipe uttered,
You heard as if an army muttered ;
And the muttering grew to a grumbling;
And the grumbling grew to a mighty rumbling ;
And out of the houses the rats came tumbling :
Great rats, small rats, lean rats, brawny rats,
Brown rats, black rats, grey rats, tawny rats,
Grave old plodders, gay young friskers,
    Fathers, mothers, uncles, cousins,
Cocking tails and pricking whiskers,
    Families by tens and dozens,
Brothers, sisters, husbands, wives—
Followed the Piper for their lives.
From street to street he piped advancing,
And step for step they followed dancing,
Until they came to the river Weser
Wherein all plunged and perished
—Save one who, stout as Julius Cæsar,
Swam across and lived to carry
(As he the manuscript he cherished)
To Rat-land home his commentary,
Which was, " At the first shrill notes of the pipe,
I heard a sound as of scraping tripe,
And putting apples, wondrous ripe,
Into a cider-press's gripe :
And a moving away of pickle-tub boards,
And a leaving ajar of conserve-cupboards,
And the drawing the corks of train-oil flasks,
And a breaking the hoops of butter-casks ;
And it seemed as if a voice
(Sweeter far than by harp or by psaltery
Is breathed) called out, Oh, rats, rejoice !
The world is grown to one vast drysaltery !
So munch on, crunch on, take your nuncheon,
Breakfast, supper, dinner, luncheon !
And just as a bulky sugar-puncheon,
All ready staved, like a great sun shone
Glorious scarce an inch before me,
Just as methought it said, Come, bore me !
—I found the Weser rolling o'er me."

VIII

You should have heard the Hamelin people
Ringing the bells till they rocked the steeple ;
"Go," cried the Mayor, " and get long poles !
Poke out the nests and block up the holes !
Consult with carpenters and builders,
And leave in our town not even a trace
Of the rats ! "—when suddenly up the face
Of the Piper perked in the market-place,
With a " First, if you please, my thousand guilders ! "

IX

A thousand guilders !   The Mayor looked blue ;
So did the Corporation too.
For council dinners made rare havock
With Claret, Moselle, Vin-de-Grave, Hock ;
And half the money would replenish
Their cellar's biggest butt with Rhenish.
To pay this sum to a wandering fellow
With a gipsy coat of red and yellow !
" Beside," quoth the Mayor, with a knowing wink,
" Our business was done at the river's brink ;
We saw with our eyes the vermin sink,
And what's dead can't come to life, I think.
So, friend, we're not the folks to shrink
From the duty of giving you something for drink,
And a matter of money to put in your poke ;
But, as for the guilders, what we spoke
Of them, as you very well know, was in joke.
Beside, our losses have made us thrifty ;
A thousand guilders !   Come, take fifty ! "

X

The Piper's face fell, and he cried,
" No trifling !   I can't wait, beside !
I've promised to visit by dinner time
Bagdad, and accept the prime
Of the Head Cook's pottage, all he's rich in,
For having left, in the Caliph's kitchen,
Of a nest of scorpions no survivor—

With him I proved no bargain-driver,
With you, don't think I'll bate a stiver !
And folks who put me in a passion
    May find me pipe to another fashion."

XI

" How ? " cried the Mayor, " d'ye think I'll brook
Being worse treated than a Cook ?
Insulted by a lazy ribald
With idle pipe and vesture piebald ?
You threaten us, fellow ?   Do your worst,
Blow your pipe there till you burst ! "

XII

Once more he stept into the street ;
    And to his lips again
Laid his long pipe of smooth straight cane ;
    And ere he blew three notes (such sweet
Soft notes as yet musician's cunning
    Never gave the enraptured air)
There was a rustling, that seemed like a bustling
Of merry crowds justling at pitching and hustling,
Small feet were pattering, wooden shoes clattering,
Little hands clapping, and little tongues chattering,
And, like fowls in a farm-yard when barley is scattering,
Out came the children running.
All the little boys and girls,
With rosy cheeks and flaxen curls,
And sparkling eyes and teeth like pearls,
Tripping and skipping, ran merrily after
The wonderful music with shouting and laughter.

XIII

The Mayor was dumb, and the Council stood
As if they were changed into blocks of wood,
Unable to move a step, or cry
To the children merrily skipping by—
And could only follow with the eye
That joyous crowd at the Piper's back.

But how the Mayor was on the rack,
And the wretched Council's bosoms beat,
As the Piper turned from the High Street
To where the Weser rolled its waters
Right in the way of their sons and daughters !
However he turned from South to West,
And to Koppelberg Hill his steps addressed,
And after him the children pressed ;
Great was the joy in every breast.
" He never can cross that mighty top !
He's forced to let the piping drop,
And we shall see our children stop ! "
When, lo, as they reached the mountain's side,
A wondrous portal opened wide,
As if a cavern was suddenly hollowed ;
And the Piper advanced and the children followed,
And when all were in to the very last,
The door in the mountain side shut fast.
Did I say, all ? No ! One was lame,
And could not dance the whole of the way ;
And in after years, if you would blame
His sadness, he was used to say,—
" It's dull in our town since my playmates left !
I can't forget that I'm bereft
Of all the pleasant sights they see,
Which the Piper also promised me ;
For he led us, he said, to a joyous land,
Joining the town and just at hand,
Where waters gushed and fruit-trees grew,
And flowers put forth a fairer hue,
And everything was strange and new ;
The sparrows were brighter than peacocks here,
And their dogs outran our fallow deer,
And honey-bees had lost their stings,
And horses were born with eagles' wings ;
And just as I became assured
My lame foot would be speedily cured,
The music stopped and I stood still,
And found myself outside the Hill,
Left alone against my will,
To go now limping as before,
And never hear of that country more ! "

XIV

Alas, alas for Hamelin !
   There came into many a burgher's pate
   A text which says, that Heaven's Gate
   Opes to the Rich at as easy rate
As the needle's eye takes a camel in !
The Mayor sent East, West, North, and South
To offer the Piper by word of mouth,
   Wherever it was men's lot to find him,
Silver and gold to his heart's content,
If he'd only return the way he went,
   And bring the children behind him.
But when they saw 'twas a lost endeavour,
And Piper and dancers were gone for ever,
They made a decree that lawyers never
   Should think their records dated duly
If, after the day of the month and year,
These words did not as well appear,
" And so long after what happened here
   On the Twenty-second of July,
Thirteen hundred and Seventy-six : "
And the better in memory to fix
The place of the children's last retreat,
They called it, the Pied Piper's Street—
Where any one playing on pipe or tabor
Was sure for the future to lose his labour.
Nor suffered they Hostelry or Tavern
   To shock with mirth a street so solemn ;
But opposite the place of the cavern
   They wrote the story on a column,
And on the Great Church Window painted
The same, to make the world acquainted
How their children were stolen away ;
And there it stands to this very day.
And I must not omit to say
That in Transylvania there's a tribe
Of alien people that ascribe
The outlandish ways and dress
On which their neighbours lay such stress
To their fathers and mothers having risen
Out of some subterraneous prison

Into which they were trepanned
Long time ago in a mighty band
Out of Hamelin town in Brunswick land,
But how or why, they don't understand.

XV

So, Willy, let you and me be wipers
Of scores out with all men—especially pipers:
And, whether they pipe us free, from rats or from mice,
If we've promised them aught, let us keep our promise.

BACON PIE

NCE upon a time there was a great magician, and his name was Picrotoxin. His wife's name was Menisper, and she was not a conjurer at all, but no more than a simple, orderly, hard-working woman. Picrotoxin, being a great conjurer himself, did not want two of the same trade under his roof. He wanted to agree with a good housewifely soul, who would wonder at him and obey him, and with whom he could forget his magic when he pleased, and drop down—or it might be, climb up—into a happy human life. They had no children, and they lived in a lone cottage together, on a great lump of a moorland hill that had a large iron beacon on the top. In the grate of the beacon an old man, named Moonseed, the only other person living on the hill, lighted a fire of nights for the guidance of ships in a sea channel full of perilous shoals, currents, and tide-ways, from which the broad back of the hill could be seen when clouds were not too low. That hill was a huge waste of stone, lichen, puff-ball, and fern ; of bog, moss, rush, horse-tail, and liver-wort, covering a tall heap of peat-bog, marshes, pools, and pebbly wastes of marl, cornstone, and red conglomerate, that rose and rose for miles about, until it came to a head wherein the clouds hung when there was any rain at hand. When the rain really came, it flooded the pools into lakes, soaked with water the great spongy marshes, and made of nearly the whole mountain a slough, over which the driving mists raced after one another, and the water plashed till only the wild ducks and the bitterns would choose to be out of doors.

Quietly on the top of this hill lived Moonseed, the beacon-keeper. Horses could jolt a wagon-load of wood and coal up the great slope in any but the wettest weather.

Moonseed had also at his service a rough little moor pony, that helped him in the carrying of stores.

Somewhere upon the side of this hill lived Picrotoxin, the immensely powerful magician, and his wife Menisper. They had no settled address, for it pleased the great man to move house on the most trivial occasions. Sometimes his house slipped down hill. Sometimes he ran it round from one side to another, much to the discomposure of his wife. For Menisper was expected to do all that a good cottager's wife ought to do: to cook, to market, to keep fowls and a pig; and it was no small trouble to her, when she came from market, with a heavy basket on her arm, home to the place where she had left her house, and found that it had pleased Picrotoxin, in her absence, to move to the opposite side of the hill. If he had carried off the cottage, and forgotten to take with it the poultry and the pig, the poor woman had to take them along with her in a search over the mountain-side. Again, if Picrotoxin wished to keep his wife in her own natural place, and to solace himself in the intervals of conjuring with that happy pastoral life to which, as a country maid, she had been born, he ought not to have turned away from her hog's lard and fried potatoes, her rich soup of oatmeal and treacle, her hard buttered dumpling, or neglected to praise her bold execution of the favourite pie of the district, made of successive layers of sliced apple, bacon-fat, and onion, thick layers and plenty of them, covered in with a stout oily pie-crust. Her pies could be smelt out at sea when Menisper was baking them ; and once a ship was wrecked in the channel below, because the pilot held his nose, instead of steering, when it was a pie-day on the hill-side. Yet Picrotoxin, though determined that his wife should market, make, and bake, was too much of a conjurer to eat the dinners she prepared for him.

This great magician had discovered by his art much that was doing at the palace, and among other matters, at what hour his King dined. Then fixing that as his own dinner-hour, when there was set before him one of these savoury tarts, he cried, "Goodwife, that is a pie for a king! The King shall have it. Up, pie, through chimneys to King! Open, doors! In, King's dinner, to us!" Instantly the pie flew up the chimney, the cottage-door opened wide, and there rushed in a steam of soup over their table-cloth, followed by boiled, and fried, and stewed fishes, and fowls, and joints of many meats, tarts, jellies, costly fruits, and a great splashing of spilt wines. "There, old woman," said the conjurer, "a fair exchange. The King has got more than the worth of all this in your famous pie. Fall to!"

"Yes, husband," said Menisper, "you praise my pie, but you don't eat it. Besides, I'd have put in the biggest onions and more bacon, and put more lard in the crust, if I had known you meant to send it to the King."

"Never mind, sweetheart," said the magician, "you shall make something on purpose for his Majesty to-morrow. I rather like the thought of changing dinners; so, henceforth, you are sole cook to King Cocculus, and we will put up quietly with what the palace cooks provide. Don't keep any of these leavings. Feed the pig with what is fit for him, and throw the rest away."

So the King's jellies, and creams, and pine-apples were mixed with his cabbage and his truffles into pig-wash, and all his meat that Picrotoxin and Menisper did not eat was thrown over the moor.

Cocculus, King of Lardizabala, lost five pounds of his weight every week: one pound through vexation, and the rest through want of dinner. There was a State dinner the first time Picrotoxin played this trick, and that was one of the things the magician knew. Cissa, the treacherous Grand-Duke of Ampelos, a person most particular about his eating, was chief guest. When the soup was set on the table, suddenly it rose out of the tureen, and dashing itself into a double current on the face of the Grand-Duke, between it and the door, flew out of doors. "Sire, Sire," cried the cooks, running into the banquet-hall, forgetful of · all proper decorum in their consternation, "all the dinner —all of it—has flown out of doors!" But while they spoke, there was an overpowering smell of onion, followed by the entry, through the chimney, of Menisper's pie, that set itself down, with a thump, between the Grand-Duke and his Majesty.

"This is strange! This is terrible!" said the Grand-Duke, shivering from top to toe. "I recommend, Sire," said the Prime Minister of Lardizabala, "that we send for the bonzes." The bonzes were sent for, and declaring, for State reasons, that the pie came out of Paradise, where it was made especially for the Grand-Duke, pronounced a blessing upon all who should partake of it. "But the crust," said his Majesty, "is very black. It is well. That shall gladden the mouths of our bonzes." So the bonzes were obliged to eat the sooty crust, and the chief guests of the King ate Menisper's apple, onion, and bacon. Whatever else was brought flew out of doors, the wine rushing abroad out of every bottle as it was uncorked by the chief butler and his men.

The pie was praised, and much was said of the delicate attention that must have been paid by the Houris to the known daintiness of Cissa, the Grand-Duke of Ampelos. The Grand-Duke himself spoke never a word; but, on the day following, sailed back in a swift ship to his own country, smelling of onions when he reached it a month afterwards, and declared war against Lardizabala.

Now, when the second change of dinner came, and the bonzes, who had eaten enough soot, being sent for, pronounced that the black and greasy tablets of potato, mixed with cubes of bacon, had been chopped by demons, Cocculus and all his Court went dinnerless. Let nothing be said of the hard ten-pounder dumpling, or of the three red herrings fried with cabbage, for which the King's dinner was exchanged on the two next days.

Picrotoxin ate well, and he drank well; for it was only on the first day that, because of what he knew, the soups, gravies, and wines were made to travel without their tureens, boats, and bottles. Afterwards, royal souptureens, bottles, and decanters lay broken about the moor in which the happy conjurer resided; and the simple-minded conjurer's wife, sure that what her husband said was right, and growing to be proud of the praise he bestowed upon her royal cookery, adopted all the hints he threw out touching pig's-fry and other dainties with which she might vary the diet of her King.

At last King Cocculus, who had found comfort in lunch, resolved to dine no more. A hundred changes of his cooks, the padlocking of dish-covers over his dishes, every device that his Cabinet Ministers were able to invent, had been in vain. There was a standing offer of a thousand crowns a day for any person who could cook the King a dinner that would lie still to be eaten. Nobody had won that prize.

One day, Menisper's pig being fat, the good housewife was forced to admire him aloud. "See, husband," she said, "with such a pig outside his door, mightn't a king be happy!"

"Off, pig, and be doorkeeper to the King!" said Picrotoxin. Menisper wept when the pig vanished; but her husband comforted her, and said, "Dear wife, I mean that you shall see your pig again; ay, and that you shall be thanked for your cookery by the King Cocculus himself, in presence of his Court and people. Lock the house door, and come out for a walk with me."

They locked up the door, and the house was immediately lost in a mist.

As they went down the hill-side, they were overtaken by a troop of knights in armour, who were carrying off Moonseed, the peacon-keeper.

"They are carrying off Moonseed without his pony," Picrotoxin said. "It is not far to Lardizabalon" (that is the name of the seaport capital of Lardizabala), "but we will ride." So the magician said three times, "C'up, c'up!" and Moonseed's little pony trotted down to them. "Take him by the head, wife," he advised. Menisper took him by the head. "Now hold him tight, while I pull at his tail." As the conjurer pulled, the pony stretched to the length of a crocodile. Then he pulled each of the pony's legs till they were longer than those of the tallest cameleopard. Then he broke a head of bulrush into three pieces, threw one piece over his head as he gave the animal the other two pieces to eat, and instantly the pony spread into a horse as stout as any hippopotamus. "Very fattening stuff that," said Menisper. "I wish I had known of it when I had the pig to feed."

"Now, wife, we are going to Court to see the pig and his King. Put your foot in my hand; here is a long arm—a long, long, long, long arm—and up you are! Now I leap after you, and off we go!"

"But how your beard grows!" said Menisper, as they jolted down hill with great strides, and at every jolt more hair seemed to be shaken out of Picrotoxin's chin.

"And how comely you are becoming!" said the con-

jurer; for with every jolt the wife seemed to be getting a
fresh pound of fat upon her bones. "You will look like a
King's cook by the time we come to Lardizabalon, and I
shall look like the Prime Minister of the Moon."

"The Moon, man! Surely you mean of the moor?"

"No, wife. King Cocculus believes there is no man on
earth so clever as himself. Therefore I will come down
upon him from the Moon. Oh, never fear, I have a great
work in hand! As for you, you shall see your pig sitting
outside the door of the state council-chamber, and you
shall be King's cook in the royal kitchen, and you shall be
thanked by the whole nation for your apple tart with onions
and bacon. Look you, here is the great city, and here
round the corner by the lighthouse is the channel that lies
underneath our hill."

"Picrotoxin! Picrotoxin! What work is it that you
have in hand now? What are you about? How everybody stops and stares at us and our great horse! How
all the other horses and carriages have to run down the
by-streets to make room for us! We take up the whole
carriage-road. I feel big, I do, and I am going to Court
as a proud woman this day!"

When they came to the palace gardens, the huge pony
stepped over the gates and lumbered over the grass to the
palace door, where he stood still. But then he was so tall
that it was much easier for his riders to alight upon the
roof than on the door-step. Therefore they stepped upon
the roof, and Picrotoxin called down to the throng of
lacqueys, who were wondering and running in and out, "Be
so good as to let my pony loose upon the lawn, and tell
King Cocculus that the Prime Minister of the Moon has
come down to him with a cook."

So the two wonderful strangers walked about upon the
palace roof, and when the enchanter came to the great
chimney of the council-chamber, "This," he said, "is our
way in." A Gold-Stick at the door was saying that a person
calling himself Prime Minister of the Moon was on the
tiles with a fat cook, and said that he was coming down to
see his Majesty, when suddenly there was a terrible clatter
in the chimney, and down Picrotoxin came, pulling after
him, not very easily, for she was a tight fit, the round
Menisper. Gold-stick ran forward at the sight, leaving

the door open, and Menisper saw that her pig sat on the mat outside.

"My chimney must have wanted sweeping," said King Cocculus to the new-comers. "What a large quantity of soot you have brought down!"

A man in armour of chased gold, and in a cloak of crimson velvet, stood before the King, and behind this man were five knights, each holding a leathern sack. Behind King Cocculus there was an open money-chest, from which a score of silken pages were about to fill the sacks. "There is exactly soot enough to fill those bags," said Picrotoxin. "Pay to your black enemy his tribute in his own coin, soot."

"What mean you, knave?"

"The Moon sees everything," answered the magician. "Be advised by the Prime Minister of the Moon, who has just brought down the right money due to Cissa, Duke of Ampelos."

"In your moony counsel," said the king, "there may be wit. Pages, put soot instead of gold into those bags!" But all the pages looked at their white doublets and their dainty fingers, to which gold might stick if it would, but soot was unsuitable. While they were hesitating, the knights closed the mouths of the bags, frowned, and clashed their swords; nevertheless the soot was in the bags, and the King's floor was as clean as the two strangers who had brought it down, and who advanced now to the royal council table.

"You are about, Sire, to buy a false peace," Picrotoxin said. "I have observed the doings of the treacherous Grand-Duke of Ampelos. It was high time for me to come down upon him."

"Thank you," said the King. "Then perhaps you will send my answer to him by this his High Lord."

"His High Lord!" cried the magician. "That ambassador in scarlet and gold was littered on the same day with your doorkeeper."

"The pig that haunts me!" shuddered Cocculus.

"This gentleman is Pork," said Picrotoxin. "If he and his five knights do not confess the cheat upon your senses, they shall be sent home as sausages in chains."

Then the ambassadors fell forward on their hands and squeaked, "It is true, Sire; we are pigs."

"I had a fit doorkeeper to wait on such ambassadors," the King replied. "But whence came that doorkeeper? Is he, too, from the Moon?"

There was a clatter of arms outside. Word was brought that the King's knights had found the person who must be concerned in the magical thieving of the royal dinners. The Beacon Hill was covered with the broken pieces of the royal crockery and bones of the King's meat. The only man upon the hill was captured; and they brought in the old keeper of the beacon.

"What is your name, fellow?" the king asked.

"Moonseed."

"Moonseed! Are you from the Moon, too?" cried King Cocculus. As he spoke there was a great crash of glass; for Moonseed's enlarged pony being upon the lawn outside, and tall enough to look in at all the palace windows, had spied his old master. So he thrust his enormous head through all the glass in the council-chamber, and began to lick the old man's hand.

"I am not awake," said Cocculus, falling back into his throne with the face of a man who is giving up a riddle. "I am in bed after a supper of too savoury pork-pie, and soot had fallen on the crust. I am asleep with the Moon shining on my face. Are these men pigs?"

The knight from Ampelos and his five attendants, each holding a bag full of soot, again fell on their hands and squeaked in concert, "We are pigs!"

"What awful horse is that?"

"He has," said Moonseed, "the eyes of my little pony; but if he be my pony, he has grown out of all knowledge."

"Is that a pig who waits outside the door?" asked Cocculus. At a glance from Picrotoxin, Menisper's pig stood on his two hind-legs, advanced to the King's chair, bowed respectfully, and said, "I am."

"Gentlemen and pigs, and Ministers of the Moon and Moonseeds," the King groaned, "pray make yourselves at home. Help! help! Somebody carry me away, or wake me!"

Then Picrotoxin advanced, and bowed low before his Majesty. As he spoke he had pig's eyes and cheeks, and a round moist snout over his beard.

Be assured, Sire," he said, "that the interests of Lardi-

Q

zabala and of your august person are being watched.
What you behold now is a great political crisis."

"Oh, dear! Oh, dear!" the poor King groaned; "my
head begins to ache."

"A State," said Picrotoxin, "may be saved in many
ways. Complexities of the political machine that puzzle a
bystander——"

"Stop!" said the King, suddenly. "Did you not say
that you had brought a cook? I see a gleam of light.
By help of that cook may I dine to-day?"

"May it please your Majesty to smile upon your cook,"
said the enchanter, bringing forward his good wife
Menisper.

"She looks," said his Majesty, "like a King's cook."

Menisper curtsied with a happy smile. "Let her command the kitchen, and produce for me to-day her choicest
dish. I ask but one dish, and that it will stand before me
until I have eaten it."

"Sire, it shall be so," said Picrotoxin.

"May it please your Majesty," then asked a knight,
"what are we to do with the enchanter Moonseed?"

"Prime Minister of the Moon, advise us," said the
helpless and bewildered King.

"Let him mount his large horse, and ride swiftly through
the land, commanding all your liege subjects to save their
bacon, and to bring it to the royal commissioners whom
you will presently appoint to buy up all the bacon in the
land."

"Buy all the bacon in the land of Lardizabala! Is
there a State reason for that too? Be it so. Prime
Minister of the Moon, do as you will, say what you will to
these ambassadors. Cook, dinner at six!"

The King retired to his inner chamber, and then trotted
after him Menisper's pig to take up a new station at his
closet-door. The envoys from Cissa, Grand-Duke of
Ampelos, were treated like pigs and dismissed. Moonseed
was despatched on the great pony to command all people
in Lardizabala to save their bacon, and also to outbid
private consumers in the price offered by his Majesty
King Cocculus for onions and apples. Menisper retired
to the kitchen and prepared her choicest dish. While
it was baking, Picrotoxin called her away to smell—

though she thought them less fragrant—the flowers in the garden.

Half an hour afterwards, a little crowd of knights and scullions, carrying a man who seemed to be in a swoon, clamoured at the door of the royal closet—"Sire! My lord! State news! A paper! A traitor!"

The King opened his door, and a little crowd rushed in, some carrying the almost lifeless stranger, one holding out the six seeds, another holding out an open letter.

"Your Majesty's dinner was baking in the oven——"

"Yes, good, yes."

"Yes, Sire, your pie was in the oven, and the new cook had gone out of the kitchen——"

"Oh," said the King. "It is to be a pie, then?"

"Yes, Sire, and nobody was by, may it please you, Sire, when this man crawled out of a large fish-kettle in which he had been hiding, leaving the lid off and his coat and hat in it, and in his coat-pocket was his pocket-handkerchief, and in the lining of his hat there was this letter."

"Yes, Sire," said he who held the seeds, "and in his hand were these six seeds, like peas. And in the letter we find they are deadly poison."

"Yes, Sire," cried two or three of the crowd who held the man, "and here is the assassin who crawled to the oven where your pie was being baked; but when he opened the oven, the stink of the pie knocked him down, and so we found him."

"What do you say?" the King cried, aghast. "The stink of the pie!"

"Yes, Sire, tremendous. We are not sure that the man will recover."

"Good gracious!" said Cocculus, with a groan of despair; "the oven-door has been left open, and I smell it myself. It may be smelt all over the palace. It is like that pie of apples, onions, and bacon that came down the chimney once or twice."

"The letter, Sire, the letter!" said the man who held it. "Somebody read it to his Majesty!"

Somebody read as follows:—

"Eminent Hog,

"The attempt you made on my behalf to poison Cocculus and all his Court, by rubbing candril-seeds

over the inside of the soup-tureens, gravy-dishes, and
decanters, on the occasion of my giving him the honour
of my company to dinner, I find to have been
frustrated by a powerful enchanter, who now fights
against me. He it was who splashed the poisoned soup
across my face, who forced us to eat that which is our
own flesh and blood, and caused our lips to have been
embittered in vain with the antidote that would have
enabled us to drink, unharmed, the candril poison. That
enchanter lives upon the Beacon Hill that is beyond
Lardizabalon, and against him vengeance is sworn by the
whole fraternity of swine of Ampelos, to which you belong,
and of which I, Cissa, Grand-Duke of Ampelos, am the
Grand Master. His time will come ; our ships are nearly fit
for sea ; and the magician on the Beacon Hill shall save from
our wrath neither himself nor the State of Lardizabala.
But first it is fit that King Cocculus be poisoned secretly ;
for which purpose I send you candril-seed, and require
that you find some place of hiding in his kitchen, and
there lurk until you find an opportunity of poisoning his
meat. I have sent threats to that king, with demands for
tribute. If he pay gold, the gold is yours when you
succeed, and will be held in trust for you by the faithful
brethren who are charged with this mission. Should you
be taken prisoner, find means to gain time for yourself.
The invasion, for which we are now almost prepared, will
turn the blood of Cocculus to dish water."

"What astonishes me most," said Cocculus, "is that
a person should have thought it necessary to add poison
to a pie like that I smell. But what ? what ? what ? I
have smelt such a pie before. Ha ! ha ! I have an idea !
Sound trumpets ; all the world shall know it."

Trumpets sounded in the palace and the court-yard,
heralds went into the city to proclaim by sound of
trumpet, "His most gracious Majesty the King of
Lardizabala has an idea !" All the people, and especially
the newspaper reporters, flocked into the squares to hear
it ; and in half an hour the words spoken in the royal
closet were trumpeted forth in the streets ; and they were
these :—

"WHOEVER MADE THIS PIE, MADE THAT PIE !"

Public opinion in Lardizabala had long come to the conclusion that political affairs were in a complex and peculiar position. The order to save bacon had been discussed hotly at public meetings; and the interference by the State with ordinary rules of trade, in buying up onions and apples at a price much above the market value, though it had been lauded highly by the Government newspapers, was denounced as profligacy by the Opposition press. But what was to be said for or against the King's idea, "Whoever made This Pie, made That Pie," none but the most wonderfully well-informed of editors could tell.

While King Cocculus was agitated with his great idea, and causing messengers to be sent for the new cook, and for her introducer, the Prime Minister of the Moon, Menisper's faithful pig, who sat at the door of the King's chamber, was seen to be shedding tears. The half-poisoned prisoner had been placed on the ground, and was there slowly recovering his breath. As he aroused he often looked towards the pig sitting outside the door. At last their eyes met, and they rushed towards each other, with loud cries of "My brother! My own long-lost brother!"

"We were of one farrow, Sire," explained the faithful pig; "pardon these tears!"

"Oh, brother!" said the hog who had been misled into the paths of crime, "I repent of all my wickedness now that I have your love to reclaim me. On your breast I will pour out a full confession of these plots." So, lying with his head between his brother pig's fore-legs, in a repentant attitude, the prisoner told, in the presence of King Cocculus, a dreadfully long story, chiefly about the part he had himself taken in the rising of pigs in the Grand-Dukedom of Ampelos, after his brother had been sold to the foreign merchant of whom Menisper had bought him when he was a tender pigling. The greatest of the hogs knew a hog who was descended from the men turned into hogs by a great enchantress, many thousand years ago, and he had got from him the name and address of that enchantress. Then, through some toils, he had found his way to her, and obtained from her a charm that would turn pigs into men. Thus all the pigs in Ampelos had become men; and rising in revolt, they had placed Cissa, the greatest hog, upon the chair of the Grand-Duke. Among themselves they had divided, with much quarrelling, the chief places of trust in the State. At Cissa's Court were greed and gluttony. From devouring victuals, the Grand-Duke turned to devouring States; and he was on the point of annexing Lardizabala, after poisoning the King at a friendly banquet given to himself, when the poisoned soup was dashed into his own face, and, by some unknown power, he was forced ignominiously to eat pig.

The penitent creature who told this and more was in the middle of a list of treacheries, when Picrotoxin and Menisper entered.

"The King's dinner is cooked and served," Menisper said.

"Prime Minister of the Moon," said Cocculus, "before I attempt to dine upon the pie that saved the State——"

"That is to save it, Sire," said the enchanter.

"That has saved it, I tell you," cried the King, impatiently; "for has it not saved me? I publicly thank this cook that you have brought me, for her morning's work." Proud woman was Menisper then. "That repentant creature and his brother may be united as one household henceforth in a royal sty. I will not punish him, or make him into bacon."

"May it please your Majesty," said Picrotoxin, "you shall prosper in pigs all your days, if you will meet as I advise you the invasion that is threatened."

"Speak, Prime Minister of the Moon!"

"Let all the coasts—except the coast of the channel underneath the Beacon Hill—be fortified with bakehouses, and mount in each bakehouse a heavy battery of iron ovens. Let the bacon that has been saved, the onions and apples that have been bought and stored in your arsenals, be distributed among the bakehouses and made into pies like that of which you know. When the enemy's fleet is seen to approach the coast at any point, let the ovens be loaded with the pies, and let the fires be lighted; let the pies bake till the ships draw near, then let the oven doors and all the seaward doors of the bakehouses be suddenly flung open. Thus drive the foe away

from every point, except the shore under the Beacon Hill;
then leave the rest to me."

"Absurd!" cried the King. "Bombard an enemy
with such a smell as that! It would be barbarous; it
would be against all rules of civilised war. But I owe
much to the pie, and I will show my gratitude by dining
on it, if I can."

The King went therefore in procession, with the usual
sound of trumpet, into his great banqueting-hall, where
the pie he knew of stood alone on the great table, and
was growing cold. "Somebody carve!" said the King.

"May it please your Majesty," said the Lord Steward,
"my health is delicate, and I dare not." Nobody dared.
"Poltroons!" the King said, "look at me." He thrust
his knife into the pie and turned pale. Reflecting for an
instant, he with a rapid hand cut a small slice out of the
pie, then turned and fled in the rout of all his attendant
courtiers and lacqueys who fled with him, pressing their
hands tightly down over their noses. He was gasping for
breath when he met Picrotoxin. "Order the batteries," he
said; "your notion was not at all absurd. If the opening
of the ovens be not enough to repel the enemy, open the
pies upon them! open the pies!"

Batteries like these, terrible to a man, might well strike
dread into the Armada of pigs. Under lead of Cissa, the

Grand-Duke, a mighty host of ships brought all the
fraternity of which he was Grand Master to invade the
coast of Lardizabala, but upon no point dared they approach land, till it was discovered that the straits below the
Beacon Hill were undefended by the batteries that bristled
everywhere else.   Into those straits at high water the fleet
pushed, and therein at low water every ship was stranded
that had not. already run aground.   The beacon-keeper
was gone, and there was no light to direct a pilot.   In the
night Picrotoxin stalked alone over the moors, and from
the summit of the hill rolled down by mighty spells cloud
after cloud that covered the lost ships with a thick darkness.
Then he gathered fernseed, and when he had filled with
it his peaked cap, let his cloak fly with the gale, and rode
in it upon a whirlwind of his own raising three times round
the fleet, scattering the seed that dropped like points of
living fire into the darkness

Among the ships word had gone forth from Cissa, while
the darkness gathered, that this was the work of the
enchanter on the Beacon Hill, who had been warring
against him, and against whom he had been warned.   The
Beacon Hill must be stormed at daylight, the enchanter
seized and killed, the finest possible position taken for a
military camp which would command Lardizabalon, the
enemy's capital.   It was so natural to these creatures to
feel themselves pigs, that they hardly knew how changed
they were in outside character when, as a vast herd of
swine, they all plunged through the water, gained the
shore, and stormed the hill next morning.   It was now
walled round, but there was an open gate on the sea front
through which the pigs rushed, with the greatest of hogs,
Cissa, at their head.   Cissa had mounted to the beacon
before the last of his army had passed through the gate,
and then the gate was shut.

So the huge hill was covered (as it is to this day)
with the finest herd of swine that any man in the world
has ever seen ; and Picrotoxin gave the whole herd
to his King.   The pigs were wild for a few weeks,
but a sufficient number of swineherds having been appointed, they were in good time brought into subjection.
Menisper was, on a day appointed for the purpose,
thanked by the King, before his Court and all his people,

for her famous pie. The nation gave her seven pigs of gold.

Thus it was that her clever husband brought her cooking to honour ; though he did not himself like to eat her pies. Many such pies have since been made from the pigs of the herd upon the Beacon Hill, for which reason, and as a memorial of the service they had done, they are to this day called Beacon Pies by many people thereabouts.

THE STAVESACRE FAIRIES

THIS is the tale of Teel the shoemaker, Whirlwig the hatter, and Surmullet the tailor.

Teel was a shoemaker, about whom very few people knew how well he understood his business. So one evening the poor fellow, slipping dolefully out of the town in which he starved, went for a walk on a neighbouring common. It was a small rough piece of broken ground, ragged with briar, fern, and furze, scratched over with deep rutted paths, drilled into with rabbit-holes, here and there scooped also into forgotten sand-pits, and dabbled with pools. At one end a steep and jagged lump of sand-rock cropped up through the brambles. On the top of the bit of rock the shoemaker sat down to think. From that height there was a view over the meadows round about the common. Behind him they sloped up into a line of bare downs, with the white chalk glimmering here and there through their green banks. Before him the rich landscape was warm with trees. Alders and great willows were clustered near the river ; oaks gathered in knolls about the slopes of the deer-park ; pear, plum, and other fruit-trees overtopped the little country-town, and all the yellow roads that led out from Stavesacre into the world at large were fringed with blackberry, wild rose, and honeysuckle hedges, broken with elms, and upon one side, beyond the bridge, raised to the rank of an avenue with lines of poplar.

Trees gathered about the quiet town so closely as to hide all but the great mossy church-tower from the eyes of Teel, as he sat on the sand-rock, with his feet dangling over its sides, and looked about him. Already the mild evening star was in the sky, the rooks were flocking to their nests in a small wood that dipped over the riverside, where the stream flowed between the farther slopes of the smooth park. The distant peal of the town-bells told the shoemaker that Hodge, Peter, and Jeff, cobblers and bell-ringers, had met for practice in the belfry before spending (prosperous men!) a social evening together in the parlour of the Sandhopper's Arms.

When the bell-ringing was over there were more stars in the darkening sky, and presently the moon rose, large and red, from behind the wood in which the rooks were sleep-. ing. A bend of the river was alight directly. All was so still that Teel heard now and then the faint creak of the insects stirring in the bushes of the common and the whirr of the night-moth as she flew by.

"Heigho!" he sighed. "I get nothing by this thinking; so I will go home to my good dame."

He was about to rise, when a young rabbit leapt into his lap. The rabbit tamely suffered him to pull its ears.

"Silly puss!" said the shoemaker; "when you jump into the lap of a man who has an empty cupboard, don't you know that you are good to eat? But never fear, small creature. As you trust me, you shall take no harm."

"Very well," said the rabbit—no longer a rabbit; for, indeed, he was a curiously little man in grey body-clothes, but without coat or hat, and with his feet quite naked. He had a tiny bundle in one hand, which he held up to Teel.

"I hope, my good fellow, I may trust you. Make me a pair of shoes out of the leather in this bundle, and return me all the pieces. I will pay you well, and bring you some more custom, if your fit is good."

"Fit good!" said the neglected artist. "Those ignorant people of Stavesacre are content to wear clumps on their feet. They fatten no less than three cobblers with their custom, and have suffered me, a proper shoe-maker, to starve. Yes, sir! I can fit a dainty foot like yours, sir, in a way to show you something of my art. Am I to send the shoes, or will your honour call for them?"

"I will call at your house for them," the Fairy said. "Be ready, if you can, at this hour, this day week."

At the appointed hour Teel was quite ready; and Till, his good wife, had been so careful to help him in obeying the wish of his Fairy customer, that not a shred of leather or thread—though it were but a shred no bigger than a morsel of a line of spider's web—was left on or below the table at which Teel had worked. All was put, with the shoes themselves, into the tiny bag. Then as they sat— too poor to afford candle—in the light that was half moonlight and half twilight, the old couple suddenly saw the little grey Fairy busy about that bag. He weighed it first in one hand, and then in ʌhe other. He opened it, took out the shoes, turned out and examined all the pieces. Then he put the pieces back, and, sitting down upon Till's spectacle-case, put on the shoes. When they were on, he got up and danced about in them to try their fit. They fitted perfectly. Advancing at last to the edge of the table, he said, " Brother Teel, I am authorised to appoint you shoemaker in ordinary to the Fairies of the Downs and Commons. Remove, therefore, to your new house on the sand-rock in Stavesacre Common where you will have plenty of custom and good pay as long as we may trust you."

" Oh, sir ! " said Till, " you may trust my old man with shoes of gold."

" He will find shoes of gold that are his own in his new house. I pay them to him in exchange for these. There is a piping hot supper also waiting for you both in your new house, so I advise you to move into it at once. You need take nothing with you. Tools, furniture, and even clothes, are there already."

Tools, furniture, and new clothes—yes. But never-theless, after the Fairy vanished, Teel and Till, indulging themselves with the extravagance of a candle, searched their house through, and filled a large bundle with house-hold treasure. There was the Sacred Book, in which they had read to each other; there were the little clothes, at which Till worked when she had been a younger (but still not a young) wife ; and the small shoes Teel made for the baby, that was still the baby to their hearts as when it was lost, a score of years ago.

Then Till had to wipe the dust from her mother's Cookery Book, given to her on her marriage. That edifying work had been neglected of late, for want of the eggs and butter, without which, in its opinion, nothing could be brought into being. But there was the mother's

He had a tiny bundle in one hand which he held up to Teel.

name, in her own hand, written across the title-page, worth all the dainties that were ever fried. Till had more relics, and the foolish shoemaker had treasures put away in drawers—dead flowers, faded ribbons. "Do you know, Till," he said, "I must have you carry to the new house the whole of your white wedding-dress that is in yonder worm-eaten old press." So off they went at last under the moonlight, he with a pack and she with a pack.

When they came to the skirt of the common they saw all the windows lighted in a neat little white house on the top of the sand-rock. When they had climbed the sand-rock the cottage-door opened to them of its own accord, and a delicate smell of boiled rabbit and onions kissed their noses. In a dainty little parlour, that dish, dear alike to Teel and Till, smoked ready for them. There were hot mealy potatoes too, boiled as few but the Fairies can succeed in boiling them ; also, there were two bright glasses set beside a foaming jug of ale. "What a sweet perfume of meat ! " said Teel. "And onion," added Till, who was so much moved by the sight of a comfortable hot supper and the smell of onion, that she wiped her eyes as she sat down.

A half-open door was opposite Teel's seat, and there was a lighted room beyond. "I must just run and peep in," said the poor shoemaker. So he ran across and peeped, and what he saw was his new workshop. There were his counter and his cases, and his shoemaker's bench, and the tiniest little tools, made with broad handles to suit his grasp. But sitting all round the shop, row behind row, were thousands of little Fairies in grey body-clothes, without hats, coats, or shoes, who cried as he peeped in, "Good evening to you, gossip. We are all waiting for you to measure us when you have supped ! "

Before Teel could answer them, there was a clatter behind him that obliged him to turn round. It was caused by the falling of a large pair of gold shoes through the ceiling to the floor, followed by a cry of "Shoes for you, shoemaker ! " Thereupon all the Fairies in the shop began to sing :—

> "Shoes ! Wonderful Shoes !
> Safe on the water, safe on the land,
> Ready to run at the word of command."

Whirlwig was a hatter, who had made felt caps for the ploughmen of Stavesacre, though he was clever enough to fit with the glossiest of hats the head even of a crocodile. He had plenty of custom for his caps; but he would have poured his earnings out as easily as he poured beer into his throat at the Sandhopper's Arms, if his wife Willwit had not been careful and honest as she was. A month after Teel had left the town, and gone to live in his new cottage on the sand-rock, Whirlwig was seeing a comrade home over the common after a supper at the club of Noisy Dogs, at which he was perpetual vice-president. On the other side of the common his friend left him, and went on to his own village. Whirlwig turned back to Stavesacre, but in the middle of the common he lay down (as he afterwards said) to think a bit. " Dame Willwitt," he thought to himself, " will say there's little enough in my pocket. Poor woman ! She don't know what a famous supper I got for my money. I'll go home and tell her of it."

He was trying to rise, when a young rabbit jumped into his lap, and tamely suffered him to seize it by the ears. " Heigho ! " cried the hatter, " here's a supper for the good dame too. I'll take you home to her, trust me."

" Very well," said the rabbit—no longer a rabbit, being indeed a curiously little man in grey body-clothes, without coat or hat, but with the neatest of small shoes upon his feet. " Very well, my good fellow, I hope I may trust your wife at least to see that you deal fairly." Then, holding up a tiny bundle, he said, " Make me a cap out of the felt in this bundle, and return me all the pieces. I will pay you well, and bring you some more custom, if your fit is good."

The hatter laughed with defiance. " Fit good ! " he cried. " Though I have been making caps for blockheads all my days, I know what I know; you shall wear, sir, what will make you feel the real use of your head. Am I to send the hat, or will your honour call for it ? "

The fairy said he would call at that same hour on that day week. The little cap was ready in good time. Whirlwig had made a careless litter of the pieces of felt cut off while he worked, but Willwit, his prudent wife, not only had gathered them all carefully into the tiny bag,

together with the new cap, she had also locked the door
of the house, and put the key into her pocket, so that her
husband could not help being at home to receive his
customer. The Fairy came as he had come to Teel, and
being satisfied with what he found, advanced to the edge
of the table, and said, "Brother Whirlwig, I am authorised
to appoint you hatter in ordinary to the Fairies of the
Downs and Commons. Remove, therefore, to your new
house by the roadside on Stavesacre Common, where you
will have plenty of custom and good pay as long as we
may trust you."

"Oh, sir!" said Willwit, "there's not a truer soul than
my old man's when he only gives himself time to consider
about what he does. But I do wish he'd make himself a
considering cap—I do, indeed!"

"He will find a considering cap in his new house. I
pay it to him in exchange for this. Supper is laid there,
Dame Willwit, for you and your children; so I advise you
to remove at once. As for your good man, he has supped
already. Everything you will want is there; you need
take nothing."

The Fairy was gone, and Willwit at once began to get
her seven children out of bed. When they were dressed,
the whole family went under the moonlight to the common,
where there was a new white house on the turf by the
roadside. The house door opened for them of its own
accord. In the snug kitchen there was a hot rabbit-pie
upon the table, large enough for all, and Whirlwig was
inclined to indulge in a second supper; but on peeping
into a second room from which light shone through the
partly open door, he found in his new shop thousands of
tiny customers, all eager to be measured without one
moment's delay. So he set to work while his wife and
children ate and drank, and the savoury steam of the pie
made his mouth water. Once he ran back when he heard
something fall to the floor in the next room. It was a
felt cap that had tumbled through the ceiling, followed by
a cry of "A cap for you, hatter!" Thereupon all the
Fairies in the shop began to sing :—

> "Cap! Wonderful Cap!
> Wear it for counsel; and when you despair,
> The advice of the Cap will relieve you of care."

R

Surmullet was a clever tailor, but a rascal; and his
wife, Smull, was no better than himself. He had lost his
trade by robbery of customers, and lived by robbery upon
the roads. He was lurking at night in the bottom of one
of the sandpits on Stavesacre Common to waylay a
traveller, when the rabbit jumped also upon his knee.
The rabbit would have had its neck wrung in an instant
if it had not changed in less than an instant into the form
of the little Fairy with grey body-clothes, a neat little cap,
and perfect shoes, wanting only a coat to be completely
dressed. When Surmullet received from this tiny customer
the order for a coat, he said that he would rather take a
coat than make a coat, but for all that he would fit the
little gentleman so that he should think he had two
skins.

Surmullet also was to finish his work in a week, and
did finish it. The little man looked grave when he came
for his coat and missed the pieces. But he, nevertheless,
formally declared Surmullet's appointment as tailor to the
Fairies of the Downs and Commons, and invited him
to his new place of business at the bottom of the sandpit in Stavesacre Common. There he would find
plenty of custom and good pay as long as he was to be
trusted.

"Trust!" sneered his wife. "One man is as safe as
another, for the matter of that. There's no man who
wouldn't own himself thief if he had on a coat of confession."

"You will find such a coat in your new house," the
Fairy said. "I'll pay it in exchange for this."

Surmullet and his wife were eager to be gone. The
bottom of the sandpit was a newly-established place of
business for them; but the advantage of a house built
there, in which they might be always lurking, and from
which they might at any time pounce out upon a traveller,
was to be secured without an hour's delay. So they went
to the common, and found that there was really a white
house built at the bottom of the largest sandpit. Going
down into it they found no supper, but a crowd of little
men, angrily waiting to be measured for their coats.
As they looked dangerous, Surmullet began measuring
directly. While he did so you may be sure that a coat

fell through the ceiling, followed by the cry of "A coat
for you, tailor!" and the song of all the little customers :—

> "Coat! Wonderful Coat!
> What you do wrongly, and what you do well,
> The Coat of Confession will make you tell."

Now the shoemaker, the hatter, and the tailor worked
hard each of them for a twelvemonth and a day, before
they had finished making shoes, and hats, and coats for
all the Fairies of the Downs and Commons. Teel worked
hard with honest will, and lived in luxury. Whirlwig
worked hard because his wife looked after him, and while
he worked the Fairies gave him famous suppers. Surmullet worked hard because the Fairies frightened him,
and every man who is not true is a coward.

At the end of a twelvemonth and a day the Fairies of
the Downs and Commons were all fitted with their new
coats, caps, and shoes, and as these articles were made of
very durable material, they would outlast the lives of the
tailor, hatter, and shoemaker who made them. Teel was
the first to finish. The house on the sand-rock vanished
when the last Fairy was shod, and the tradesman to the
Fairies went back with his old wife to their cottage in the
town. They took with them nothing but what they had
brought thence, except the golden Shoes of Safety. A
month afterwards, Whirlwig, the hatter, came back with
his wife and seven children, richer for all his work only by
the Considering Cap; and Surmullet returned next, with
the Coat of Confession on his arm.

They had all been kept so closely to their work, that
they had never been outside the white houses, invisible to
other eyes, in which the Fairies had supplied their wants.
They had been completely and unaccountably lost out of
Stavesacre. Their houses remained vacant, because new
people never came into that quiet place, and the settled
inhabitants were so entirely settled, that a Stavesacre man
never so much as thought of moving from one house into
another. When, as it rarely happened, anybody went
away from Stavesacre, somebody painted on a window of
the house he quitted that it was To Let. Then it remained empty until natural increase of population in the
place itself would, in the course, perhaps, of many genera-

tions, cause another tenant to be reared. The process was a very slow one. In the half-century before the time of which this story tells, the increase of the population had been only from two thousand one hundred and five to two thousand one hundred and eleven.

When Teel and Till came back into the town, and said they had only been as far as the common, where they had spent the year in shoemaking for the Fairies, Stavesacre said that was a fine tale, but no doubt they had their reasons for being secret; and opinion was divided as to the way in which Teel came by his gold shoes. A month afterwards, Stavesacre looked out of window to see Whirl-wig and Willwit, his wife, tramping in again with their seven children. He, too, said that he had been no farther than the common, where he had been making caps for the Fairies, and was only the richer by a Considering Cap for his pains. The only persons who believed that story were Teel and Till, and Dame Till lost no time in holding consultation with Dame Willwit, and comparing their experience of Fairy patronage.

"I am told," said Till, "that those ne'er-do-wells, Surmullet and his wife, were lost out of town soon after you. Has he been in the same employ, I wonder?"

While the two women talked together, Whirlwig came downstairs in a rusty blue coat, a stained and soiled red waistcoat, and high walls of shirt-collar about his cheeks. "I am going to sup at the club," he said to his wife as he went out.

"Ah!" sighed Willwit; "the Fairies gave him a Considering Cap, and he always has refused to put it on. A poor man, with a wife and seven children, needs to put on his Considering Cap before he goes to sup at the club; but he shall wear it after he comes home. I will put him to bed in it to-night."

"A famous notion, gossip," said Dame Till. "But what my man is to do with his shoes I wish I could see. He hasn't a fault to be mended, bless his old heart!"

"Or a sorrow to be cured," said her friend, "when you are by."

But Till looked into the empty air, and her fingers strayed towards a lock of baby hair that had lain folded in paper for a score of years upon her bosom.

Willwit took her by the other hand, like a kind gossip as she was, and said, "Yes, though it be twenty years ago, it must be hard to miss your little Clary. And you had but her!"

"If we had but her grave to kneel over!" mourned the good Till. "She may be living with the thieves who stole her, and they may have made her one of them!"

"If she be alive, there is still hope that you may find her. Truly, dear friend, the man would walk on shoes of gold who brought her back to you."

"On shoes of gold!" Till cried. And leaping up, she clapped her hands for joy. "Oh, neighbour, neighbour, let me go!"

"Husband!" she panted, when, out of breath with the haste she had made, she got home to her old man; "put on those Fairy Shoes of Safety, and go out to find our child. My heart tells me they were given you for that."

"But whither shall I go?"

"Put on the shoes and go—'Safe on the water and safe on the land, ready to run at the word of command,' the Fairies said they were. Then bid them carry you to Clary, if she be alive."

"You are right, and I am gone," said Teel. While he was gone, Till went to the old locker, in which she treasured as a relic her white wedding-dress.

At the word of command, the shoes carried Teel swiftly, lightly, through the town. They ran, without touching ground, down the slope to the river, crossed the surface of the water without wetting a sole, and sped over the sward of the deer-park to the wood by the far slopes of the winding stream. The autumn leaves were falling on its sheltered paths, but the wonderful shoes did not stir or tread upon a fallen leaf as they sped on, causing their wearer to flit like a shadow through the underwood, already damp with night-dew. At last, Teel struck into the thickness of a massive oak, and entering its substance, stood still, in the very heart-wood of the mighty trunk, that clipped him about like a cloud.

The brighter for that veil around it and above it was the mossy nest over which Teel now stood still. Here it was that the Fairies of the Wood, who stole her, held his little Clary cradled. Here she was sleeping happily, in form

not a day older than when she was lost, soothed by singing from a choir of green wood-fairies, who were her
attendants.   But when Teel snatched her up, and fell to
kissing her, the Fairies sang :—

> "Playfellow Clary, nice to steal,
> You must go home with Father Teel.
> Clary will be our playfellow for good
> If father don't leave his Gold Shoes in the wood."

Teel instantly stepped out of the shadow of the oak,
and took his shoes off.   Their gold rose in a mist that ran
along the ground and spread into the trees, until the
autumn leaves dropped, yellow and clinking, upon paths
that had become strewn with gold.   The gnarled trunk of
the oak was solid enough when Teel turned his back
upon it.

So, without stooping to pick up any of the gold through
which he walked, and without flinching when his naked
feet trod among thorns, the old shoemaker went through
the forest.   Slowly, and trembling with joy, he went
through the forest, bearing upon his arms the sleeping
infant.   It was a long walk home, and there was the bridge
beyond the poplar avenue to be crossed outside Stavesacre,
for which reason his way must be through the main street.
But the stars were all out when he reached it, and half the
town was already abed.   Few saw the old man limping
with torn feet over the stones as he went homeward by the
light of the crescent moon and of the stars, pressing, with
shrivelled, knotted hands, the tender sleeping child to his
warm heart.   .

Till saw him from afar, and ran to him through the night
shadows in her yellowish-white wedding-dress.   She had
been holding solemn festival in this attire, sitting alone in
her poor room, and so awaiting the return of Clary.   If
she thought of an old time, she had not thought it would
come back to her so perfectly that Clary would be Baby
Clary still.   She was a yearling child when lost, and as a
yearling child she was returned into her mother's bosom.
Age had not hardened the true heart that welcomed her.
It was a dainty sight to see the old dame crooning with
love as she wept fast tears over the child that smiled up at
her from the lap of muslin and old lace and limp white

satin bows. Till pressed its nose into the wreck of the
great true-love-knot upon her bosom, and got her thin grey
hair into confusion with its golden curls, as she sat lip to
lip with it in her agony of joy. Meanwhile, her old man,
kneeling before the newly-lighted fire, stirred in their single
pot a baby-mess with one of his thin hands. His other
hand moved with a wandering touch about his wife and
child.

Presently the child was to be fed with a wooden spoon,
and grasped the spoon as it was coming to its mouth.
Immediately the wood was gold. They were in no joy
about that, but in some concern lest there should be an
objectionable change made in the gruel. No, that was
excellent. And Clary throve like any other child; was
healthy, happy, natural, except that she would sometimes
murmur a strange Fairy music in her sleep, and that, when
touched by her, wood became gold.

By noon next day so many planks, beams, window-
frames, and door-posts of the shoemaker's cottage were
transmuted into shining gold, that gossip Willwit held her
breath when she ran in with something of interest to tell
to gossip Till. We know what there was to be told by
Willwit. What she had to say to Till was that her good
man Whirlwig, waking up that morning with the Considering Cap on his head, had sat up in his bed, and poured out
such a stream of wise reflections on the headache he had
got, and on the responsibilities he had got; on the
necessity of getting a new coat for the boy Daniel, and new
shoes for Heartsease, and a new gown for Willwit; on the
devotion and prudence of his valuable wife Willwit and his
own past wastefulness; on the propriety of instantly re-
signing his place as Vice-President of Noisy Dogs; of
clearing out his shop, and making a great stir, if possible,
to procure increase of custom; on the possibility of saving
enough for the purchase of a small pony-cart with which
he could go in search of customers to the surrounding
villages; on the cost of a cart and of a pony; on the
average rate of his possible week's earnings in Stavesacre,
and on the average weekly cost of a sufficiency of meal,
of meat, of butter, of eggs; on the advantages and
disadvantages of keeping a pig, and his own powers of
building a pigstye; on the number of years it would take

to turn by economy a pig into a cow; on the best thing to be done for little Sorrel's cough, and the cause of that pain in the side his wife had been complaining of; and so on, and so on, that he was another man. He had sold ten caps that morning; he was inventing, as a speculation of his own, a grand official hat for the next Mayor of Stavesacre. He had already found her money enough to get a leg of pork and stuffing for their dinner.

"I wouldn't have my good man lose this industry," said Willwit; "no, not if he got, instead of it, your child's wonderful power of gold-making."

"I don't care for the gold-making," said Till, "though I suppose it makes us very rich. That old chair you sit on, now it's made of gold, must be worth something. Take it home, gossip. Nobody need be poor in Stavesacre if this is to last with Clary; but it's so like a disease, that I shall be glad enough to see her cured."

When she said that, a green dwarf with a very long nose peeped in at the door. "Oh, good morning, dame Till," he said. "If you don't wish that child of yours to infect any more wood with a jaundice, let her walk round the room three times in the gold Shoes of Safety. Here they are. If you are in the mind to make that use of them, keep them; if not, let them be cast back into the wood yonder, where your good man left them." The dwarf threw the shoes into the room, and vanished.

Till put little Clary's feet into the shoes directly, and began to guide her tottering.

"Think what you do," said Willwit. "The child's power will give you never-ending wealth."

"I want my own natural and healthy little Clary," Till replied.

"But won't you wait till you have advised with your husband?'

"As to Clary, and all else, my Teel and I are of one heart."

So Clary pattered three times round the room in the gold shoes. After the first round, there was no sign of amendment, for all the wood in the house not changed already became gold. After the second round, everything that was made of cotton, hemp, or flax, the child's clothes, all the linen the two women wore, and their poor cotton gowns, changed into cloth of gold.

"I fear to go round again," said Till. "The disease grows stronger, and the dwarf may have meant only to mock me. Yet I will have trust."

So she went round for the third time, and after that there was no change, but there was not a splinter of wood left in the house with which to try whether the desired change in the child really was effected. The women, dressed as they were in gold from head to foot, dared not go out of doors to fetch a stick. It was lucky for them that at this moment the knave Surmullet and Smull his wife stepped in.

They were then coming in from the common, and as they passed Teel's cottage in the empty country street, were the first to notice the golden window-frames and door-posts, and the brilliant gold door of Teel's cottage. Inside, the room was like a gold mine, with two golden women in it and a golden child.

But a passing boy or two soon spread the news, and all the town had presently turned out to look at the shoe-maker's cottage, with golden beams and posts, and doors, and golden thatch. Surmullet and Smull had been hearing wonders inside, while they looked greedily about them, and Smull had fetched a fagot from the yard to put in the child's hand. It remained wood. "A pretty game you have spoiled," she said. "My worthy husband also had a Fairy gift, and who knows what may come of it. Put on your coat, good man."

Surmullet put on the Coat of Confession which he had brought in on his arm, and suddenly began to tell of all his rogueries. In-doors and out-of-doors, all Stavesacre was there to wonder and listen. Surmullet seized upon every man he had cheated or robbed, and made a thoroughly clean breast of his offence; but he was astonished at the good nature with which all his confessions were received.

When Teel came home with the shoe-leather for which he had been to the tanyard two miles down the river, he found himself suddenly seized by the mob of townspeople before and about his cottage, lifted upon men's shoulders, and beset with a great shout of "Teel! Teel! Teel for

the next Mayor!" More astonishing still were the shouts
of "Bravo, Surmullet!" Though Surmullet was telling
half the town that he had robbed and cheated it, yet there
he was, speaking the truth. He who went out a year and
a day since, a sneak whom no man trusted, and who
trusted nobody,—he who was known to be a thief when
he used all his cunning to get credit for honesty,—was
now held to be honest when he manfully confessed all
that was in him, though the all was bad.

Now, the end of the story is, that Surmullet, finding
comfort in his Coat of Confession, ceased to be the coward
that he had been. He grew to be fearless in speaking the
truth, and, from being true in word, soon became true in
deed. By shifting his coat slyly and whenever he could
to other men's backs, he found that other men, forced to
speak all the good and evil that was in them, commonly
turned out better than almost anybody else expected. The
sensation of being trusted was to Surmullet himself very
welcome; and even Smull was content to stand with her
husband in the good books of her neighbours.

Whirlwig became the most considerate and painstaking
man in the whole world.

Teel and his wife were the richest people in or out of
Stavesacre, after they had given gold away to Whirlwig, to
Surmullet, and to every poor neighbour. There was
built for them a fine house in the deer-park, where they
loved, all their days, the kindest and prettiest of daughters.
Teel wore the Mayor's cap that Whirlwig had distinguished
himself by inventing. In the second year of his mayoralty,
he gave his wonderful Shoes, and, in the same year,
Whirlwig and Surmullet, who no longer needed magic
help, gave also their Cap and Coat, to be held in perpetual possession by the town-council of Stavesacre.

The Shoes, Coat, and Cap were kept in a strong
tower, and committed to the keeping of six faithful
warders. Whenever an offence was committed in the
town, an officer of justice, putting on the Shoes, commanded them to bring him face to face with the offender.
Instantly tracked and seized, the culprit was brought
into the presence of the Mayor. There all the witnesses,
and the offender himself, wore, when they gave evidence
of what they knew, the wonderful Coat of Confession.

The whole truth about everything that related to an offence being thus presented to the Mayor, that Magistrate put on the wonderful Considering Cap, and arrived at the wisest possible decision of the case. There being no escape for any Stavesacre criminal while the Cap, Coat, and Shoes were there to secure his capture and conviction, nobody played the rogue; and the Stavesacre men lived for a century with so little necessity for keeping their eyes open that they became sleepier than ever.

So it happened that one day all the six warders who kept the apparatus of Stavesacre justice were asleep together in the porch of the tower. When they awoke, Cap, Coat, and Shoes were gone, and half the houses in the town—bolts and bars having long fallen out of use—were robbed that night. The thieves were great grand-children of Surmullet, and as they crossed Stavesacre Common with a wagon-load of plunder, they threw into one of the pools a bundle, which contained not only the Considering Cap and Coat of Confession, but also the golden Shoes of Safety; for, although these were of solid value, there was great fear of their Fairy power.

Whenever the pools are dragged on Stavesacre Common, if that bundle should be found, let it be forwarded immediately to the Lord Chief Justice.

FAIRY SONG

A lake and a fairy boat
To sail in the moonlight clear,
And merrily we would float
From the dragons that watch us here!

The gown should be snow-white silk,
And strings of orient pearls,
Like gossamers dipp'd in milk,
Should twine with thy raven curls!

268

THE BAG OF MINUTES

I

TIME ON HAND

 NCE upon a time there was a youth, named Trigonel, who was a grief to his mother, because he had never in his life eaten hot meat. As an infant in arms, hot meat was not his food, and when he could use his legs he was abroad at work or at play, so busy or so idle, that he never came to dinner till his meat was cold.

Dame Peaflower, Trigonel's mother, was a proud and particular woman. It was her noon of glory to set a hot dish in the middle of her table at the very moment when the sun—that hot dish on which all the flowers feast—stood in the middle of the day. For the sun to stand still at noon would not have been more unnatural than for the potatoes in the pot of Mistress Peaflower to need another minute's boiling when the clock struck twelve. Keeping hot is overcooking. "Better," she said, "let meat be cold than overcooked." Papilion, her husband, was of the same mind; and little Vetch, her only daughter, being helpful to the mother in the house, and being indeed the person who peeled the potatoes, always was on the spot when she ought to be eating. But of her one son, Trigonel, it was the single fault that he was always behind time in coming to his dinner.

Yet this Trigonel was a brave, stalwart lad; able, in hour of need, to bear the whole weight of the house upon his shoulders. Father Papilion, who was a woodcutter, chopped his foot one day with a false stroke of the axe. He was then confined to his house for many weeks; not while he got well, but while his wound got worse and

269

worse, until at last his life was nearly at at end.   Trigonel
worked with the strength of two men in the forest.   In
many hours of the night he was his father's watchful nurse.
He found odd moments, too, in which he could make
mirth and sing, with a voice cracking into manly rough-
ness, delicate songs for his small sister Vetch, whose joy
of childhood was not to be quenched because there was a
day of sorrow on its way to her.   The young man was
true in short, to everything but his dinner.

Happy are they who in youth have some acquaintance-
ship among the Fairies of the Hours.   Aster, the noon
Fairy, was Trigonel's good friend.   She had come to him
in his childhood, when he rolled on his back among the
cowslips of the meadow.   Then she appeared, and always,
like the sheen of a maiden in gold armour, with long locks
of golden hair.   A plume like a flash of light waved over
the diamond helmet beneath which glanced her blue eyes,
more radiant than all.   To other sight than that of
Trigonel she was a ray, and nothing more.   At mid-day,
Papilion and Peaflower gave their minds to their meat;
so that they did not see, as they must have seen had they
but dined at half-past twelve o'clock, the sunshine that
at noon, even when all the upper air was thick with fog
and sleet, would glitter daily for a little while about their
boy.   He had told his parents often and openly enough
that he stayed from his dinner to talk with the Noon
Fairy; but they only grieved that he should joke upon so
serious a matter as the being late at meals.

Trigonel stood under a green oak in the autumn
wood, leaning against the mighty heap of fagot bundles
that he had prepared since sunrise.   The light of his
Fairy shone on his brown face and dingy clothes, and
made the fagots glow as if they were ablaze.   Grasshoppers chirped in the light, butterflies fluttered through
it, and the cups of the golden acorns overhead gleamed
like cut jewels.   Aster sat at the youth's feet, with her
helmet off.   She held between her fondling palms the hands
from which the axe had fallen, and was dazzling
him by looking up into his face.

"Farewell," she said.   "You are a man.   Work henceforth by yourself.   Each of my days, remember, is but
for an hour, and yet you will be giving life to me all the

hours through, while you are brave and open as the noon."

Trigonel laughed. "Am I to add twenty-three hours to the one that is your life? It is but fair, then, that you should beg me a spare minute of your father. You have told me that he is a great magician, owner of the sand-heaps by the border of the endless sea, where each grain of the sand is a minute, and each drop of the flood an everlasting age. Surely the old man would not deny his daughter one spadeful of sand. You know that you want to give it as a keepsake to your friend."

"Ah, me!" sighed Aster; "but you ask that as a keepsake which may cause you to forget me. Wear in your cap my better gift, this crystal; it will be a star to me while you are true; and take care not to wear it in the sun if ever you and honesty be parted. For the other gift, say nothing. My father, who flies by unseen, grants you your wish."

Aster slid back into the sun. The incredulous youth, with a cheery laugh, looked upwards, shaking his black hair at her, and waving with both hands his farewell as she flashed from sight. Then, being left alone, he turned his face towards his dinner.

There was a narrow belt of moor between the forest in which Trigonel cut wood and his father's cottage. The sun was hot on the dry turf, and there was a dropping fire among the pods of the whin-blossoms that were scattering their seeds with the pop of a Fairy cannonade. Suddenly the air was chill, the wind screamed through the forest, and the forest itself was not to be seen. Overhead shone the sun, there was blue day over the cottage roof, beyond was a far prospect over field, and copse, and stream. But Trigonel looked back upon the blank of night, through which the wind rushed wailing and sobbing. Mightier than the wind was presently a sound as of the stroke of hugest wings by which the air had been thus beaten to tempest. Then the roar ceased, the storm rolled back, and the great giant Time, with a face high and hard as a mountain-top, and with his beard rolling like a cloud among the clouds, stood still over Trigonel. One huge arm he upreared, and with the gesture of a reveller, swept his great hour-glass through the upper sky.

"Spill! spill!" cried Trigonel. "Crack me a hole in your glass, and give me of your sands."

Father Time fixed his eyes on the youth, but said nothing. Putting one hand into the robe about his breast, he drew out what seemed to be a leathern purse well filled, and dropped it at his feet; then, with a frown, spread his wide wings again, and passed on in the hurricane he raised. When Time beats with his wings in angry flight we may be thrown by the wild weather he makes, as Trigonel was, unexpectedly upon our faces. Trigonel, when the darkness passed and left him in the sun again—while it obscured the distant prospect of field, copse, and stream—perceived with joy that he had fallen so that his nose struck into a sandbag. Cruel or kind, Father Time had granted him his wish, and had presented him with as much as he could carry on his back of that choice sand in which the grains are minutes. Trigonel's heart was lighter than his step as, shouldering his bag, he slowly tottered on to his cold dinner.

II

TIME WASTED

BUT the dinner was not cold when Trigonel entered the empty kitchen. It was the second hour of afternoon, and the old white hen, who should have smoked at twelve upon the table, was a black hen, smoking by the fire in company with her new kindred the cinders. It was dull company, for in the ashy grate the coals had been a good deal put out by the boiling over of the saucepans. The clean dinner plates were still upon their shelf.

"Little Vetch! Mother!" the youth cried in terror as he entered. But there was no answer. Dropping his sandbag heedlessly upon the floor, and without staying to close the cottage door, Trigonel hurried up the ladder to the sleeping-loft. There was his father dying. Vetch, poor maid! trembling, weeping, fondling, lay on the bed nestled to Papilion's panting breast, and at the bed-head knelt the mother, with her whole soul fixed upon her husband. Trigonel, kneeling beside her, put his strong, rough arm about her neck, and bowed his head upon the coverlet.

"O, boy! it snaps my heart," the mother said. "Thirty years my good man, and more life the more love. O, for a little, little more time; till we go together. O, for a little, little time! But a few minutes are left him."

"Minutes, mother!" Trigonel cried, jumping up. "A little time!" At the word he was down the ladder. In the room below he fell upon a select party of porkers that had found their way in, and were thrusting hungry snouts into his treasure bag. There never was a man yet who secured himself a little spare time but a part of it was eaten by the pigs.

Trigonel seized a handful of the sand as the pigs took their leave. They were none of them the better, he saw, for their meal. Time, he thought, is a thing to hold and not to swallow. Hurrying back, therefore, to the sick-bed, he pressed some of the sand into Papilion's failing grasp. It was clutched eagerly, and in that instant life flowed back upon the dying.

Death-bed life was in this way prolonged. It soon appeared that while Papilion had in his hand some of the sand, he was the master of so much Time as he held. A grain of the sand vanished with each minute that went, but till the bag was empty the old man might live. For many years he could be kept thus balanced on the point of death.

Dame Peaflower soon put a check on the loose handling of the precious grains. Counting them into sixties and double sixties, she had them sewn up carefully into small one-hour and two-hour bags. Of these some were again stitched together into twelve and twenty-four-hour packets. Had her husband's life depended only on her punctuality in keeping him supplied with Time, it was secure. But it depended also on his own grasp of the Fairy gift. In a little while he became weary of the days beyond his span, impatient of the fist for ever clenched that his wife tied up like a pudding when he dozed, lest the hand loosened in sleep might let his life slip through its fingers. Therefore, one day, when Trigonel and Vetch were both gone to the wood, and when his dame was nursing him, Papilion, raising his head from his pillow, kissed her quietly, and while he thus took her attention slipped the freshly-supplied twelve-hour bag out

s

of his palm into her bosom. Then he sank back with a smile that never changed.

"He was quite right," afterwards said Peaflower to her son. "I'd seen myself, dear as he was and is, his life had been kept too long to the fire. It isn't only meat that can be overdone. If I were you, boy, I would throw away that sackful of leisure. Strict to time and ready to the minute is worth any heap of odd minutes to spare."

In the old days, when the kitchen clock might have been set by the ways of its mistress, it had never come into the mind of Dame Peaflower to tell even her son that she was a punctual woman. Punctuality was nature to her—no more talked of than digestion by the healthy. Now, however, she made daily assertion of her good old principles against the heap of odd minutes that tempted her. They were so handy. For the sands that had added minutes to the life of which the time was out, gave also to healthy people time outside the common day. Sixty grains held in the hand melted into an hour, of which no record was kept by clock or sun. If little Vetch wanted two hours of play instead of one, she took a sixty-grain packet of Trigonel's sand ; went out at eleven, played for two hours, and yet was home again at noon to dinner. If Madam Peaflower had a day's washing to get through, she would hold a linen bag of sand between her little finger and her palm, while she rubbed in the suds with the other three fingers and thumb. It was not easy work, but a day's washing had been got through in that way, upon one occasion, between eleven o'clock and one minute past eleven, when the poor Peaflower was so tired and weary that she would much rather have gone to bed than cooked the dinner. The sand being at hand, no little delays were heeded. There was always time for everything. At one second to twelve it was not too late to roast an ox before the clock struck. Always time for everything was on its way to become no time for anything with the most punctual of living creatures—and how tired she was! Although the clock took no note of her added work, she felt it in her bones. The Fairy-sand gave time, not strength, beyond the common bounds. Then, too, if she was tired, how fagged was Trigonel! That young man, eager to earn for his mother and sister silk attire,

The Bag of Minutes 275

sometimes would make his arms ache with twelve hours of chopping between breakfast and dinner. And when he did come home to dinner, very likely he would find his mother fast asleep upon the floor. Always oppressed by fatigue, she was apt to drop asleep suddenly and unexpectedly. Even when she had in her hand the Fairy-sand, it would then slip from her hold, and the hours of the day would march in procession over her, till Trigonel came home and woke her up. Little Vetch, too, when she had overplayed herself, would drop about the house like a fly in November. Sometimes even Trigonel the brave, who was so haggard that he looked like an old man, went off into a sound morning sleep over his woodcutting. Then, if by chance it happened that his mother and Vetch were snoring on the floor at home, the sun might set before they all came to themselves, and wondered whether they had had their dinner.

Vetch was the first to find that the natural day had the right number of hours for her. While her mother and her brother were still worrying and wearying themselves, she, meddling no longer with the Fairy-sand, budded and blossomed into the full beauty of her maidenhood. The mother's housekeeping had fallen into such confusion of hours, that the cheerful and busy daughter took that charge out of her hands. It was Vetch now who, setting her ways by the sun, kept up a wholesome order in all household affairs; who made out the time of the true noon. by setting on the kitchen table the meat she herself had cooked; and who sought to lessen the unruliness, not only of Trigonel, but also of the good Dame Peaflower herself.

"Mother," she said, one day, when they were shelling peas together at the kitchen table, "Poppy, the ploughboy, knows a great deal."

"Ah!" said Peaflower.

"What do you think he told me yesterday?"

"Well, I think I can guess."

"No," Vetch answered, with a bright smile and the flicker of a blush; "you guess nothing important. Poppy and I only talk about important things." While she spoke, Trigonel entered hastily, crying out, "Where's the sand, mother?—be quick!"

"Why, what's the matter, boy?"

Trigonel, with a large packet of sand in his hand, and the whole bag on his shoulder, had only time to say, before he hurried out—

"Grand notion of Poppy's! Ducks for dinner? I shall be back in the cracking of a peascod!"

III

A FORTUNE MADE IN NO TIME

POPPY had simply been suggesting, as a confidential family friend, that Fairy gifts have nothing at all to do with ordinary life. The sand in Trigonel's bag probably was worth a thousand gold pieces a grain to somebody. He had heard of a King who would have given his throne for two minutes of time. If kings frequently made such offers, Trigonel might furnish his kitchen with a fine set of a dozen thrones, instead of the four old oaken chairs that his father had chopped out of the forest. Magic tools could be meant only for working upon magic stuff. Dolt of a Trigonel! To get no more out of his Fairy-sand than a few silver crowns more profit by his wood-cutting! Let him shoulder his bag of minutes, and hold some of the sand tight in his hand, while he looked out for great adventures. Let him always have sand in his fist, and he might, if he did not rest too easily content, step out of his door to come back with his fortune made in no time. So he did.

That is the Prince Marattin who comes galloping across the plain, where there is a distant prospect from the cottage-door of field and copse and stream. Field and copse and stream—and mountains where there were no mountains last night. The plain was being changed into a valley among high and tumbled rocks, while Prince Marattin spurred for life towards the one opening still left on the side of the forest.

"Out of the way, bagman!" said the Prince, as Trigonel, standing before him, seized the reins. But that youth, taking the horse by his right foreleg, thrust a four-hour packet of sand between the hoof and the shoe, and then,

The Bag of Minutes 277

flinging his sand-bag across the horse's neck, himself jumped
up behind his gracious Highness.

"I am in peril of life ! Down, fellow !" the Prince cried.
"Never mind that," Trigonel answered. "Take a good
grip of my bag that lies before you, and no matter what
your peril is, you shall get out of it."

The Prince, who was in danger enough to grasp at a
straw, fastened, of course, at once upon the sand-bag.

"Now," Trigonel said, "be easy, my lord. Our time's
our own." The Prince Marattin and his horse were as
white as the miller with long scampering through all the
dust they raised. Trigonel, now sitting behind his Highness, wiped a large piece of his back with his coat-sleeve,
and saw that he wore copper armour. "Only copper !" he
said to himself. "You poor halfpenny Prince ! Where
shall I find the Crown Prince who wears silver ?" Marattin
saw that, although his horse had changed its pace for that
of a mere beast of burden, not another stone was added to
the ring of rocks, so he said nothing until they had passed
through the opening towards the forest. Over that they
saw the giants striding, as men stride over grass, every one
with a lot of mountains on his back.

"Wonderful man !" said Marattin then. "You have
helped me through the prison wall these enemies of mine
were building, and have brought me to where they will rain
mountains over us till we are crushed. How shall I thank
you ? "

"A giant helps me who is stronger than them all," said
Trigonel. "Amble on ; we have time." The army of
giants stood like a wilderness of sublime statues, every one
with the sign, and no more than the sign, of life and
motion in his limbs, as the horse stumbled among the
patches of trees, crushed and trampled by the great feet
treading over them, with Marattin, Trigonel, and the sand-
bag all on his back.

"Now," Trigonel said, when they had passed from
between the thickest pair of giant legs, and were toiling
over a great hillock of foot, "my lord, the Bagman will
bid you good-day. I must shoulder my bag and begone."

"Not leaving me to ruin——"

"No ! for your horse and copper armour I will give you
two hours to escape with. You are a king ? "

"Since yesterday!"

Trigonel did not like the fellow. The cold of his heart struck through his eyes; his long, pointed moustaches were like bayonets, and under his mouth there hung a beard like a false tongue.

"Very well," said the youth. "If you want another two hours, have them. Take my cap and leathern jerkin. Give me your horse and copper armour, and we part."

So the Prince went on his way afoot in cap and leathern jerkin, with a two-hour packet of time clenched in his fist. Trigonel took his gracious Highness's address and trotted away, with his sack before him and the copper on his back.

Always taking care that there should be plenty of spare time in his hand and plenty tucked between one of the horse's front hoofs and his shoe, Trigonel travelled at his leisure. He went forward till the helmets of the giants, when looked back upon, appeared like distant mountain crests; and there was a large city before him, out of which had been brought, by a great crowd, a knight in armour, covered with dust that the crowd raised. He had a rope tied round his neck, and sat in the hangman's cart. As Trigonel rode up to him, the Knight began to cry with might and main, "Behold the enemy! He of the copper armour is Marattin! Seize him, and let him tell you that I am his enemy and not his spy!"

"I wear Marattin's armour," Trigonel said, taking off the helmet. "But whoever knows him may see that I am not he."

The Knight, leaping out of the cart, ran forward to seize Trigonel's hand, and said, "Great hero, have you vanquished him? Shout, people, for the suppressor of Marattin!" And the people would have shouted themselves thirsty again for much less than that. Trigonel put his hand on the Knight's shoulder to answer him, and saw that here was a man dressed in silver armour. "Only silver!" he said to himself. "You poor Crown-Prince! Where shall I find the Sovereign Emperor who wears nothing but gold?" But he spoke to himself so that he was overheard.

"That Emperor is my father," said the Silver Knight. "Of course you wish to carry your good tidings to him."

"At once," said Trigonel, giving time to the Silver Knight. "The people will not lose a minute, though we ride for a month and leave them standing here. Borrow that mare out of the hangman's cart, let me see to her shoes, and ride with me to the country of the Emperor, your father."

So Trigonel rode with the Silver Prince into the city, leaving the crowd exactly as they found it; every listener in it with his ear turned; every one who spoke or hallooed with his mouth still open, his gesture fixed, or the cap he had thrown still in the air.

"We had made undersea gangways," said the Silver Prince, "out of my father's island into most lands round about. Suddenly coming up into this city by a path just opened, I was taken for a spy of Marattin, whom I hate, and against whose treacheries all men are watching. I believe him to be now surrounded by the giants that will crush him; yet if you yourself are not his vanquisher, how came you by his armour?"

"Never mind," Trigonel answered. They had passed through a mountain cavern near the city walls, and were now traversing an endless tunnel, lighted by towers open to the sky. To each of them there was an ascent by winding terraces. "May we not mount one of these towers?" From the battlemented summit of the first they climbed Trigonel and the Prince looked out over the sea. A stiff breeze caught their helmet plumes, and the salt spray broke over them. A dotted line of towers led their eyes to a white streak on the horizon.

"That," said the Prince, stretching arm and finger to it, "is the country of my golden father, which strikes root through the foundations of the sea, and becomes neighbour to all nations."

The way seemed to be long to the dominions of the Emperor in Gold. At last they were reached, and Trigonel restored to a magnificent father the young Prince whom he had saved out of the hangman's hands.

This Prince was but a younger son. Eldest son of the golden Lord was the illustrious Duke (the name of whose rank has been corrupted into Duck) of Diamonds. The Duke of Diamonds was paved with precious stones from top to toe, and wore by his side a sword of many jewels beaten into a blade at the forge of the Fairies. Trigonel, open as noon, told all his story to the King, confessing candidly that he had come abroad to make his fortune. He had it in copper, when he bought for one hundred and twenty grains of sand the armour of Marattin. He had not asked for it in silver when he saved the Silver Knight, because he learnt that the Emperor in Gold was his father. Now, however, he owned that he felt partiality towards the Duke of Diamonds.

"Well," said the King, "say no more. I will not buy your sand, because we are in this land already a hundred years ahead of the rest of the world, but you shall go home in a suit of armour like my eldest son's, and that alone is worth a common dukedom. Possibly, you have a sister?"

"Sire, I have."

"Then shall my son, the Diamond Duke, who wants a wife, ride home with you himself, and if he should like your sister, he will marry her."

So it was done; and as this is no traveller's tale, I need not describe how they made the journey. Trigonel, dressed in diamonds, rode beside the Diamond Duke, who was mounted upon a great piebald horse in sapphire harness. They were both shouting "House, ho!" outside the cottage of Dame Peaflower, before Vetch, with her dainty little thumb, had scraped the peas out of the shell she was cracking when her brother stepped into the sun to make his fortune. Mother and daughter hurried to the threshold; but the Diamond Duke, when he looked at Vetch, immediately saw that she would be the best wife in the world for him. So the first words he said to her (and she was the first person to whom he spoke) were, "Marry me." But Vetch had her fortune made already in the love of her dear oracle, Poppy, the ploughboy. Therefore, she said, "No, thank you," to the Duke of Diamonds. Dame Peaflower explained to the Duke that Poppy, although only a ploughboy, knew a great deal, and had on this very occasion been her son Trigonel's adviser.

"Better still," said the Duke. "We in our land want a wise Vizier quite as much as I want a wife. Poppy knows a great deal. Poppy's advice has clothed your son in diamonds. Fetch Poppy, and he shall be our Minister of State. The tender little Vetch shall be his wife. You, sir, who have saved my life, shall be my friend, and we will all take care of the good mother. Let us dine together, and then start."

Vetch was willing to go if Poppy thought he would like a State Minister's business as well as ploughing. Poppy was sent for, and the affair was settled. So the Widow Peaflower sat down at noon to her dinner of ducks and green peas, with the betrothed Poppy and Vetch, one on each side of her. Her ducks were carved by the Duke of Diamonds himself. But Trigonel, who was gone out to feed the horses, had not come in when the ducks were cut. His eye had been caught by a well-remembered flash descending swiftly from the sun, and lost behind the mountains that now made a valley of his native plain. The flash was Aster, the Noon Fairy, ablaze with wrath, having in rigid grasp her downward-pointed spear.

When Trigonel exchanged his cap and jerkin for Marattin's armour, he had left in his cap, too thoughtlessly, the crystal which his playfellow, the Fairy, had set in its front. Over Marattin's forehead it had clouded into a dull black, and when, under the noonday sun, the wicked Prince was about to kill a beggar who demurred to his demand of free gift of the broken meat he carried, suddenly the magic crystal stretched into the semblance of a black, lean hand, with knotty joints and cruel nails, that beckoned vengeance down. Against him who had dared to wear on his false front the crystal of the Noon Fairy, Aster herself struck the spear. Marattin died thus of a sunstroke.

Then the appeased giants went back to their caves, leaving the mountains they had raised as records of their wrath; and Aster, playful as of old, but with a whisper of rebuke, appeared again to Trigonel, who had his crystal back, clear as at first.

Again, therefore, the youth had missed his midday dinner, but he dined at one o'clock, and afterwards was ready to depart, with Peaflower, Vetch, and Poppy, to the wonderful land, where the Duke of Diamonds would be their bosom friend. There is nothing else to be told, except that before starting, Trigonel, by the advice of Counsellor Poppy, scattered his bag of minutes to the winds, and ever since he did that, grains of spare time, seldom to be caught, are thought to have been dancing upon puffs and eddies of wind up and down the world.

THE WHITE DOE OF RYLSTON

FROM Bolton's old monastic tower
    The bells ring loud with gladsome power;
The sun is bright; the fields are gay
With people in their best array
Of stole and doublet, hood and scarf,
Along the banks of crystal Wharf,
Through the Vale retired and lowly,
Trooping to that summons holy.
And, up among the moorlands, see
What sprinklings of blithe company!
Of lasses and of shepherd grooms,
That down the steep hills force their way,
Like cattle through the budded brooms;
Path, or no path, what care they?
And thus in joyous mood they hie
To Bolton's mouldering Priory.

What would they there?—Full fifty years
That sumptuous Pile, with all its peers,
Too harshly hath been doomed to taste
The bitterness of wrong and waste:
Its courts are ravaged; but the tower
Is standing with a voice of power,
That ancient voice which wont to call
To mass or some high festival;
And in the shattered fabric's heart
Remaineth one protected part;
A rural Chapel, neatly drest,
In covert like a little nest;
And thither young and old repair,
This Sabbath-day, for praise and prayer.

Fast the church-yard fills;—anon
Look again, and they all are gone;
The cluster round the porch, and the folk
Who sate in the shade of the Prior's Oak!

And scarcely have they disappeared
Ere the prelusive hymn is heard :—
With one consent the people rejoice,
Filling the church with a lofty voice !
They sing a service which they feel :
For 't is the sun-rise now of zeal,
And faith and hope are in their prime,
In great Eliza's golden time.

A moment ends the fervent din,
And all is hushed, without and within ;
For though the priest, more tranquilly,
Recites the holy liturgy,
The only voice which you can hear
Is the river murmuring near.
—When soft !—the dusky trees between,
And down the path through the open green,
Where is no living thing to be seen ;
And through yon gateway, where is found,
Beneath the arch with ivy bound,
Free entrance to the church-yard ground ;
And right across the verdant sod
Towards the very house of God ;
—Comes gliding in with lovely gleam,
Comes gliding in serene and slow,
Soft and silent as a dream,
A solitary Doe !
White she is as lily of June,
And beauteous as the silver moon
When out of sight the clouds are driven,
And she is left alone in heaven ;
Or like a ship some gentle day
In sunshine sailing far away,
A glittering ship, that hath the plain
Of ocean for her own domain.

Lie silent in your graves, ye dead !
Lie quiet in your church-yard bed !
Ye living, tend your holy cares ;
Ye multitude, pursue your prayers ;
And blame not me if my heart and sight
Are occupied with one delight !

'Tis a work for sabbath hours
If I with this bright Creature go,
Whether she be of forest bowers,
From the bowers of earth below;
Or a Spirit, for one day given,
A gift of grace from purest heaven.

What harmonious pensive changes
Wait upon her as she ranges
Round and through this Pile of state,
Overthrown and desolate!
Now a step or two her way
Is through space of open day,
Where the enamoured sunny light
Brightens her that was so bright;
Now doth a delicate shadow fall,
Falls upon her like a breath,
From some lofty arch or wall,
As she passes underneath:
Now some gloomy nook partakes
Of the glory that she makes,—
High-ribbed vault of stone, or cell
With perfect cunning framed as well
Of stone, and ivy, and the spread
Of the elder's bushy head;
Some jealous and forbidding cell,
That doth the living stars repel,
And where no flower hath leave to dwell.

The presence of this wandering Doe
Fills many a damp obscure recess
With lustre of a saintly show;
And, re-appearing, she no less
To the open day gives blessedness.
But say, among these holy places,
Which thus assiduously she paces,
Comes she with a votary's task,
Rite to perform, or boon to ask?
Fair Pilgrim! harbours she a sense
Of sorrow, or of reverence?
Can she be grieved for quire or shrine,
Crushed as if by wrath divine?

Comes gliding in serene and slow,...... A solitary Doe!

For what survives of house where God
Was worshipped, or where Man abode;
For old magnificence undone;
Or for the gentler work begun
By Nature, softening and concealing,
And busy with a hand of healing,—
For altar, whence the cross was rent,
Now rich with mossy ornament,
Or dormitory's length laid bare,
Where the wild rose blossoms fair;
And sapling ash, whose place of birth
Is that lordly chamber's hearth?
—She sees a warrior carved in stone,
Among the thick weeds, stretched alone
A warrior, with his shield of pride
Cleaving humbly to his side,
And hands in resignation prest,
Palm to palm, on his tranquil breast:
Methinks she passeth by the sight,
As a common creature might:
If she be doomed to inward care,
Or service, it must lie elsewhere.
—But hers are eyes serenely bright,
And on she moves—with pace how light!
Nor spares to stoop her head, and taste
The dewy turf with flowers bestrown;
And thus she fares, until at last
Beside the ridge of a grassy grave
In quietness she lays her down;
Gently as a weary wave
Sinks, when the summer breeze hath died,
Against an anchored vessel's side;
Even so, without distress, doth she
Lie down in peace, and lovingly.

The day is placid in its going,
To a lingering motion bound,
Like the river in its flowing—
Can there be a softer sound?
So the balmy minutes pass,
While this radiant Creature lies
Couched upon the dewy grass,

Pensively with downcast eyes.
—When now again the people rear
A voice of praise, with awful cheer !
It is the last, the parting song ;
And from the temple forth they throng—
And quickly spread themselves abroad—
While each pursues his several road.
But some, a variegated band,
Of middle-aged, and old, and young,
And little children by the hand
Upon their leading mothers hung,
Turn, with obeisance gladly paid,
Towards the spot, where, full in view,
The lovely Doe of whitest hue,
Her sabbath couch has made.

    It was a solitary mound ;
Which two spears' length of level ground
Did from all other graves divide :
As if in some respect of pride ;
Or melancholy's sickly mood,
Still shy of human neighbourhood ;
Or guilt, that humbly would express
A penitential loneliness.

    " Look, there she is, my Child ! draw near
She fears not, wherefore should we fear ?
She means no harm ; "—but still the Boy,
To whom the words were softly said,
Hung back, and smiled and blushed for joy,
A shame-faced blush of glowing red !
Again the Mother whispered low,
" Now you have seen the famous Doe ;
From Rylston she hath found her way
Over the hills this sabbath-day ;
Her work, whate'er it be, is done,
And she will depart when we are gone ;
Thus doth she keep from year to year,
Her sabbath morning, foul or fair."

LA BELLE DAME SANS MERCI

A BALLAD

I. O WHAT can ail thee, knight-at-arms,
   Alone and palely loitering?
The sedge has wither'd from the lake,
   And no birds sing.

II. O what can ail thee, knight-at-arms,
   So haggard and so woe-begone?
The squirrel's granary is full,
   And the harvest's done.

III. I see a lily on thy brow,
   With anguish moist and fever-dew,
And on thy cheeks a fading rose
   Fast withereth too.

IV. I met a lady in the meads,
   Full beautiful—a fairy's child,
Her hair was long, her foot was light,
   And her eyes were wild.

V. I made a garland for her head,
   And bracelets too, and fragrant zone;
She look'd at me as she did love,
   And made sweet moan.

VI. I set her on my pacing steed,
   And nothing else saw all day long,
For sidelong would she bend, and sing
   A fairy's song.

VII. She found me roots of relish sweet,
   And honey wild, and manna-dew,
And sure in language strange she said—
   " I love thee true."

T   289

VIII. She took me to her elfin grot,
    And there she wept, and sigh'd full sore,
And there I shut her wild wild eyes
    With kisses four.

IX. And there she lulled me asleep,
    And there I dream'd—Ah! woe betide
The latest dream I ever dream'd
    On the cold hill's side.

X. I saw pale kings and princes too,
    Pale warriors, death-pale were they all;
They cried—" La Belle Dame sans Merci
    Hath thee in thrall!"

XI. I saw their starved lips in the gloam,
    With horrid warning gaped wide,
And I awoke and found me here,
    On the cold hill's side.

XII. And this is why I sojourn here,
    Alone and palely loitering,
Though the sedge is wither'd from the lake,
    And no birds sing.

THE MAGIC MACKEREL

THE MACKEREL DISCOVERS SOMETHING IN HIS LINE

IT is not every fish that knows how to give a dancing-party. The Mackerel does not dance; he sings, and enjoys music of every sort except a catch. Therefore he does not attend the fancy balls of my Lord Shark, which are so fine that they throw all the sea into commotion.

My Lord Shark fattens upon hospitality. He asks his meat to dine with him; introduces affably the Whale to the Shrimp, and the Pike to the Gudgeon; heads the revels jovially, and sends everybody home, who does get home, so full of the good things of the sea, that the tide rolls with his praises. Some there are who do not get home, but they cannot complain.

Once upon a time, my Lord Shark gave one of his fancy balls. The fishes, in preparing themselves for the revel, had used up everything they could find in their masquerade store, and were still only half dressed. Gale and Whirlwind, therefore, were commissioned to send down many more shiploads of frippery. The said firm, which drives a roaring trade, busied itself to such good purpose for its customers the fishes, that this one particular ball was the grandest ever given under water.

The small fry that were permitted to look on made walls and roof to the great dining-hall. Kept in square, head over head, by a detachment of Sword-fishes, glittering eyes and golden noses of seven hundred and seven million million of Pilchards formed the lofty walls. Those eyes and noses belonged only to fortunate possessors of front places in the great mob eager to see the feast. Many of the distinguished guests liked to eat bits of the wall as much as any other delicacy offered for refreshment; but holes made by their nibbling were filled up instantly by the exulting outsiders, for whom front places were thus procured. The roof of the ball-room was a floating cloud of those small beings which sometimes appear as fire upon the surface of the wave. It was a joke of the Whale's every ten minutes to break from the dance into the outer sea, and then come tumbling back into the ball-room through the roof, with his great mouth open, swallowing the candles; for the myriads in the roof served also as candles at the feast they covered in. I know no more than that, in some such fashion, a whole palace was made for the occasion, of rooms scooped out of the crowd of little fishes, miles broad and miles deep, that thronged to see the fun. Except what he had of Gale and Whirlwind, who are well-known purveyors of meat to the fishes, besides being establishers of the great frippery store under the sea, my Lord Shark's feast came with the crowd that admired it, and the guests who were to entertain each other.

The costume worn at this fancy ball displayed numberless treasures of the deep. Lord Shark had made himself a chain of state from the skeleton hands of good men lost in a December tempest. He had wrapped himself in a gay coat, that was the three-coloured flag of their wrecked vessel; but as it did not keep him comfortable, he thought of enlarging it before his next ball with some patches bitten out of other flags. My Lord had covered his tail with an odd red cap, much dirtied, and had wriggled till his nose was set fast in a gilt brass crown, which had in some way fallen among the fishes. Being nearly stifled by this, he was obliged to gasp so much that his teeth were constantly on view. Still my Lord Shark he was, and the feast was his. Two Cuttlefish, who had covered themselves with more slime than belonged to them by nature, flaunted in goose feather. These creatures waited near my Lord's jaws, and whenever they saw that he was preparing for a snap, darkened the water round about him with their ink. For the Shark—to inspire confidence among his guests—declared that he ate nothing, and wished none to see him fixing his teeth in his prey. A circle of Sprats surrounded this great creature, for he was glad when he looked at them to know how great he was. There were some Sprats who had been present at the breaking of a barrel of pitch, and being stained—for the pitch stuck—of the colour of Whales, they believed themselves to be a sort of Whale, and as they swam, half split themselves with struggling to blow water-spouts out of their noses.

Distinguished among the company there was the Crab, who kept a stall or grotto of men's bones, and who had filled his grotto with old nails and chips of wood, crosses and whips, and chains and curiosities in bottles. He had a sceptre from the broken figure-head of an old war-vessel fastened to one of his forelegs, and this he trailed behind him in the mud as he crawled round and round his stall, in anything but a straightforward way, begging of every fish who seemed to be of consequence that he would please to remember the grotto. A free kind of Sword-fish fell into a passion with this Crab, ran at him, and turned him over on his back, at the same time knocking his grotto down. Then there came swimming through the holes they made in an old three-crowned hat, files of Sardines, who ran away with the clog on the Crab's leg, and so left the poor creature free to scramble quickly out of sight.

But the Mackerel saw none of the gaiety and had part in none of the Shark's feast. He stayed at home for a good many different-sized reasons, and one great reason—that he was too busy. For years he had devoted his whole mind to a question of magic. He had been occupied intensely with the study of that mysterious line which, till this day, wit of man or fish never availed to decipher—the line written in strange letters on the Mackerel's back. Clearly these are the varied letters of some words of mystery. In a strange language writing is traced on the back of the Mackerel, and it is even underlined in evidence of its importance. Now, it happened that our Mackerel, who had been studying his own back for a hundred years in a glass borrowed from a Mermaid, read the first letter of the magic line at a time when the revel of the Shark's great fancy ball was shaking all the water round his cave. And in the moment when he knew what was the interpretation of the first letter, his tail-fins grew into legs having feet each with a thousand toes, and his gill-fins stretched themselves into arms having hands each with a thousand fingers.   Music had been his sole refreshment in the intervals of work.   A good-natured Siren used to bring her harp and sing with him.   Sometimes, when she meant soon to come back, her harp had been left in a corner of his cave.   There it was at that moment, ready to be touched, and the exulting Mackerel, taking it between his feet, swept his two thousand fingers through its many strings.   Then music, such as no ten-fingered creature ever made, brought all the Sirens to his door.   A magnifi-

cent Cod-fish, rolling by on his way to the fancy ball, pushed through the Sirens, and looking in as he passed, said, "Not bad for a Mackerel!"   But all the little Pilchards, who, like the Herrings, have music in their hearts, ran to the wonderful harper when the sound of his song reached them.   Off and away went, therefore, the walls of the ball-room.   After the walls ran the guests, till, in a little while, there remained only, in open water, my Lord Shark and his black Sprats.   My Lord, for want of better meat, snapped at these creatures, made a wry face as he crunched them, and then spat them out.   For Sprat and pitch sauce disagreed even with him.

II

MORE IN THE SAME LINE

ALTHOUGH there may be more fish in the sea than ever came out of it, there never was another fish so bold as the Mackerel, who, popping his head above water, hailed a fishing-boat to carry him to shore. "Is it a Mackerel?" thought to himself Filarete, the fisherman. "Can a Mackerel hold up a long arm, stretch a finger, and cry, 'Boat, ahoy?'" Of course this fisherman did not know how this fish was studying his letters with advantage to himself. The first letter he learned gave him a thousand fingers and a thousand toes. The interpretation of the second letter on his back having now flashed upon him, he was able to speak in a thousand tongues. As most fishes are mute, the greater number of these tongues were those of men, and beasts, and birds. "My talents are drowned in the sea," said Mackerel; "I care not for a fishy reputation. Why have my tail-fins become legs, except that I may walk upon the land? To the land I will go, being on fire to extend through earth and air the fame that has already circled through the water." So, as he meant, nevertheless, to go on studying his back, he tucked under his arm the Mermaid's glass, bought for a song. He took also his new thousand-stringed harp. It was made for him by the Sirens, of hair from their own tresses, stretched over the shell of that crawling thing of the deep which once put the chiefs of men into its purple livery.

The Mackerel was looking for a boat to carry him over the surf to the shore, when he hailed the young fisherman Filarete with "Boat, ahoy!"

"What do you want! What are you?"

"I am the famous Doctor Mackerel Pescadillo, linguist and composer. Take me over the breakers. I have business ashore." As he spoke, Doctor Pescadillo reached the side of the fishing-boat, and putting up an arm, seized, with a many-fingered hand, the boatman's oar, and jumped in cleverly.

"Legs too," said Filarete; "and you stand upright! Business ashore! I think you have." Then he entangled him in eight or ten folds of his fishing-net. " You and I will have business together, my fine fish." And he began to amuse himself, as he pulled eagerly to land, with crying, " Walk up ! all alive ! " already fancying himself the prince of showmen, " All alive ; the Mackerel is now upon his legs, and speaking. Now's your time ! Be quick ; for the miracle of nature is engaged to marry the Randan of the Pacific Ocean's Grandmother, and is going off directly in a fly ! " While he spoke, the boat occupied his attention, for he was backing her across the breakers. Away darted the Mackerel when she was safely beached, and scampered singing up the shingle.

With a thousand fingers upon each hand, knots are very soon unpicked. Pescadillo had not only unpicked himself a way out of the net, but had unpicked every knot in the whole mesh ; so that when he leapt out of the boat, Filarete's nets were become a litter of loose string. The Mackerel ran faster than a swallow flies, and yet the fisherman gave chase ; for the mischievous fish, instead of running out of sight, often sat down or lay down, feigning sleep, and never started off again until the hand, stretched out to seize him, was within a scale's breadth of his body. For he was resolved that Filarete should be his follower

They ran till dusk, when they got to the top of a mountain, which they had been climbing all the afternoon ; for it had pleased the fish to try his friend's wind to the utmost. On the mountain-top were ragged points of granite, but the central peak was a smooth table on which twenty men could stand. The Mackerel then slipped into a hole under a peak, while the fisherman, distrusting his feet, sat down to use his eyes. He was too hungry to sleep, and watched well until morning, when he observed, where he had lost sight of the Mackerel, a gleam as of water in a cranny of the rock. He had been drenched in the mists of evening, and had seen the moon half the night through. He had heard odd music after sunset, as if a thousand or two of tiny fingers had been harping The ridiculous Mackerel had sung also sentimental songs about the stars.

Then, as dawn approached, when the poor fisherman was shivering with cold and hunger, the Mackerel, still full

of sentiment, as he was empty of all other meat, was heard
singing :—

" Now like the tender hope of fish, the doubtful morning breaks,
    Scarce venturing to thrust a beam upon the sullen flakes
    That stretch across the East, as though they gathered there to bar
    The passage of the coursers of the sun's triumphal car."

"Tooraloral la!" said the fisherman, "but I will venture a thrust on your flakes with something handier than a
beam, my good friend." The Mackerel was at the bottom
of a deep cleft in the rock, where he could not be reached
by his friend's arm, and he had turned his hole into a
fountain of sentiment, because that was the most nauseous
thing he could produce for the vexation of his adversary.
But Filarete saw a bush growing near the Mackerel's
retreat, and felt that he could produce what would be
more stirring than any nonsense verses. He tore off,
therefore, a long straight bough, rapidly stripped it into a
small pole, and began savagely to thrust at Doctor Pescadillo. As he did so, he found that the gleam from the
cleft was not of water, but of looking-glass, in which the
Mackerel seemed to have been admiring himself while he
sang. The glass he smashed, but the owner of it ran up
his stick almost into his hand, leapt over his head, and,
with his music-shell tucked under one of his arms, had
climbed the sharpest pinnacle of rock before the fisherman
turned round to look for him. The Mermaid's glass was
broken when he had almost made out the third letter of
his line.

"Well," said Filarete, "I'll starve you out, though I
can no more catch you up there than I can reach yonder
mackerel sky."

Mackerel sky! Pescadillo stretched his legs and spread
his arms, and gazed up at the clouds that wrote his line
over and over again on shadowy mackerel backs far overhead. His eyeballs started forward; he stood on the tips
of his two thousand toes, and spread abroad into the air
two thousand fingers, as if they were about to clutch; then
read aloud with a low voice, at which the mountain quaked,
the third of the letters in his mystic line.

In the same instant a thousand dishes of choice food
smoked on the table of the mountain-top. Close to the

right hand of Pescadillo there was floating in the air the meat he liked best, in a shining dish. Filarete's favourite dish came also to his hand. "Now let us breakfast," said the Mackerel. Filarete was already breakfasting. Fish and fisherman stood where they were; the right thing came always at the right time from the table to the hand of each. When they had both eaten enough, the breakfast vanished; but the fisherman said to the fish, "My lord, I am your servant. While you can command such a table as that, I know how great and good you are, and I will follow you about the world."

"I take you, man, into my service," said the gracious Mackerel. "Now tell me what is yonder city by the lake? There is the sea behind us, and the mountain-peaks are to the right and left. I am not for the sea or for the mountains. I shall go down into that city—what is it?"

"The city, my Lord Doctor Pescadillo, is the city of Picon, by the Lake Picuda. It is there I sold my—may I say in your worshipful presence—fish. The way from the sea is by yonder ravine. The lake is always bubbling, and produces only bubbles. Little corn or fruit will grow on the plains, and these wild mountains, as you see, are barren. The people of the city live, therefore, almost entirely on what we poor fellows get out of the sea. They seldom have enough to eat; but you will feed them. Not in your own worshipful person, no. Yet you run risk until they find out what sort of a fish you are."

"There is a king there, I hope," said the Mackerel.

"My lord, there are a hundred kings, each with ten daughters. The country, being barren, is so hard to govern, that it takes a hundred kings to make anything of it."

"Very good," said the Mackerel. "I will go down to those kings and offer marriage to their thousand daughters."

III

THE LAST OF HIS LINE

THE principles upon which Doctor Pescadillo had established his first happy attempts to read the writing on his back having helped him to three letters, enabled him thereafter to make quick and easy progress in research. When he and his Squire reached the landward foot of the mountains, they were hungry again; but the Mackerel had only to repeat the discovered third letter upon his back, and a new feast of a thousand dishes smoked upon the ground before them. Still, also the slightest freak of appetite in master and man was so well studied, that each had under his hand exactly what he wanted, at the moment when the notion of it came into his head. When they had eaten, being foot-weary with yesterday's race and the morning's scramble down the mountain's side, and, furthermore, lazy with fulness of meat, the wayfarers lay down on their backs and looked up at the sky, wishing for a coach to come and carry them into the city. There was still Mackerel enough overhead to engage the attention of the Doctor. Was it possible that thus, when half asleep, he seized the true reading of two letters at once? The tremendous possibility caused him to leap to his feet. He tried one of them—the fourth of his line—and instantly a thousand horses, harnessed to a chariot, galloped by. They halted when the chariot was abreast of Mackerel and man. Their mouths were free; there were no reins to guide them; and it was noticeable that when any of the magic coursers put their heads to the dry ground and opened their mouths, corn or hay ran up between their teeth, and little water springs welled up where they were thirsty. "The other letter," thought the Doctor, "must be right since this is right; but as I get what I want by the thousand for each letter, and don't yet know anything more that I want, let me keep it by me for a little while."

It is in common kindness to be expected that the person to whom this story is told should be told also what is the sound of the letters, that, when spoken, will produce at once a dinner, or an equipage on this liberal scale. But the letters are those of a dead language that was never living among ordinary men, and known only to a most ancient race of sorcerers, whose mouths were like the mouths of fishes. The last survivor of that race—a thousand thousand years ago—upon the day of his death caught a Mackerel, the only kind of fish having a mouth exactly fit for the pronouncing of his language. In dark

letters he wrote with his finger on the fish's back a line of
power as he died. The letters of this line, and of course
also the line itself, only the mouth of a Mackerel can
utter. It is for that reason that they cannot be told in
the story.

Pescadillo understood already a thousand tongues,
among which tongues of horses were included. He learnt
therefore, at once, from conversation with his stud, that
he might trust them to do as he wished ; and by address-
ing them all clearly in their own language before starting
upon any journey, he afterwards knew how to save himself
all trouble of explanation when upon the road. As they
galloped into the city of Picon by the Lake Picuda, there
was a commotion on the pavement, and a rush of bright
eyes to the windows. The two eyes of a lovely Princess
looked out of each of the ten windows of each of the
hundred royal palaces. As horse after horse galloped by
in the same traces, and still no coach, but still more
harnessed horses followed, first there was a cry of joy for
horse-riders, because clearly this was the troop of a grand
circus entering the town. Then, as there came by still
horses and horses, the people cried there were too many
horses, for the land did not yield corn to feed them, and
even if these riders brought so much corn with them, they
should give it to the people, who were hungry. At last,
when the streets were full of the horses, there appeared
the chariot they drew, and in it was a common fisherman,
with a small fish. "Yah!" cried the mob. "Do you
want all those horses," cried the kings in chorus, "to
bring only one fish to market?"

The Mackerel endeavoured with his harp and song to
still the uproar, but in vain. There was no help for it ;
he spoke his reserved fifth letter, and cried "Silence!"
There fell instantly upon the town a stillness as of night
in the great desert when no wind stirs. Not even the
rasp of a breath or the scrape of a foot was heard, though
men seemed to be raving, shouting, and stamping quite as
much as before. Now, therefore, the wonderful music
was to be heard, and by it a few women were soothed.

The horses, being at rest, began to feed heartily upon
the corn they got out of the stones on the road, and a
rush was made to their mouths. But the wise Doctor

spoke his third letter, and there appeared the thousand dishes of hot meat, dancing about without hands to carry them, and thrusting themselves, ready carved, under everybody's hand. While the people fed—every one getting the dinner he liked best—the Mackerel played music, and hoped within himself that the same letter by which he had enforced silence would have power to unloose from its own spell. It had. By uttering that letter, the most fortunate of fishes could stop any sound at will, and let it go again when he thought proper.

A creature that could give such dinners had his own way entirely in the city and land of Picon. The hundred kings deposed themselves for love of him, declared him sole king, and themselves his viceroys. He changed the next letter he read into a thousand palaces of wonders, and in each there was a study, walled with looking-glass, so that he worked with comfort at the writing on his back. Every new letter he learnt to utter crowned with thousandfold fulfilment the wish of the hour. The thousand Princesses vied for his love; but he began to see that he could not be happy with a thousand wives. His last letter, except the very last, he gave to the wish that the one thousand dear Princesses could be all rolled into one.

Then there was a sight to be seen! Royal Princesses tumbling out of windows and doors, rolling about the streets like balls, every two that came together lost in one another, till the thousand had all rolled together into one colossal damsel. Her the poor little fish was very proud to marry. He did not think himself small, and yet, being small, a large wife was entirely to his fancy. Even in common life we see the shrimps of men marrying whales of women. This couple was married in great state—the fisherman being groomsman to the Mackerel, and all her hundred fathers standing by to give away the bride.

The wedding ball was so magnificent beyond belief that King Pescadillo, in his brilliant court, surrounded by his hundred kingly fathers-in-law, could not help thinking of the old days under water, where so much was thought of the Shark's ball, and when the friends of his youth laughed at him for staying at home to learn his letters. As he thought this, he looked at himself in the great mirrors on the wall. There was the one last letter nearest to his legs.

His flush of triumph so quickened his wit that he could read it at a glance, and whispered it unconsciously while he was wishing my Lord Shark were there to see what a state ball Lord Mackerel was giving. He looked up, and saw the ball-room walled with glass, behind which were a thousand sharks in sea-water glaring upon the company. The company was in extreme delight at this clever addition to its entertainment.

Then the little Mackerel's heart beat with exultation. "Something," he said to himself, "I know not what, is near. This is my wedding-day, and on this day of all days I have finished reading the inscription on my back, letter by letter. If the power of the single letters be so great as to fulfil wish after wish, and tempt me on till I learn all, now that I know all, what will be the strength of the whole charm!"

Ah, cunning sorcerer, last of your line, you fellow who died a thousand thousand years ago, and on your last day wrote upon a fish's back the word that would give you life again when it was spoken, you had reason for being liberal in your rewards to the fish that would spell out that word for you!

The Royal Pescadillo stood upon the stool before his throne, and spoke the letter that compelled strict silence. Then, with panting sides, dread at the great unknown issue of his adventure tempering his triumph, he gasped out the entire magic word; and at the word the giant sorcerer, with a great hairy face, of which the beard trailed behind his feet, entered the ball-room door. This might be right, thought Pescadillo, though his little knees knocked at each other, and the thousand fingers of each hand twitched nervously. The cruel sorcerer advanced to the poor little fish, seized him, and thrust him into his great mouth as the first morsel to be eaten in his second course of life.

The first and last. He should not have been cruel. With his two thousand little fingers Pescadillo fastened to the hair about the monster's lip, and as he hung there he dug with his two thousand little toes into the monster's throat, so that he could not bite; he could do nothing but cough and choke. And the wise Mackerel held tight. He would not be coughed up, though he was almost blown off his legs by the tremendous coughing. All the company had run away; nobody had stayed to see how the brave little Mackerel fought out his battle in the sorcerer's mouth, till the great wretch, in a fit of choking, tipped over his own beard, reeled heavily against the glass walls, and broke through into the tank where all the Sharks were swimming.

The Sharks soon finished the battle, and with a large sorcerer to eat had no eyes for the little morsel of a Mackerel, who seized his opportunity to slip away, and ran back with the stream of water to the sea from which it had been raised by magic channels.

And so Mackerel got safely home again. In all his life he never read another line, and he warned all his relations to get through their lives as merrily as they were able, without ever inquiring what they carried on their backs. "Not for thousands," he said, "would he himself have been so curious had he known everything when he began his studies!"

WILL O' THE WISP

GET you home, you merry lads:
    Tell your mammies and your dads,
And all those that news desire,
How you saw a walking fire
Babes as soon as they can lisp,
Used to call me Will-y-wisp
If that you but weary be,
It is sport alone for me.
Away : unto your houses go,
And I'll go laughing, *Ho, ho, ho!*

HIMPEN HAMPEN

(*Robin Goodfellow Goes*)

BECAUSE thou layest me himpen hampen
I will neither bolt nor stampen:
'Tis not your garments, new or old,
That Robin loves : I feel no cold.
Had you left me milk or cream,
You should have had a pleasing dream:
Because you left no drop or crumb,
Robin never more will come.